OFF ROCK

KIERAN SHEA

OFF ROCK

TITAN BOOKS

Off Rock
Mass-market edition ISBN: 9781785653735
Electronic edition ISBN: 9781785653391

Published by Titan Books
A division of Titan Publishing Group Ltd
144 Southwark Street, London SE1 0UP

First mass-market edition: March 2018
1 2 3 4 5 6 7 8 9 10

A CIP catalogue record for this title is available from the British Library.

Printed and bound in the United States.

THIS ONE IS FOR DOC.

"*A galaxy is composed of gas and dust and stars —billions upon billions of stars.*"

CARL SAGAN

"*OK, boys—let's go make a withdrawal.*"

JOHN DILLINGER

PROLOGUE

To begin with, hypersonic atmospheric re-entry at a forty-five degree angle was supposed to be about holding down your lunch, not fighting for your life.

But there Jimmy Vik was.

Fighting.

For his fucking life.

As the inner-system transport shuttle *Sultana* bellied past the Kármán Line of Earth's upper atmosphere, the sweeping drag of 1600-plus Celsius compression hellfire scored past its ludicrously thick, silicate windows. While the blistering cacophony outside couldn't be heard within, the penetrating reverberations grew louder and louder still until a deafening roar drowned out almost every other sound: the shimmying squeaks, the pressurized squeals, the whimpering moans of the other twenty-six passengers jackhammering up and down in their cheap ergonomic seats.

Oddly enough, most of these passengers hardly noticed Jimmy and the muscle-bound goon whom he met on the Neptune Pact Orbital duking it out in the center aisle. Not exactly a shocker, really. Scrunchedshut eyes and foxhole prayers on atmospheric re-entry? Despite conventional assurances, the routines of commercial space travel in the twenty-eighth century had pretty much iced whatever was left of the life insurance industry.

Often Jimmy Vik wondered why the engineering brains who pioneered long-distance space travel didn't just figure out a way to keep passengers returning to Earth fully sedated until their hot little heels were back on the planet. Sure, the phony bureaucratic orbital-trade interdictions and dutiable commodity inspections, all the lip-service decontamination protocols, and the messy process of filing passengers' complaints, but—*c'mon*. It'd been *three hundred and fifty years* since the first successful Mandelbrot skips to the h-Class mesoplanetary expanses. If the whole wearisome, ducks-and-drakes affair had been properly upgraded from some half-baked carnival ride, given his circumstances, Jimmy might have even stood a chance.

Once more the goon sprung at Jimmy with the feral, unrelenting release of a jungle cat. Doing his best boxer's weave, bobbing from side to side, the sad fact was Jimmy's movements were wholly comical in the increasing onslaught of turbulence. Like a hoisted safe slashed free from its tackle, the goon's gloved knuckles connected with Jimmy's opaque bubble visor with such force that his whole body nearly hinged backward at the hips. Thankfully the polycarbonate visor didn't give or split, but still—such was his attacker's power.

Son of a—

A stiff jolt pitched Jimmy and the goon end over end in a brawling embrace, and crashing into the rear area of the cabin Jimmy's attacker quickly seized the advantage. A crippling barrage of blows—explosive shots, relentless and tight.

Right-left! Left-right!

Bam! Bam! Bam!

Jimmy lost count, but on what was likely the eighth punch his entire left side ruptured apart in a crackling streak of fireworks. While functional, shuttle passenger spacesuits weren't exactly robust in the body armor department and instantly Jimmy sensed something skeletal had gone south. Definitely a rib. Maybe two. Unable to slow down his breathing, each draft of air felt like he was pulling a gust of molten glass into his lungs. Jimmy tucked in his elbows and despaired.

Usually he could hold his own when it came to brawling, but as vicious as his assailant was Jimmy realized a few more good shots to his sides and he'd be all but finished. He pictured his insides anatomically—organs pulped and oozing like so much spastic, living shish kebab.

Skewer of ruptured spleen take your fancy?

Coming right up.

The galloping, superheated snarl outside the shuttle's fuselage built to an earsplitting pitch and, regardless of the sophisticated insulations, the temperature inside the *Sultana* spiked. Sweat flashed down Jimmy's face and tears of frustration welled in his eyes. Time slowed, and the oncoming horror of drowning in his own blood became so real Jimmy wondered if he'd be conscious when he met his end.

Truth was, Jimmy had had his close shaves with death before. Certainly a bunch of near misses as a surface specialist for the interstellar mining companies, and definitely that time he contracted food poisoning from the pillow crab hollandaise on Panus-28, but even before that—way back when he was just a scab-kneed rugby rat running around Vancouver's waterfront slums—the flirty, black scrim of death always seemed to find him.

One time, despite his late parents' never-ending warnings, Jimmy slipped from a pile of rubble while horsing around the scrap heaps above the city's seawalls and only by sheer, dumb luck did he survive. Like a scabbard, a piece of corroded steel had been pried loose from its fittings and as Jimmy fell past, the rusty hook of metal snatched him out of the air by his belt. Then too, hanging by the thin strip of buckled canvas around his waist, did Jimmy perceive time's salient, slow spell as the Grim Reaper loomed close. Even now he distinctly recalled, hanging fifteen meters above the harbor shallows, thinking that if the fall to the rocks didn't kill him, the toxic swill flooding the Strait of Georgia certainly would. Fortunately for him, though, that afternoon Jimmy had been with some of his rugby friends. Scrumming up as a team, his rough-and-tumble peers quickly came to his aid and hauled him up like an anchor.

God, what Jimmy wouldn't give for a few of his old rugby friends now.

But Jimmy Vik didn't have any friends. Not anymore.

Then again... maybe it's best not to get ahead of ourselves.

1. THE GLEAM UNFORESEEN

Roughly twelve months earlier in the Kappa Quadrant on a Cyclopean-Class moon known as Kardashev 7-A, Jimmy Vik was busy planting the initial hardware for a controlled mineshaft demolition and idly considering the merits of offing himself.

Soloing in small planetoid mineshafts made you ponder all sorts of odd things. Deliberately sabotaging your own spacesuit, inexplicably releasing an airlock… strange, meaningless snippets of bizarre android porn. Still nursing the tragic resonances of a hangover, and dehydrated, Jimmy pushed these dark introspections aside and tried to focus on the work at hand. Being seven hours into his shift, he was cold and way past cranky. Anyone would be hard pressed to argue against it: solo rigging demolition inlays for mineshaft closure just plain sucked.

But then Jimmy found the pocket.

At first he thought—*no way. No freakin' way*— he had to be seeing things. Jimmy knew that raw fatigue, isolation, and a lame nitro-oxygen mix in your auxiliary O_2 processing stores could sometimes do that to you, mess with your head. But the more he examined the crammed deposit directly in front of him the more the smudged, dense, yellowish gunk looked like the real deal.

Gold.

Jimmy checked the elapsed time reverse-projected on his helmet visor. Unless there was a significant emergency like a cave-in or equipment malfunction, he wasn't supposed to check back in with Azoick Surface Operations Command Center until the top of the hour. Jimmy was just one of dozens of surface specialists doing any number of assorted final tasks on the small planetary object's sandblasted surface, and unless you were a long way off from station (some shift assignments required temporary camps away from base or the use of tram delivery circuits), check-ins more often than not were just primal grunts over the comm link to acknowledge that you were still on task. Since Fifty-Seven was just under two kilometers from base, the shaft wasn't considered to be a high observatory locale, so there was no reason to go off all half-cocked about what he'd found—at least not yet.

Jimmy holstered the portable drill he'd been using to mount his inlays. Taking a needle scraper from a flapped pouch on his spacesuit, he scratched away at the loose shale around the imbedded mass and flecks of dust swirled outward like blown cinders from a long-dead campfire. Working steadily, in no amount of time he was able to clear a good patch for closer study. His pulse raced. Sandwiched between two soft layers of gazillion-year-old silicate, the pocket was a corker—a peanut-shaped vertical scar as thick and as long as his thigh.

Extensive bore analytics, trace maps, and secondary diameter scans of the SPO's contours indicated that the majority of ore and precious metals on Kardashev 7-A had been stripped out already. Azoick's extended twenty-six-month expedition to the moon had gone over schedule by eight weeks, and the remaining two hundred-plus service personnel were there strictly for regolith sifting and final site closures. Like most major mining concerns, when defining final parameters for its spoliating missions Azoick concentrated its efforts on planetary areas that held the greatest potential for yield. Deep space operations were expensive, but on balance a well-targeted mission stringently managed could offset expenditures with its yield. So far, Kardashev 7-A's bounty had been about average. Some larger veins of iron, nickel, precious cobalt, with sporadic pockets of osmium and scattered yet-to-be-identified materials. It was weird, but very little gold, if any, had been found. So what Jimmy was looking at was incredible. The gold pocket must have slipped past every single one of Azoick's scanners somehow.

By contract, employees were required to report all deposit anomalies no matter what the size—precious metals in particular. At the helm of a publicly traded company with multi-world reach, the top muckety-mucks at Azoick certainly weren't stupid. The echelon calling the shots knew all too well the temptations for workers to take even minor amounts of precious materials were an unfortunate downward corollary to the industry and, as such, dire penalties were enforced across the board for theft infractions— including long-term incarceration and sometimes medical experiments, depending on the value of the pilfered materials and the circumstances.

At thirty-five, Jimmy was still reasonably fit, but for some time he'd been feeling burned out and far riper than his years. He dreaded putting a finger on the specifics of his general malaise, but often he lay awake during his sleep cycles ruminating that maybe, just maybe, he'd frivolously wasted the better part of his life.

Grievously Jimmy theorized that perhaps he'd made a tactical error when he dropped out of school at seventeen. While clever and inquisitive, he had at the time found the dogged regimentation of his poorly funded provincial school back home in Vancouver stifling. His teachers felt he was bright enough, but being bright enough Jimmy was also able to recognize the whole education system was designed not to teach but to impart a sort of addled, confused resignation. It didn't help that his school was of a pious bent and offered little in the way of training its students to think independently. When he announced to his mother and father that he'd had enough and up and quit they totally freaked out. How, his parents demanded, could he, their only son, expect to survive? Jimmy argued he could learn more on his own, and when he further informed his parents that he'd passed the advanced physical and mental assessments for long-term, interstellar trade work, it was as if he'd smashed their hearts into a thousand pieces.

In almost two decades since, Jimmy had broken his back for deep-space mining companies, and if someone pulled together a list of all the outfits he'd worked for there'd hardly be one left out. Nation-state conglomerates like Telesto Energy Solutions, Iset-Belyayvev Metalurgical, and Consolidated Ruthenium, and much later the bigger independent corporations like Dyno Excavation, Lo-Bo Core LLP, and now Azoick. After all that time making shareholders and backslapping company fat cats rich, Jimmy now questioned if he had anything to show for it. Creaky knees and a double arthroplasty for two nearly annihilated rotator cuffs? A pitiful health pension and paltry savings account that could easily be snuffed out by the next financial downturn? With his being in space for years at a stretch with plenty of idle time between skip deployments, it was no wonder that most of two decades had slipped past Jimmy in a hazy, dull blur.

It hadn't been all bad, though. When he first started out in mining, Jimmy really loved the freebooting lifestyle. It beat the mother-loving pants off grinding out his days in some low-wage service job back home in Vancouver, and the allure of distant space travel promised a degree of excitement. Like most glamorous appeals, however, with time working space turned out to be as zestless and prosaic as anything else. Still, the work was physically demanding, and Jimmy liked that. Working as a roughneck made him relish playing hard even more when he rotated back to Earth or Mars between deployments. But, alas, after a time, even those high-spirited shenanigans grew stale. Inevitably one day you rolled out of bed and discovered the whole aggregate of your life had shifted. Obsolescence was bearing down on you with a capital O and you started second-guessing yourself. Jimmy likened it to that old story about the frog in the pot of water, or perhaps a cruel, mixed-up game of musical chairs. He tried hard not to dwell on his growing disjunctive unease, and attempted to blot it out with distractions, intoxications, medications, and the like, but the idea that he'd foolishly turned down a blind alley plagued him to no end. Even if he survived a few more calendar flips without significant injury, with their increasingly stringent physical evaluations Azoick might crunch the numbers and soon assess him as a liability, and then where would he be? A gray-temple washout on a fragile financial scaffold with nothing but a deep, black crevasse of nothing yawning below? Damn.

But now luck, Lady Luck in her glorious rhinestone stilettos, eye shadow, and creamy "Come here, big boy" smile was serving up a hot goblet of possibility.

What if he could get some of the gold back to Earth undetected? Maybe it wasn't too late for him to turn the rest of his life around after all.

Dangling there in near zero gravity, Jimmy thought about that for a while.

For about a half hour, actually.

Goddamn... a real life.

True, with the potential consequences it was balls-out loony to even toy with such an idea. For the better part of his life Jimmy had at least tried to play by the rules, but this much gold with the extended market evaluations—it might make it possible for him to forge a whole new existence.

A raft of possibilities tantalized.

Could he actually live out his days in relative leisure?

Perhaps he should take just enough to retool his credentials and get work in some other field that could afford him a decent, quiet lifestyle. Jimmy imagined canny maneuvers of frugal nuance. Maybe he could invest the gold's value into something tangible, like one of those fancy new Peruvian grotto-condos along the peaks of the Cordillera Real that they'd been advertising like crazy on the imported media streams. Yeah, all that cool neo-classical, white faux-marble… that might be sweet. Perhaps Jimmy could find work as a bartender and roast out his days serving frilly cocktails poolside with a view of Lake Titicaca. Maybe he could even find a well-scrubbed girl and finally settle down.

"Specialist Vik? This is Azoick Surface Operational Command Center. We're noticing a heart rate uptick on your biometrics. Can you elaborate on this, over?"

The woman's voice over the comm link jerked Jimmy right out of his fantasies.

Leela.

"Specialist Vik, I repeat, this is ASOCC. Please respond, over."

Jimmy rubbed the heel of his glove over the yellowish smear in the shaft wall. He'd the presence of mind not to immediately convey what he was seeing over the comm. It was weird, but prior to setting out hours before he hadn't seen Leela Pendergast's name on the work-cycle roster. Dimly, Jimmy wondered what happened to his usual supervisor, Dickerson.

"Dickerson? Is that you? Man, your voice has changed."

"Bonehead," Leela replied tersely. "This is JSC Pendergast. Senior Surface Coordinator Dickerson seems to have come down with the flu, over."

Jimmy kept wiping away at the gold. "Oh, in that case, please convey to SSC Dickerson my best wishes for a speedy recovery. Since I know you're all about formalities, JSC Pendergast, this is Specialist Vik on site in Shaft Fifty-Seven. I'm having some difficulty with my drill power, over."

At twenty-eight, Leelawati "Leela" Pendergast (or Pain-in-the-Ass as she was sometimes referred to out of earshot) was a petite, freckle-peppered brunette who happened to be Jimmy's former flame. Love's labor's lost, the two had broken up a couple of months before and since the breakup their working rapport was what pop psychologists might label as delicate. To avoid contention on the job, Leela and Jimmy agreed not to overlap their work shifts whenever possible. Naturally he didn't like to talk about it, but whenever Jimmy was pressed for the reasons why he and Leela had split up he explained that they'd dissimilar ideas about where their relationship was heading. A pat answer and perhaps intolerably clichéd, but the essence of it was true. Leela had more expectative designs, and reprehensibly Jimmy claimed he did not. It wasn't his finest hour as a human being, but he'd been the one who put the kibosh on things.

Staunchly industrious and resolute, Leela Pendergast was seven years younger than Jimmy and had come up through the Azoick ranks. Despite her rather diminutive size, Leela had made her bones as a surface specialist, but then later steamrolled her way into jockeying a knuckleboom loader. With a chancy eighteen to twenty percent casualty rate, operating a knuckleboom loader was perilous work. However, unlike most of the other operators Leela stuck with it because she knew getting a knuckleboom master-rating would reflect well on her higher aspirations. She parlayed her attention to detail and nerve into a Junior Surface Coordinator position.

Over the comm link, Jimmy endured a sluice of crackling static and then a sardonic huff. "Difficulty with your drill power, huh? I'd say that's a pretty common ailment for an old gravel-crusher like you. Can you clarify the nature of the issue for ASOCC?"

Jimmy pocketed his needle scraper. "Switching to auxiliary power. Hang on just a sec."

Hell, the last thing he needed was hassling from his ex-squeeze. Jimmy tugged his portable drill from his tool belt and toggled the trigger twice close to his helmet so Leela could hear the whir. He seated the drill back in its holster.

"Portable drill power is now good, ASOCC.

Recommencing hardware inlay work, over."

"Acknowledged. So, are you feeling up to snuff, Specialist Vik?"

Jimmy brushed the surface of the pocket and retrieved his needle scraper again.

"I'm sorry, ASOCC, could you repeat that?"

"ASOCC is concerned about your physical status, over."

"Just the power issue, but we're good now, thanks."

There was a momentary pause before Leela continued. "Well, I must say it is kind of odd. I've got your biometrics here tracked back and there's nothing, just routine sixty-eight BPM and then it was like somebody goosed you with an icicle. By the way, you're out of water and your O_2 draw is kind of heavy too."

Jimmy took a second to compose himself. "How're my readings now?"

"Better," Leela answered. "Obviously the H_2O and oxygen losses can't be helped, but your BPM looks like it's leveling off. Come to think of it, I never bothered to ask you: Do you have a history of heart trouble in your family, Specialist Vik?"

"Uh, that's a negative, ASOCC."

"Oh. Well, maybe you're just under the weather—again."

Huh?

How the hell did Leela know he was hungover? Damn, Jimmy wondered if his heart rate was jack-rabbiting again. He told himself to just chill out.

"Moons are devoid of weather," he offered. "So

ASOCC's assessment of Specialist Vik is also a negative at this time."

"You're sure?"

"See, this is what happens. Certain individuals get bumped up over us lowly peons and sitting behind a cushy desk all the time they forget what it's like to actually bust their butts for a living. Specialist Vik is attributing heart rate flux to too much hard work."

The overwrought and deliberate emptiness over the comm link was something to savor.

"Is that an attempt at humor, Specialist Vik?"

"Not at all, ASOCC."

"Yeah, well, I suppose there are always health concerns with someone of your age."

Jimmy was thankful that, due to recent tightfisted Azoick cutbacks, his spacesuit was not equipped with a live bodycam. With his left hand he held up his middle finger and kept scraping away at the yellowish smudge with his right.

Hell hath no fury...

Leela continued, "Incidentally, be advised: We're getting some significant emission interference with the communication relays at this time, so count this as your hourly check-in. Finish up whatever you're doing and return to base via tram in thirty as scheduled, over."

"Copy that."

Jimmy turned the comm link's volume all the way up and waited until he was certain that Leela had moved on to rattle someone else's cage. Only when he heard her exquisitely bitching out some dolts in processing control about a poorly reset sorter did he feel he was well and in the clear. After drifting up and down and scratching for a few more minutes, Jimmy then came to an abrupt decision. The decision felt terrifying and exhilarating at the same time, one of those rare, crystalline moments when one straddles the rails of fate, a massive leap into the unknown.

Jimmy craned his head up and doused his suit lights. Like an inverted telescope, the sudden blackness of the shaft's chasm soared upward and the entire frozen cyclorama of stars and distant planets shined down upon him.

Long ago, he had gotten over his awe of deep space. But given the surging quandaries of their humdrum lives he knew when most people back home or on Mars did contemplate the ruthless absurdity of the greater cosmos, more often than not, and no matter what transcendent shield they stubbornly clung to, the universe scared people shitless. Call it what you will—existential paradox; celestial sucker punch in the abstract—the soul-crushing, never-ending void really put one's inconsequentiality into perspective. Hey, he wasn't a party-pooper. Jimmy would be the last one to tell you that there wasn't any divine plan. But, honestly, he knew the universe was indifferent to your plight. You say plane of immanence? Get real. The universe was just one gigantic brutal fact. It didn't care about your troubles, about whether your missing schnauzer came home or whether you lived or died, and it certainly didn't give a damn about what you stole.

Drawing his Miyakawa X8700 laser cutter from a second spot on his tool belt and picturing the gold pocket as a big, soft slab of yellow cake, Jimmy Vik leaned in and began to cut.

2. BOSS LADY BOOGIE

Ninety minutes later Leela Pendergast found Jimmy in one of the grimy cylinder showers in the ASOCC central locker room. Jimmy was just preparing himself for a long overdue shave when he sensed Leela's eyes boring into the back of his head like a couple of laser cutters.

"So, what's the status on Fifty-Seven?"

Jimmy sighed. Tilting his chin upward into the chemically purified mist, he allowed the water's lukewarm spray to soften his whiskers as he slid a palm beneath a dispenser attached to the wall. The dispenser splorted out a dollop of dense body soap and he rubbed it all over his face. A diehard fan of antiquities, Jimmy was a straight razor guy and his blade was a gift from his late father. German-made, the razor was probably the only thing he had left of the old man save for his chromosomic amalgam. Angling the blade at twenty degrees like he was taught, Jimmy stretched his skin tight and stroked downward.

"What do you mean, the status?" he said.

Leela rapped her knuckles on the shower stall's housing. "The inlay hardware, genius. How far along are you? Lay it out for me so I can adjust the closeout schedule and finish up Dickerson's logs. We're looking at, what? Half a shift before we can consider it primed?"

"More like four," Jimmy answered.

"Four?"

"Yeah, it's all flaky down there, you know? It's like every third screwbolt I sink there's a crack or chink of some kind and I have to start all over again. That's why the juice in my portable drill kept petering out. It's like taking two steps forward and one step back. Pretty frustrating."

Jimmy flipped the excess soap from his razor. Working quickly, he shaved the rest of the lather off his face and cranked the shower's controls counterclockwise for a refreshing rinse. He then killed the flow, folded his razor, and wiped his eyes. Shying away from giving Leela the full pendulous frontal, Jimmy stepped into a drying stall to his right and sensors detected his height and weight. Noisy, compressed air blasted his lanky frame. He plucked his black boxer shorts from a nearby hook and tugged them on.

Leela squinted. "Did you try spacing the hardware out?"

"What do you think?"

"I'm asking you."

"Yeah, of course I tried spacing the hardware out."

"And still the screwbolts aren't holding?"

Jimmy traipsed to his open locker to retrieve the rest of his clothes. He stashed his straight razor in his

Dopp kit, pulled on a threadbare thermal T-shirt, and stepped into one of his long-sleeved, canary-colored jumpers, the one that had nearly all his past mission patches on the sleeves and back. The mission patch for Kardashev 7-A station covered one of the last available spaces on his right shoulder—a shrunken, stitched image of the massive Azoick station. A symbiotic cluster of five interlocking multi-decked, geodesic vertical takeoff and landing structures, the Azoick station was collectively referred to as "the spiders." Each "spider" was independent, linked by multiple passageways and corridors. There was ASOCC operations, material processing, life support and gravity production systems, and shipping and storage. The last spider was the smallest of the bunch and elbowed out almost as a tumorous afterthought: residential. In addition to staff quarters, the residential spider housed the station's canteen and a woefully outdated medical deck. Post rock-reap, all five connected VTOL structures would retract their legs and lift off simultaneously from K7-A's surface for retrieval and eventual repurposing. Instead of personnel names (which were too many, seeing that operative populations fluctuated in around two hundred), the circumference of the Azoick mission patch bore the company's trademarked logo—an arrow-in-midflight with a blowhard tagline in Latin, the deadest of languages:

RELIQUUM HODIE USURPAMUS™
Claiming the Future Today

Jimmy slumped. "Cripes, what do you want me to say here, Leela? This isn't, like, my first rodeo, you know. I've been at this a lot longer than you, and I think I know how long a job is going to take. I'm a professional."

"Oh, I know you're a professional," Leela replied, hooking her fingers. "But what I really want to hear is that Shaft Fifty-Seven is ready for demo and final seal. No one at the other shaft sites seemed to have problems with flaking. And extending the completion forecast to four shifts? I'm sorry, but I just can't have it. Fifty-Seven is the last site to be finished before everything's done."

Jimmy rolled his shoulders. Man, maybe it was a side effect of downing too many pints nearly two-dozen hours ago, but his back had been aching a hell of a lot lately. Maybe it was just dehydration. He made a mental note to drink some water with extra electrolytes when he got the chance. He zipped up his jumper. "Hey, can I ask you something, Leela?"

"What?"

"Why do you like them so much?"

"Like who?"

"Azoick," said Jimmy. "I mean, really, what the hell have they ever done for you, huh? Oh, sure, they gave you a nice promotion, a small bump in currency units and shares. But, seriously, the last time I checked there are over twenty exploration licenses and proprietary claims in this sector alone. I mean, do you really think Azoick cares about all your dotted I's and crossed T's?"

"You trying to be cute?"

"Hell, I thought I was trying to be vivid. Anyway, the company is used to closeouts running long. You really need to lighten up and let people do their jobs."

Fists balled on her hips, Leela wormed her head from side to side. "Gee, Jimmy, I didn't know we were going to have a good cry or I would've brought along my hanky."

Jimmy stared at her. Even in her tooled cherry-colored cowboy boots, Leela was at least a foot and a half shorter than him and he needed to step back a bit to fully take her in. Once again, her brown eyes caught him a little off guard. Although the two of them were no longer an item, he'd be damned if the way she was looking at him right now didn't turn him on. Leela always looked pretty hot when she was all fired up and cracking the crop, and right then she had him cornered. All around them, dozens of men and women milled about in various states of undress while high along the surrounding locker room walls several VDT screens played prepackaged, outdated media streams. Most in the locker room seemed to be watching a playback recording of the Catatumbo Fire and Iberian Front football match. Like a colony of wasps, the players flitted to-and-fro on the pitch. Jimmy vaguely wondered if any rugby highlights would soon be on.

"Listen," he offered, "make it four shifts and I promise you Fifty-Seven will be good to go."

Leela shook her head and added a melodious lilt to her voice. "Well, I suppose I could always assign the work detail to someone else…"

Jimmy's stomach iced. At once he regretted not covering up or disguising the gold pocket back in the shaft and cursed himself for being so careless. Leela's suggestion of someone else taking up the inlay detail was not something he'd counted on. With the pocket exposed as it was, if someone else took over the assignment it would be a lock they'd notice the gold vein and find a sizeable chunk of it missing. Jimmy adopted an air of nonchalance.

"Like who?" he asked.

"I'm thinking maybe one of those two Chinese brothers could handle it."

Jimmy drew back. "Those guys? Good luck with that, hon. Those two are colossal blockheads."

"That may be," Leela said, "but combined, those two colossal blockheads are also half your rate."

"Oh, sure, but take a peek at their files. The real reason those Chinese guys are half my rate is because they've botched routine work like inlays before. Hell, you know as well as I do that those two got kicked from the Athena Cupala project back on Europa because they blanked on procedure and nearly wiped out an engineering crew along with some scouts looking to get their supersymmetry service badges. Just because they keep to themselves and you can't understand a word of Jianghuai Mandarin doesn't mean they're going to get it done any faster or safer. Look, Leela, I've got this. I gave you what I thought was a fair estimate. Four shifts and I swear to you Fifty-Seven will be ready for blow and closure. And don't give me that compromising the schedule crap. Everybody here knows you pad your timelines."

Leela's face flushed. "I do not pad my timelines."

"Oh, really?"

"Wipe that grin off your face, Jimmy, or I swear to God I'll—"

"You'll what? Put it down in my file? Nice. Real nice. Another itty-bitty Azoick star for you."

"Jerk."

"Wow, you used to find me charming."

"Not anymore."

Jimmy faked a long shiver and snapped his Dopp kit closed. "Sheesh, why're you so uptight about all this, huh? Have you even checked with Dickerson? Dickerson is my usual supervisor and he's got seniority. Dickerson never gets worked up over shift extensions."

"I told you. Dickerson has the flu. The latest is he's blowing ballast from both ends so now I have to cover his workload on top of my own. God, Jimmy, four shifts to complete a standard demolition inlay? That's a crock and you know it. I mean, who do you think you are?"

Jimmy finger-raked his damp hair. Slowly he massaged the back of his neck with one hand and tried to gauge the level of Leela's nitpicking hostility. Based on their fleeting intimacy, he knew that if he leaned on her too hard, Leela had surprising combustibility. Actually, Jimmy used to get a kick out of winding her up. Sometimes he used to tease her until her cute little ears grew dark. Still, he needed to back off.

"All right," he said, "how about, mmm, three shifts?"

"Three? The best I can go is maybe two."

"C'mon, be reasonable."

"*C'mon, be reasonable…*"

Man, the petulance.

To bloat out the moment, Jimmy looked up and pretended to be engrossed in the sped-up play on one of the VDT screens. "Fine," he said with a sigh, "two shifts. Is the boss-lady all happy now?"

Leela didn't respond and took a few measured steps toward him. As she drew near, Jimmy looked down and locked eyes with her once again. Like back when they were sleeping together, Leela looked at him as though she was trying to tweeze a loose wire or defective part out of the back of his skull. Such a heady intensity. Her eyes were one of the first things he ever noticed about her. When they first met at a deployment briefing on the Neptune Pact Orbital, her eyes just *grabbed* Jimmy and wouldn't let go. It seemed ages ago, but he recalled how he sat there dutifully listening to the Azoick wonks blabber on about the Kardashev 7-A metric ton projections and knew it was only a matter of time before something between them would reach a boil.

Breaking into a diffident smile, Leela socked his shoulder and put her weight into it. The punch hurt and left a dull ache. Admittedly, Jimmy knew he deserved worse.

"That's what I like to hear," Leela said. She added a jibe as she sidled past him. "Guess it's good to have a shower, huh? Clean out the pores. If anything, it probably makes you feel a lot better."

Jimmy rubbed his shoulder. "A lot better than what?"

"Don't play dumb with me, mister. Over the comm link I could hear it in your voice, and now that I see you up close I know the score. Barking at the moon, that hangdog look…you're not a kid anymore, Jimmy."

Jimmy drifted back to his locker. He pretended to sort his gear and waited until Leela took the hint and finally flounced off. Out of the corner of his eye, he saw her ponytail switch and disappear as she took the corner. Once she was good and gone Jimmy let out a long breath of relief.

It could have gone either way with Leela, but a long time ago Jimmy learned a valuable lesson.

Back when he was a kid in Vancouver, he and his rugby pals used to panhandle after pickup games in order to score enough loose change to buy and share large wax paper cones of greasy fried potatoes. When you were a rugby kid and begging for a handout, panhandling had only one rule: if you don't ask, you don't get. Jimmy knew it didn't hurt to try. The two agreed-upon shifts were a gift.

It was what he had hoped for anyway.

3. THE DISTANCE, PERSISTENCE, AND INSISTENCE

Eight minutes later and back at her console at ASOCC, Leela plunked down in her chair and took a sip from a mug of smoky lapsang souchong tea long since grown cold. Hefty and deep, the mug was a gift from Jimmy, and she liked it not because he'd given it to her but because the mug was formidable and had the words LEELA'S ROCKET FUEL in pink glitter stretched along its side.

Inserting a bone-conductor mic into her ear, Leela stared out of ASOCC's long jalousied transoms. Lit by effulgent floodlights, the pewterish expanse of Kardashev 7-A's surface beyond—with all its sharp-edged hoodoos, hogbacked catenae, and barren plains—was a hoary dead ringer for the front lawn of hell. Unforgiving, frozen, and harsh, it was a constant reminder that Leela was glad she no longer made her living out on the surface.

Setting down her mug, she absently ran a finger along the spines of several stacks of hardcopy three-ringed binders surrounding her console area, long overdue for re-shelving. She procrastinated at putting the backup paperwork away because she liked to hunker down behind them and disappear from her ASOCC colleagues. During her breaks, when she didn't hit the gym to push herself on the machines, Leela enjoyed reading whatever trashy bestseller was making the rounds while huddled inside the armature of her binder garrison. She was so tiny that her coworkers would occasionally inquire where she was and invariably Leela would have to shoot up an arm to announce her presence, a signal flag raised from the trenches.

Hitting the space bar on her keypad, Leela activated her console screens. Like roller blinds going up in a half hoop of cul-de-sac houses, one by one the screens came online and soon she was half encircled in a tawny array of graphs, readings, and assorted analytics. The screens' warm colors gave her freckled cheeks a cozy glow, but they offered little in the way of tangible heat. While Azoick claimed they did their best to make things comfortable for management in ASOCC, no matter how many layers Leela wore she always felt a chill.

After pulling on a dingy pair of fingerless wool gloves, she slapped a three count on her cheeks to bring herself into focus, blew into her cupped hands, and got to work.

Two hours later, when she finished with her tasks and completed deciphering Dickerson's half-finished and utterly horrendous logs, Leela shut down all her screens except for the largest one centered directly in front of her. Tapping her bone mic, she then audibly requested James Barclay Vik's file from the station's central mainframe. In scarcely a second a three-dimensional image of Jimmy appeared in front of her, naked from the waist up.

Sliding across the screen from the right, Jimmy's Azoick dossier materialized in a sidebar as neon green circles highlighted Jimmy's known physical identifiers: two mottled scars from his shoulder surgeries, a blotchy birthmark just under his left nipple in the shape of a fishhook, and a non-cancerous pair of moles on his collarbone. Unlike practically all of the other mining staff on Kardashev 7-A, the rest of Jimmy's upper body was unsullied save for a sparse delta of chest hair. Like her, Jimmy was one of those eccentric sorts who eschewed florid skin-embossings and tattoos.

Leela frowned.

Goddamn you, Jimmy.

Goddamn that raffish smirk cranked on your lips like you think you invented it. Goddamn those lashy blue eyes of yours straight to hell.

Leela debated whether she should make an annotation to Jimmy's file, but then pointedly shook off her hesitation. Now that she was a JSC, it was her responsibility to stay on top of any and all slackers, even ones she used to sleep with. Vigorously pecking her keypad with two fingers, Leela quickly updated the file's comment section. She added her name and ID number at the end along with the date—Earth time, per Azoick regulations:

Surface Specialist Vik demonstrated an inability to deal with unexpected occurrences within the scope of

standard shaft demolition procedures. Disrespectful
manner—unsubstantiated, excessive alcohol
abuse suspected. JSC-Pendergast, L. -54776823 /
3.22.2778GMT

Leela held the tip of her index finger above the
ENTER key and felt a tightening in the pit of her
stomach. It seemed vindictive of her to add that second
sentence, but she pressed the ENTER key anyway.

There, that'll show him.

Since their breakup, Leela thought she'd done her
best to tamp down her resentment toward Jimmy.
Yet, despite her best efforts, deep down she knew she
was failing. The thing was, for the life of her she still
couldn't figure out why Jimmy had hit the brakes
on their budding relationship. One day out of the
blue, bang, it was over. Sitting there with Jimmy's
torso rotating before her, Leela closed her eyes and
summoned up the exact moment of their breakup
with uncanny clarity.

It was a Tuesday (whatever that meant out in
space) and her day off. She'd gone down to Jimmy's
quarters toward the end of his scheduled sleep cycle
to surprise him, and as a wakeup token she'd brought
along a cup of black coffee and a foil-wrapped
toasted bagel smeared with raspberry jelly from the
canteen. It was Jimmy's favorite breakfast. When at
last he opened his hatch, Jimmy looked her right in
the eye and without fanfare calmly announced that
they were through. Speechless, Leela thought at first
he was pulling her leg, but when he shook his head

and crossed his arms she knew he wasn't. It was all so unexpected and bizarre.

Jimmy was always a talker. Frankly, it was one of the things that had first attracted Leela to him, the way he was always telling stories and narrating his day, how he drifted off into funny, third-person tales. Frequently he'd start off with the phrase *"Did I ever tell you about the time…"* and then riff on from there. Jimmy had this wonderful way of milking trivia and mixing facts with fancy that was wildly entertaining. Leela herself wasn't much of a talker, and she half-anticipated a long, rambling excuse for why he was calling it quits at least. But all he ended up saying was that he was sorry and that they were finished.

His exact word.

Finished.

At the time Leela tried not to fall apart. Gathering the affected coils on her emotionally swamped deck, she demanded to know if there was someone else or whether she had done something wrong. Jimmy told her no, adding that the mature and responsible thing for them to do henceforth (*henceforth!*) would be to adjust both of their work schedules to avoid as much contact as possible. Of course, much later Leela regretted throwing the hot coffee and toasted bagel at him, but in the heat of the moment she wasn't having any of it. She was angry and she insisted that Jimmy let her inside to talk it out. When Jimmy shut the hatch on her and threw the lock it sent her through the proverbial roof.

Damn it. Leela wasn't some besotted, doe-eyed

schoolgirl. She wasn't so inexperienced to think she was actually swooning head over heels for him or anything, but what the hell? The two of them *got along*. They made each other laugh (which was rare for Leela with anyone), and their lovemaking was inventive and satisfying. Jimmy did this powerful roll with his pelvis that never failed to push her over the edge, and when they shared time together they honestly seemed to get a blast out of each other's company. When you were working in space for extended periods of time and under uncertain conditions, having things like that was like hitting the damn jackpot. Yeah, their personality contrasts often seemed extreme, but people always say opposites attract, don't they? Leela felt their connection compelling. It was edgy and fun, and she missed it.

Leela eased back in her chair and rubbed the cold tips of her fingers on her temples. She was painfully aware of her dispositional tics so once again she wondered whether she'd pushed Jimmy too far. Leela didn't like to think about her overly assertive attitude, but whenever she spoke of the future and life outside mining Jimmy's demeanor would change. He'd turn inward somehow and a look of gimlet cynicism would brim in his eyes. Maybe she shouldn't have pressed the idea of him shooting for a promotion—but hell! At nearly ten years her senior Jimmy's lack of professional drive was beyond perplexing. To be content as a surface specialist with all of his know-how? She believed she was justified in arguing he ought to strive for something better. Something with legs. System guidance or perhaps photometry analytics—anything other than dangerous surface work. For him to still be mulishly wailing away at rock at his age was nuts.

One time during one of her rather epic jeremiads on his professional obstinacies, Jimmy just laughed at her.

"But I like the risks!"

"Oh, stop it," Leela replied. "No one likes the risks, Jimmy. To say you like exposing yourself to that much danger on a day-to-day basis is just—"

"Cycle."

"What?"

"It's cycle-to-cycle, not day-to-day. There are no days out here in space, remember? Only object surface time. Days are for back home on Earth, not moons."

"Whatever. It's like you saying you like cleaning a loaded gun two inches from your forehead."

"Wow, now there's an image."

"I'm serious, Jimmy. You know the statistics."

"That I do."

"Sooner or later something will go wrong."

"It might, but then again it might not."

"But it could be the simplest thing," she argued. "The tiniest lapse of judgment and that's it. You're done. It might not even be your fault. Somebody else could screw up. There could be a malfunction or an accident. Everybody's luck runs out eventually. What's wrong with having a little ambition?"

Jimmy said, "Well, for one thing, I think ambition is kind of overrated."

"Are you making fun of me?"

"Not at all. Look, I realize ambition has been good for you, Leela. And really, I'm happy you have plans, but you're the exception not the rule. I've bounced around this industry for a long time. Present company notwithstanding, in all that time I've found that only insecure, elitist wonks have to be defined by what they do. Granted, being a surface specialist isn't the noblest of professions or the best paying, but so what? It's a paycheck. I've got other interests. And in the long run the endgame is the same for everybody. You're born. You live a while. If you're lucky, you get to have a few laughs along the way and then it's over. Why can't you accept that? Why can't you accept me for who I am?"

His ambivalent outlook was, in a word, infuriating.

Leela opened her eyes and lowered her hands. After accessing Jimmy's file again with a few keystrokes, she scrolled down to the comment section and slowly tapped the DELETE key on her keypad to adjust the entered field.

Surface Specialist Vik demonstrated an inability to deal with unexpected occurrences within the scope of standard demolition procedures. JSC-Pendergast, L. -54776823 / 3.22.2778GMT

Leela shut down the file once more and finished off the last of her cold tea. A staccato buzzer sounded, and the long transom shutters in front of her started to close. She checked the time. Regulations specified that between operational shift cycles, the SPO's days and nights ostensibly, the transom shields were to be closed to prevent unnecessary radiation exposure and wear and tear. Leela popped up her head from her binder bunker and looked around. She hadn't noticed, but once again she was the last one still on duty at ASOCC.

When the last of the transom's slats finally clanked into place, she stood and found herself recalling a time when she and Jimmy witnessed a terrible accident just outside the ASOCC spider. The mishap occurred only a day or two after they had first stepped off the intimacy ledge, and they happened to be in the same airlock vestibule. Jimmy had just finished suiting up because he was scheduled to relieve another surface specialist, a wooly-bearded bear of a Russian by the name of Chesnevsky.

In a libertine flash of yearning, Leela had snuck down to the vestibule under the pretense she needed a little lip-lock action to get her through her shift. Jimmy, of course, was happy to oblige. He removed his helmet and swept her into his arms. It was just as he pulled her close for a kiss that there was an explosion.

Azoick later classified the accident as a negligible chain-reactive occurrence. After being dropped off by one of the surface trams, Chesnevsky was making his way back to the outer staging areas for the ASOCC airlocks when a turbine strut on a conveyor over a hundred meters away overheated and ripped apart. Chesnevsky hadn't even realized there'd been an explosion, but in the airlock's vestibule Jimmy and Leela felt the concussive, rumbling wallop through the soles of their boots. In the outer airlock proper, both of them plastered their faces side-by-side at the airlock's dilated outer aperture and watched helplessly as a piece of shrapnel the size of a beagle sailed toward the unsuspecting Russian. The shrapnel's flight seemed to take forever, but finally the fragment struck Chesnevsky square in the head. Later internal investigations by Azoick revealed that the integrity of Chesnevsky's helmet had initially remained solid, but knocked down and dazed, the big Russian knew something was wrong. After getting to his feet, Chesnevsky started hotfooting it back to the outer staging areas like he was being chased by a cloud of killer bees.

Inside the airlock, Jimmy wheeled at Leela and screamed at her to get out and seal the inner vestibule. Leela didn't argue, and even now she could still recall the nauseating hitched strands of panicked Russian over the comm link just as Jimmy secured his helmet to his spacesuit. Powerless, Leela sealed the vestibule's inner door and watched on an adjacent monitor as Jimmy quickly ran through his final checks. Jimmy pounded on the door waiting for the chamber to equalize, but in the next instant it was too late. Twenty meters from the outer staging area Chesnevsky's visor splintered apart and crumpled inward like a squeezed egg.

Later Leela told Jimmy that she had nightmares about what happened. She grew teary and explained how she imagined it was Jimmy who'd died out there instead of Chesnevsky. At the time, Jimmy was putting the finishing touches on his HMS *Victory* model—Lord Nelson's flagship from the late eighteenth century. The model had taken Jimmy close to three months to assemble and the mizzen mast rigging still had him vexed.

"Jimmy? Say something."

Jimmy only looked at her and smiled. "Hand me that tube of glue, would you?"

4. BLUE EYES, SCRUTINIZE

After Leela went back to whatever obscure, tedious drudgery JSCs like her did, Jimmy took his rucksack from a hook inside his locker, slipped the straps over his shoulders, and plodded his way back to his quarters.

It was a ten-and-a-half-minute, ant-farm-like slog from the ASOCC locker room out to the residential spider. Following a long mazework of interconnecting ramps, gangways, and ladders, Jimmy kept his head down for most of the way lest he run into somebody and end up having to talk with them. The gold sample he'd cut from the shaft was stored in a pint-sized, radiation-proof container at the bottom of his ruck. Carrying the pilfered chunk on the sly was giving him a serious case of the heebie-jeebies.

Most thought that Jimmy had gotten a bad deal in the housing lottery when he first arrived on K7-A because he drew a living unit at the very bottom of the residential spider. His quarters were in a longish oubliette formerly used for utility storage next to the spider's fragmite waste incinerators. The fact was, even with the nearby incinerators' excessive heat and occasional tremors Jimmy embraced the monkish seclusion of his lonely, hothouse domicile. With all his years in space he'd pretty much had his fill of the grab-ass ambiance of the regular residential offerings. Most of the time those upper honeycomb quarters could be downright crazier than a jailhouse. The screaming, the latest bassed-out Kryp-Bop song volume at eardrum-piercing decibels, the primal slap of men and women balling their brains out to ward off boredom—all of it imbued Jimmy with a dull, cheerless weightiness. He saw the separation from his colleagues as a blessing, a refurbished troglodyte hideaway carved out just for him.

As narrow as the erstwhile storage room was, Jimmy did his level best to make his quarters comfortable. Fastidiously he arranged most of his things on a shelf along one wall to give him a clear path to a bathroom installed at the far end. The last thing you wanted when you got up in the middle of your sleep cycle to take a leak was to crack a shin on something that should have been stowed better. Upon entering, the first manner of items Jimmy set up on the left was his wardrobe. Fairly basic. A couple pairs of boots and a pair of trainers, a week's worth of fresh jumpers, skivvies, and some casual leathers to go home in, all of which hung on a rectangular rig of thermoplastic resin. After that came Jimmy's desk area and his small collection of knickknacks, his HMS *Victory* model and three lush terrariums with Black Mondo Grass, ferns, and stubby mushrooms on a long shelf above. His bunk came next, followed by a small space he reserved for stretching. The bathroom was behind a falcated partition of frosted plastic at the far end.

On the wall opposite these items, Jimmy took to taping up things. Some unindustrialized landscapes of Earth and rugby heroes mostly, but sometimes he liked to tack up passages from something he'd read or colorful samplings of artwork. It was a necessary nuisance, but he had to change these taped-up things quite frequently as the heat from the incinerators next door tended to yellow and curl the posted edges after a while. On the artwork front lately he'd been reading a lot about early hyperviorealism and a trio of printouts adorned the wall. The first picture was of two men bare-knuckle sparring in an alley as a baby with large black sunglasses levitated above them. The second was of a fever of long-extinct stingrays inside a shimmering, metallic wave. Lastly, the largest picture of the three wasn't exactly a favorite, but the artist's subject fascinated Jimmy. The picture was a full-color painting of a *doppelgänger* of a famous reactionary pundit. The pundit, a woman, was blonde and nude and she sat on a plain wooden chair as she held a blood-soaked dressing to her stomach. A pragmatic mugwump at heart, Jimmy didn't throw in much for full-contact, political hullabaloo, but he did find the utter bankrupt look of compunction in the *doppelgänger*'s eyes riveting.

Once inside, Jimmy slapped the lock home to seal the hatch and flipped on the lights. Generally he preferred to use just a small lamp at his desk or the soft terrarium lights for illumination as the flickering industrial overheads gave him a headache, but he felt a full glaring radiance was needed to properly study the sample he'd cut from the pocket. As he passed his desk, a quick wristband swipe under a tri-pod reader initiated his personal workstation screen. Jimmy dumped his rucksack on his bunk, rummaged inside—and drew out the sample in its latch-sealed tumbler. Bringing the tumbler back to his desk, he sat down and got to work.

Like most hardnosed outfits, when it came to what you worked on and looked at on your personal workstation screens, Azoick could fit all of its concerns about your personal privacy up a single, dead gnat's ass. By providing each employee on site with an integrated state-of-the-art workstation system as part of their housing package, Azoick had reserved the right to routinely scour any and all drives for security purposes. As a policy, it was ridiculously ineffective. Azoick wouldn't cop to it publically, but they were keenly aware that almost everyone on station possessed illegal graphometric processor chits able to block their scrutiny via pico-flex encryption. Regular inspections failed to uncover these chits because they were A) so thin and B) so small they could be disguised as almost anything. The processor chits also left no traceable signature. Jimmy had adhered his illegal chit to the face of a playing card, and with five and a half petabytes' worth of capacity his was one of the least powerful on the market. After pulling a rubber-banded deck of cards from a drawer in his desk, he selected the card that held his secreted-away chit—the old chin-muffled self-lobotomizer, the King of Hearts.

Laying the card face up on his desk just below his activated workstation screen Jimmy mumbled a few lines from "O Canada" to engage a voice-stress frequency, and the processor chit instantly synced up with his system. His first manner of business was pulling up the latest three Earth-year market evaluations for gold, and then he skimmed some research datawells for a metallurgic assaying procedure as a brush-up. Soon feeling up to speed, he retrieved a timeworn geological testing kit covered in olive-drab moleskin from another desk drawer on his lower right. Jimmy had bought it on a lark and rarely, if ever, used it. After removing the gold sample from the tumbler with the kit's tongs, he tested the gold using a Mohs Scale hardness tool and got a solid 2.8 reading.

Encouraging.

Nitric and hydrochloric acid swabs came next and then he weighed the sample on the kit's tiny digital scale. The results proved to be positive as well. Satisfied, Jimmy shut down his workstation, dropped the sample back in the tumbler, and replaced the King of Hearts back in the deck.

He held the tumbler up to the overhead lights.

No doubt about it. The gold was the genuine article. So now what? How was he going to get all that gold back to Earth undetected?

He'd no idea.

Jimmy got up and paced the length of the room. No one knew about the gold yet, and as that was the case he still had some strategic flexibility. If he changed his mind, he could still come clean on the discovery, return the sample to the shaft and announce the find after his next shift to make things look good. No one would suspect a thing. A fortune would be lost—that much was certain—and it would be another regret on top of many, but he'd be safe. Naturally, Jimmy understood Azoick would likely steal his thunder and claim the pocket was something they'd had a premonition about all along, but at least he wouldn't end up in the slammer or worse.

His conscience badgering him, Jimmy lay down on his bunk and brooded. Stupid conscience. Didn't someone famous once say cowardice and conscience were the same thing? If Jimmy sided with taking the high road and chose to report the find, who knew what could happen? With any luck his status with Azoick would take a constructive turn for the better. The company might even choose to offer him a low-level management position. Funny, Leela had always wanted him to shoot for something like that. Toeing the company line and keeping things humming along—the prospect made him not just uneasy but mildly depressed. No one ever made their mark by being complaisant and following the rules—holy hell, where had all that gotten him? Nowhere. So was that his destiny? Being another company-man schlub buried alive in the toil of insignificance? He'd almost decided to give in to this resignation when an idea came to him in a rush.

Wait a second, Jimmy thought, get all that gold back to Earth undetected?

Why, he *did* know someone who might know a thing or two about that.

Sitting up, Jimmy checked the time on his wristband.

The next major meal service in the residential canteen was scheduled to start in a half hour.

5. ALLUSION COLLUSION

Fifteen minutes later in the canteen up on deck one, Jimmy found Jock Roscoe at a round baize-topped table holding court with a trio of paper-pajama-clad machine-op greenhorns fresh out of stasis from their Mandelbrot skip. Gliding up and standing just off behind the gathering, Jimmy went unnoticed by Jock as he was busy stacking thirty-two black *Pai Gow* tiles in a square plastic box in front of him. Jock snickered.

"Piece of advice, boys. Next time you're looking for a game, stick with something easy like Warlord and Scumbags. Because frankly? You really kind of suck at this."

None of the greenhorns looked amused.

"It's not fair," the largest of the three men said. "Hell, I'd me a gut feeling about your fading ass the moment we sat down. It was you who wanted to play this stupid bunco game instead of shooting dice."

The other two greenhorns sulkily murmured agreements. Jock resumed stacking the *Pai Gow* tiles in the box and let the newcomers get a good look at his bulging eyes.

Bred in Brisbane's platform housing projects, Jock

Roscoe would never be called a handsome man. Rawboned, short, and with every available inch of his hairless, flyweight epidermis tattooed with a hodgepodge of cross-cultural symbols, Jock prided himself on giving the distinct impression that he was an overgrown, long-nosed weevil and at least half a draft shy of sane. With his spikey teeth and tombstone-colored eyes, his appalling halitosis and rank bodily odors often added to this impression.

"Is there a problem?" Jock asked.

The three greenhorns simultaneously looked at each other and then with the subtlety of rousted cattle scrambled to their feet. A few assorted heads in the canteen registered the commotion, but most promptly went back to their own business. The greenhorn who initially spoke speared a finger.

"You're nothing but a lousy cheat!"

Jock sighed. "Look, mate, you're new here. Seeing that you're still in your stasis PJs and not seasoned in Kardashev 7-A affairs, let me clue you in on something. First off, on my cold bitch of a dead mum's soul I am not a cheat. Craven degenerate, absolutely, but a cheat? Never. Out of the goodness of my heart I showed you three how this game worked and after you won a few rounds I believe you were all hot for it, were you not?"

"Yeah, we were, but—"

Jock held up a hand. "But nothing. Because of said enthusiasm I merely suggested—suggested, mind you—that a little side action might make things more interesting. Now then, if I recall, you three agreed to that. But see, that's just the thing. Once a good piece of wagering starts, inevitably that reliable old temptress comes along, the very same hag that's undone men since we crawled out of the ponds. You may think you're beyond Lady Greed's wiles, but present evidence appears to be to the contrary. Now, to my second point." Jock hiked a thumb toward the patch glued onto the breast of his jumper. "You see that division? The one printed under my name?"

"What? Shipping?"

"Yeah, that's the one."

"Big whoop. So what? What about it?"

"Well, here on this rock that is, in fact, a big whoop. Maybe the biggest whoop to a bunch of winging sooks like you. Short of it is, I'm what you'd call indispensable around here. As the Frogs like to say, I'm *Kardashev 7-A's very own débrouillard. A go-to man and Guy Friday when folks on station are hankering for a fix.* Right now you may think you won't need someone like me, but clock some time on this godforsaken hunk of stardust or wherever Azoick is sending us next, and I bet you'll see things differently." Jock tapped his temple. "Think about it, all right. You want a lid of deep-hallucinatory ganja from the vertical solar farms back home in Finse? Pirated files with interactive footage of your favorite pop idol taking Mayan reed bondage to the hilt? How about a jar of black market pickled eggs or perhaps extra time on your monthly comm window allowance, eh? Extra time on your comm window allowance is always good for checking on whether your sweetheart is throwing up her ankles now that you're good and properly fucked." Jock picked up a glass of gin at his elbow. "Trifle with me, compadre, and there's at least half a dozen roughnecks behind you waiting on special orders that might have a problem with that. Now then, do me a favor, will you? Take it on the heel and toe and fuck off."

Looking around, the three greenhorns saw plenty of brawny sorts stirring about in the canteen, and while none seemed to be looking in the table's direction specifically, the hard-bitten faces of the men and women seemed to give them pause. Jock played it frosty. Flagging an airborne server drone, he ordered a refill, and when the drone sped off the trio of greenhorns picked up their duffle bags from the floor, turned, and slowly slinked away.

Jimmy swept forward and plopped down across from Jock. "Guess that was a pretty good pull, huh?"

Jock finished stacking the *Pai Gow* tiles in the box and threw back the rest of his gin. "Well, you know how these new hires are, Jimmy. All bandy-muscled and dimmer than dirt. It would be a shame not to lighten their pockets."

Jimmy glanced over his shoulder. "So how much did you take them for?"

"Why? What's it to you?"

"Call it curiosity."

Jock shook his head. "You know, they say a dose of that didn't work out so well for the cat. To slake your curiosity, I took them for a hundred a pop."

Jimmy whistled. "Nice. Units or shares?"

"They're newbies," replied Jock, "so currency units, unfortunately."

Jimmy looked over his shoulder again. Standing at the canteen's chevron-shaped bar, the three greenhorns were cracking their knuckles and giving Jock the stink eye. Jimmy turned back. "Still, a hundred each, that's not too shabby. I think you're lucky they moved along, though. The chippy one? He's looking ready to throw down."

Jock growled mirthlessly, "Oh, boo-hoo. Me getting pounded by a bunch of punters like that would be the least of my problems."

Unfortunately, Jimmy understood the usurious difficulties Jock was alluding to. An unrepentant gambler and fond of long-shot bets, Jock Roscoe was throat-deep in debt to The Chimeric Circle—a diverse, felonious enterprise with multiple planet and outer systems reach. Cutthroat and loosely organized, The CC was reputed to sink its brutal beak into just about every illicit scheme imaginable, and with its far-reaching talons enforce a measure of brutality that some believed challenged man's worst atrocities. The CC was involved in the usual sordid rackets: gambling, extortion, political kick-backing and its mushy, peculating sideshows. But recently it had also sidestepped into crisis speculation and new world commodity manipulations. With no definable central command structure to point to, no one really knew exactly how big The Chimeric Circle actually was, how it got started, or even who ultimately was calling the shots. One paranoiac theory suggested that the whole syndicate had been launched from a polymorphic virus that had infected a deep-space probe back in the late twenty-first century. Understandably, Azoick regulations prohibited outside contact with any criminal organizations or persons, but with Jock Roscoe even those with management responsibilities turned a blind eye because of their own self-interests—that is, what Jock could get for them. Most also steered clear of bringing up his problems with The CC, but Jimmy really didn't have an option.

"So I take it you're still treading water."

"Oh, are we the best of mates now or something?"

"Just making conversation, Jock."

"Oh? Well, here's some conversation for you then. Get stuffed."

"Wow, grouchy."

Jock slapped the table and the *Pai Gow* tiles rattled in the box. "You're goddamn right I'm grouchy. The vig those Chimeric Circle buzzards are squeezing my grapes with... I mean, every time I think I'm nearly clear I learn from one of my contacts on the inbound ships that their cast of deviants has hacked into my scrambled accounts to remind me—in one of nine different languages, mind you—just how far I'm behind in their precious book." Jock pinched his thumb and forefinger in the air to illustrate. "They're like leeches. Pick one off and another five of the noxious buggers latch on. I swear I'm doing all I can but sometimes it's like a full-time job muddling my accounts back home to keep them from cleaning me out."

"So how far are you down?" asked Jimmy.

"Far enough," Jock replied pettishly. "God, you want to know what really galls me about those savages? There's actually even a rumor running around that one of their connected ilk might be here on station."

Jimmy almost laughed. "Here? On K7-A? No way."

"That's the buzz."

"But how?"

"Beats me. Like I said, I keep trying to throw them off my accounts, but every time I turn around I get word from inbounds dropping out their skips that those bloodsuckers are all over me. There are moments when I think if I don't cover my debts soon, I might be out of business, and I mean in the permanent kind of way."

Jimmy mulled it over. He was skeptical. Sure, The Chimeric Circle had their grip on Jock and they had their notorious rep to uphold, so they'd certainly brutalize him, maybe break his legs or hack off a finger or two. But cut off a positive revenue stream altogether? It seemed foolish. And it was hardly a secret that Jock was the sort of man who liked to embellish his woes. However, Jimmy needed Jock's help, so he mortared together some sympathy.

"Damn, that's rough. Hey, that server drone just shot off with your order. When it swings back let me pick up your tab."

Jock's eyelids drooped suspiciously. "Whoa, time out. Jimmy Vik buying me drinks? Since when is generous spelled with a 'J'? Must be something on your mind."

"Sort of."

"Ah, I thought as much."

"But it's different than the usual stuff I've talked to you about."

Jock nodded. "Oh, I see. So, what? No kiddie toy or weed this time?"

"Huh?"

Jock muttered, "With you, Jimmy, it's always some obscure knickknack or some hard-to-find fungus you want to try growing in those little glass fishbowls of yours."

"They're called terrariums, Jock."

"A waste of time and money is what they should be called. True, like the rest of the pikers here on station you occasionally spring for some righteous tabs of lab-grade opioids, but I'd bet anything you're looking to score some hard-to-get plant or another fancy-schmancy model. You still working on that sailboat contraption I bent over backward to get you?"

"You mean the warship? Yeah, I finished putting that together a while ago."

"Huh. Well, to each his own, I suppose."

The server drone returned with Jock's gin, and Jimmy swiped his wristband over the drone's code reader. After requesting that Jock's tab be shifted to Jimmy's own food and beverage account, the drone inquired in an automated voice if there was anything else Jimmy desired, perhaps something to wet his whistle. There was a musty alloy of stale cumin, imitation garlic, and overused lard in the air, and the canteen crowds were growing noticeably thick.

Jimmy said, "It's fiesta period, isn't it?"

Hovering in mid-air and employing a suggestive, feminine voice the drone responded, "Affirmative—canteen fiesta period until nineteen hundred hours, Object Surface Time."

Jimmy frowned. His stomach was still way too fluky for food, let alone the dyspeptic outcomes of hot meat paste, rehydrated salsa, and imitation cheese. He requested a tall seltzer on ice and when the drone sped off toward the bar's drink service area, Jock studied him. Jimmy didn't say anything until the service drone returned a minute later. When he took his seltzer from the open salver portion beneath the drone's bib he raised his glass to Jock, who lifted his own drink and set it down.

"All right," Jock said. "Time to quit mincing around and for you to say your bit. If this isn't the sort of thing we've usually attended to, what sort of thing are we talking about here then, eh?"

Notching his voice lower, Jimmy eased forward and rolled his drink between his palms. "Well, it's not a thing so much as a process. See, I don't need anything brought in this time, Jock, but I think you're probably the right person to help me with getting something out."

The intimation kicked Jock into gear. "Okay, I'm reading you. So, um, are we talking about a personal item?"

"In a way. Just how hard is it to get something off rock?"

Jock cupped his elbows. "Well, let's see. With personal effects Azoick regulations say strongboxes are limited to just over four and a half kilos, right around ten pounds. Like anything there are always ways around that, but if what you're looking to move is awkward in dimension or if it's of excessive weight, certain arrangements will have to be made. What're we talking about exactly?"

"I'd like to leave that blank for now."

"Blank?"

"Well, it's a lot heavier than four and a half kilos, that's for sure."

"And it's of a personal nature?"

"Yup."

"Hmm, mysterious. Okay, there's some wiggle room with certain payloads when the scows eventually skip in and repurpose the spiders, but that'll take some time. And more than a few palms need to be greased along the way, if you know what I mean."

"I'm down with taking care of whatever is necessary," Jimmy said.

"Good. That's good."

"As long as those getting greased stay in the dark."

"Hey, what kind of bloke do you think I am?"

"Don't take this the wrong way," Jimmy said, "but one I barely trust."

Jock laughed and snapped his teeth. "Ah, good man. You're no dummy. Nevertheless, you're tapping me with this because you're in a pickle and I'm your ace."

"Mixed metaphors, but sure. That's about the size of it."

Just then a group of workers trundled past the table and Jimmy paused long enough for them to move along. When Jimmy looked across the table again he noticed Jock's eyes were overcome with a wanton glaze.

"Oh, my bleedin' stars…"

Turning his head to follow Jock's line of sight, Jimmy saw the reason for Jock Roscoe's abrupt state of intense distraction. Across the canteen, a tall woman with long, luxuriant blonde hair was making her way toward the bar with sashaying elegance. The blonde's height topped out close to six feet, and even though she was wearing a set of white paper stasis pajamas, her hourglass curves seemed to mock a pneumatic, overdrawn ideal. With her heart-shaped face and smooth alabaster skin, whoever she was she'd a lot of necks in the canteen torqued.

"Now that bird is a feast for sore eyes," Jock said reverently.

"She new?"

"Oh, yeah," Jock replied. "New like dew. Came in on the same skip transport with those three greenies I just fleeced."

"Striking."

"Striking? That's the understatement of the millennia. That goddess be thirty-six, twenty-three, thirty-six, mate."

"Dang, you know her measurements already?"

Jock's face flattened. "Jimmy, I haven't had my bloody ashes hauled in so long it's beginning to feel like I'm freakin' married."

"So what's her deal?"

"Well, that one's no rookie out of the interstellar training camps, that's for sure. Goes by the name Kollár, Piper Kollár. A subcontractor originally from Buenos Aires, I believe. Hairdo's a classic bottle-job, sorry to say, but she's a freelancer on Azoick's new agenda for outsourcing the solar wind parasols on these lesser moons."

"She's a scab?"

"Yeah, but, hey, scabbie or not, don't let the gorgeous looks fool you. Nobody gets to be an engineer in the PAL without being meaner than a snake."

"The PAL? You mean she's in the Pan-American Legion?"

"Was, mate, was. I earwigged a few details on her just after she arrived and the word is she resigned her commission after half of her brigade got wiped out in North Africa hydro-rationing conflicts."

"No way."

"Way. And get this. Back on the Neptune Pact Orbital before she made the skip out? The word is that juicy tomato totally routed a couple of guys who thought she was easy pickings. Practically yanked the cartilage right out of their throats barehanded. Nothing like a near fatal tracheotomy to ruin your day."

Jimmy turned again and watched as the woman eased into a seat at the bar. "And she's still here freelancing?"

"What of it?"

"I don't know. I mean, after pulling a stunt like that on the Neptune Pact Orbital, how can she still be subcontracting for Azoick?"

"Beats me. Perhaps smoking hot scabs with supermodel looks get special treatment."

All in all it was interesting, and certainly the new arrival was nice to look at, but what Jimmy really needed to do was to guide the subject back to his own pressing concerns.

"So, to what we were talking about…"

"Oh, yeah," Jock said. "That."

"What's the largest thing you've gotten back to Earth undetected?"

Jock took a tight sip of gin. "Well, let's see… of a personal nature? I believe it was this little arrangement I threw together on the Tallal-27 satellite construction extension six or seven years back."

"This was before you signed on with Azoick, I take it."

"Right. Some turbine welders looking for a quick payday managed to misplace a bunch of copper connectors, and we ended up disguising it in some hollow ion tubing for the skip back."

"And that worked out?"

Jock shuddered. "God, that little venture was nearly a five-star cockup from the get-go. Even with their fancy, polymathic degrees those turbine welders couldn't keep their mouths shut and we nearly all got pinched. I suppose the backend more than made up for it, though."

"So how much?"

"How much did I clear?"

"No, how much weight."

"A little over a hundred kilos."

Jimmy was impressed. "That's incredible."

Jock grinned. "True, but enough of my bragging. I'm sure what you're talking about has to be a lot less than that."

"Maybe."

"Maybe?" Jock hooked his fingers in the air. "Well, *maybe* I should just finish my free drink and *maybe* I should tell you to find your own way."

"Hey, I didn't mean to rub you the wrong way, Jock."

"Perhaps not, but let's get something straight here, all right? There are things that come across as on the up and up and there are things that just don't. You're telling me this is of a personal nature, okay, but you're not giving me any specifics. Running anything off rock presents significant risks. Yeah, and with significant risks can come big rewards, but I'm not about to lay out my meat on the block for just any old endeavor."

"Well, it's a lot less than a hundred kilos, that's for sure."

Jock took another sip of gin. "Okay, so when are you done with all this K7-A mumbo-jumbo?"

"I'm not scheduled for leave until after spider repurposing, but I'd like to arrange to move the material in question sooner because I plan on getting myself fired."

There was a tiny blepharospasm of Jock's left eyelid as he held a pause. "From Azoick?"

Jimmy tapped at the mission patch on his shoulder. "Uh, hello?"

"What the… Why the bloody hell do you want to get yourself fired?"

"When you learn more about what I want to move I think you'll understand."

"Oh, I will, will I?"

"Yeah, definitely."

Jock's inquisitorial mien told Jimmy that he'd probably said enough. For better or worse, the initial hook had been planted. Taking a scorching swallow of his seltzer, Jimmy stood.

"Look, there are too many ears here so I tell you what. Finish your drink and meet me in my quarters in half an hour, okay? I promise I'll fill in all the blanks for you then."

"Here you go. *Tres platos de fiesta*. Three fiesta plates."

Appalled, Piper Kollár stared down at the plate the bartender had set in front of her. In all her years of growing up in Buenos Aires' squalid Port Sud seaside slums and later working as an engineer for the Pan-American Legion she'd been forced to eat some ghastly slop, but even so the greasy pile on the plate bordered on offence. Nestled atop a bed of rice that looked like a heap of frozen maggots, the soggy tortillas resembled a pair of blown-out, muddy diapers left out in the rain.

"What's this?" Piper demanded.

After wiping his fingers on his apron, the bartender pulled a toothpick from his mouth and replied matter-of-factly, "Why, that's your order. Three fiesta plates. Protein-fry tacos on converted rice."

Piper looked at the bartender incredulously as her two solar parasol compatriots tucked into their plates with the famished gusto of convicts. The bartender turned and set about pouring three quick drafts of ale into red plastic cups. As he set their drinks down in front of them, Piper pushed her plate away.

"Bring me something else," she said.

"How's that?"

Piper snapped out an arm and grabbed the bartender's wrist. "I said, bring me something *else*."

The bartender squirmed. "Hey! I don't make the stuff, I just serve it, man. You got a complaint about the fare I suggest you take it up with Azoick."

With force, Piper yanked the bartender toward her. The speed rail beneath the bar sang out with a clatter of bottles as she tightened her grip. "I don't think you heard me," she said. "See, I've just finished up a hell of a long skip in stasis. While this puke might not bother my associates here, I'm not inclined to poison myself. Bring me something else."

"But it's fiesta period!"

"So?"

"It's all we've got!"

Piper twisted the bartender's wrist until he let out a mousy, high-pitched screech. The hold was a technique Piper had used countless times and one that, through severe pain, could focus even the most stalwart of opponents. Paunchy and weak-chinned, the bartender was definitely not taking up any real estate in the stalwart category.

"You feel that?" she asked. "That's concentrated stress on your radius and ulna bones. I can snap these like a couple of stiff twigs and rip out your shoulder like a drumstick if I want to. Eight to nine weeks recovery time on the fracture, maybe longer if I dislocate your shoulder." Piper let the bartender register the dark simmer in her eyes. "I can't imagine anybody of either sex finding you the least bit appealing, so I'm thinking if I hurt you it's going to put a real crimp in your love life. So here's an idea. How about we start over. What's the possibility of getting a little fresh-cut fruit?"

The bartender blustered. "Are you putting me on?"

"No."

"But we're in space!"

"Canned then," Piper said. "Pineapple would be nice."

"I think there's peaches."

Piper imagined the spongy, flesh-like texture. Peaches weren't a personal favorite, but she could eat some peaches. "Are they diced?"

"No, I think they're sliced in syrup."

With a magician's flourish—*ta-da!*—Piper released the bartender's wrist. "See, was that so hard? Bring me a bowl of peaches rinsed, drained, and patted dry. And a shaker of chili flakes for sprinkling, chop-chop."

Cradling his arm, the bartender hustled off as Piper spun around on her stool. Scanning the canteen and draping an arm behind her, she picked up her cup of ale and studied the back of the head of a man sitting at the same table as Jock Roscoe. Both men were conversing with hunched shoulders and Piper supposed that under normal circumstances that was probably a good thing—a rapt, private chat in a public place. It could mean Jock Roscoe was conducting business, the kind of business that up until now had kept the parasitic sleaze-ball from becoming a dark, runny stain.

While on the SPO at the behest of Azoick for their parasol study program, Piper Kollár was also on Kardashev 7-A moonlighting as an agent for The Chimeric Circle. Like her straight work as a freelancer, her supplemental status with The CC was technically in the capacity of a subcontractor, a lucrative sideline that bridged certain, say, rifts in her personal finances. Her efforts with the illicit organization were something Piper fell into via an old confederate from her time in the Pan-American Legion who happened to now be her fiancé. One day shortly after their engagement her fiancé asked her if she was interested in making some quick bank leaning on a couple of hot-shot investment VIPs who'd fallen behind on their commitments to The CC. Given their illustrious economic status and ascribed breeding, the ne'er-do-well VIPs felt above the accelerated charges attached to their teaser-loan rates. At the time, Piper of course knew what The Chimeric Circle was and that her fiancé dabbled in occasional muscle work for them. Awaiting her first solar parasol contract, both she and he were a bit thin in the wallet as they'd just put a down payment on an apartment, so she said sure, it sounded like a hoot, why not? When her fiancé came down with a bug he asked her if she could handle the job solo and Piper agreed. And when Piper showed up to lay down the law The CC was so impressed by her ferocity they ended up putting her on retainer. Coaxing and neutralization tasks were what they called it. Piper and her fiancé found The Chimeric Circle's employment of innocuous euphemisms to be a real scream.

After her shellacking of those two sexist jerks back on the Neptune Pact Orbital, Piper's handlers with The CC made sure all the arrangements to get her to the Kardashev 7-A station were green-lit with Azoick. The pay for her parasol work was totally on the level, but her real work on the SPO entailed a probable contract hit on Jock Roscoe. According to The CC, Roscoe was nothing but a cheap, small-time hustler and had become a problem—some pushback on an outstanding gambling debt with a claim of insufficient funds. Piper's handlers confirmed Roscoe's claim of poverty was a sham, that he'd been playing a shell game with his accounts back home, and that The CC was doing all they could to extract what they were due. The thing was, if dodging payments wasn't bad enough, Roscoe actually had the balls to become more and more vocal about his problems with The CC. Word had gotten back to the organization that he thought their endeavors to make him pay up were woefully pathetic. Given the arrogant bravado on top of his reneging on payment, The Chimeric Circle felt a correction was in order.

Hence Piper.

Her fiancé was surprised and a bit miffed when he learned she'd accepted the possible liquidation gig. With the cover work and the twelve-month roundtrip out and back to Kardashev 7-A a postponement of their nuptials was needed. But the two were shooting for a private yet expensive atmospheric-gondola ceremony above Mars and, while he was disappointed, after her fiancé learned how much Piper would be paid for the contract kill and her parasol work he saw the sense of it. While the time apart might test their relationship, the combined beaucoup compensation would more than cover their nuptials and their honeymoon, and reduce the mortgage on their new apartment by more than half.

Piper watched as the man sitting at the table stood, while behind her the bartender returned with her bowl of peaches. As the man who was sitting with Roscoe moved toward one of the canteen's exits, Piper turned around, picked up her fork, and pointed.

"Hey, who's that tall drink of water heading out?"

The bartender followed Piper's fork and set down a shaker of pepper flakes along with some napkins. "Oh, him? That's Jimmy, Jimmy Vik. Runs around with one of the station management busybodies, Leela Pendergast. I'm not sure, but I don't think Leela and Jimmy are much of an item anymore."

Out of habit, Piper memorized the names. On enforcement jobs for The CC, you never knew when dropping a name or two could come in handy.

Leela and Jimmy. Jimmy and Leela.

Jimmy and Leela sitting in a tree, k-i-s-s-i-n-g...

Adorable.

After lazily seasoning her fruit with the shaker, Piper stabbed a soft slice of peach.

6. THE PITCH AND THE PACT

Forty minutes later, when Jock Roscoe finally knocked on his hatch, Jimmy leapt up from his bunk and banged his head on the shelf above.

Rubbing his scalp, he took a second and reminded himself to just relax. At this juncture Jimmy still had everything in hand. No one except him knew about the gold, but still, his taking the next step and sharing what he found with Jock held tangible, perilous weight. To Jimmy it felt like he was about to pull a pin on an enormous grenade.

Jock Roscoe certainly was an oily one. Earlier in the canteen he'd intimated that trusting anyone, even someone like himself, was a bad idea. But seriously— what choice did Jimmy have? There was no way he could get any amount of gold off of Kardashev 7-A by himself. Jock's connections and expertise were essential. With his shaky footing with The Chimeric Circle, it seemed that Jock was at least primed to take such a chance. Coming to his quarters was a good sign. Nevertheless, a sense of mild dread spread through Jimmy. If he gauged stealing the gold wasn't worth the effort, Jock might choose to sell him out to Azoick's higher-ups in order to shore up Jock's own tenuous prospects. It was common knowledge that Azoick often awarded substantial bonuses to snitches, and while he didn't know precisely how much Jock owed The CC, a whistleblower bonus might prove to be a better play for Jock.

Jimmy then remembered the words spoken back in the canteen.

With significant risks come big rewards...

Damn right.

Freeing the lock and opening the hatch, Jimmy greeted Jock and waved him inside. After locking the entry, he watched as Jock moseyed half the length of the room and looked around.

"Lordy, hotter than a hog brazier in here, eh?"

Jimmy shucked a thumb. "Fragmite incinerators. They're just on the other side of the wall. Noisy and a bit on the smelly side from time to time, but the heat's good for my terrariums." He rubbed his chin. "Listen, man, I'm sorry to have to do this, but I've got to frisk you."

Jock looked at Jimmy as if he had just asked for a big, sloppy kiss.

"You've got to do *what*?"

"Hold up your arms."

Groaning, Jock rolled his eyes theatrically and then raised his skinny limbs out to the side. "Bloody hell. In all my years, some shale chipper looking for me to help him out, this has to be a first. God, what kind of Judas do you take me for, Jimmy? I make my side living on trust, and trust isn't a one-way proposition, I'll have you know."

Jimmy finished giving him a quick pat down. The fact was, Jimmy wasn't looking for concealed weapons, as such things were forbidden under Azoick regulations and harder than hell to come by; he was searching for possible miniature recording devices. The reason for meeting still hadn't been fully disclosed, and shrewd as he was, Jock might record their conversation to avoid future problems and maybe sell him out to Azoick for his own benefit. Truth was, Jimmy hadn't a clue as to what kind of recording device he was looking for, but he made a big show of patting Jock down anyway. Stepping back and waving a hand, he apologized.

"Sorry, man, but up until this point it's your word against mine in all of this. Like it or not, you have a reputation for trafficking in opportunity. Take it as a compliment."

"Fair enough," Jock replied.

Jimmy gestured toward his bunk. "Have a seat."

Jock sauntered down the narrow room. He paused to examine the pictures tacked up on the wall, the naked blonde *doppelgänger* with the stomach wound in particular, and then sat on down on Jimmy's bunk. Following him, Jimmy reached up to the shelf above his desk. Tucked behind his HMS *Victory* model he'd a bottle of single malt Scotch stored in an imitation green leather box. The box was sealed with a shiny silver clasp, and he reserved the Scotch for special occasions—something to help gild his reflections whenever he had a really bad day, like his birthday.

Opening the case and looking at the bottle, Jimmy paused for a moment and marveled at the embossed age printed on its label.

Fifty-seven.

It was the same number as the shaft where he'd found the gold.

Was it an omen?

Jimmy didn't believe in such things. Like horoscopes and organized religious flimflammery, he saw omens as nothing but interpretive, superstitious fantasies for knuckleheads who believed in enigmatic cogs beyond themselves. Good or bad, it was an amusing coincidence for sure, but seriously, an omen? C'mon.

"Up for a taste?"

Jock stared at the bottle in Jimmy's hands. "Ooh, for a glass of that I'd unzip my jumper right now and be your Mary. Where'd you happen to score that bottle of happy? You rob a senator or something?"

Jimmy shook his head and looked for a glass. "Actually, I picked this up on one of my extended leaves back home on Earth. I'd a delayed connection on Kaffeklubben Island in Greenland, and there was this major gale macking offshore that kept all of the outbound flights grounded. To kill time I cleaned out some tourists there to pay their respects at the Arctic battlegrounds. There was a duty-free shop."

"Poker?" Jock asked.

"Nope. Bridge."

"Get out. Who plays bridge for stakes?"

Jimmy bunched his shoulders and let them drop.

Finding a glass, he removed the bottle's stopper and poured two and a half fingers' worth. "I guess I do. My parents liked to play when I was a kid, and they used to cajole me into sitting in when one of their regulars dropped out of their semi-weekly kitchen game. The tourists were up for some side bets on penalties, and anyway it worked out pretty well for my partner as well, so not too many feathers got ruffled. Cheers."

Jimmy handed the glass to Jock and put the bottle back in the case. He left the box open on his desk and after excusing himself he crossed and entered the unit's bathroom. He removed a loosened panel in the wall and, balancing it on the edge of the sink, he then lifted out the radiation-proof tumbler with the gold sample from where he'd stored it earlier. Holding the container up so the chunk of gold could catch some light, he caught a glimpse of himself reflected in the tiny round mirror over the sink. It was strange, but Jimmy detected something different in his eyes. A spark of life perhaps had returned.

Here goes nothing…

Walking back out into the room, Jimmy casually tossed the tumbler onto the bunk next to Jock. The container bounced once on the mattress, rolled, and the gold inside tapped the tumbler's dense glass with a sharp plink. In the midst of testing his single malt, Jock turned his head and looked at the tumbler. Close to a half a minute passed, and an impatient bubble threatened to burst from Jimmy's chest.

God, what's taking him so long to respond?

Jimmy hadn't exactly rehearsed what he was going to do if Jock passed on the deal, but even with the station's artificial gravity it was taking a mighty long time for the other shoe to drop.

"Is that what I think it is?" Jock asked eventually.

Jimmy nodded. "Yeah. I'm sorry, but by my showing you this you are now an accessory to a capital one corporate offense."

Jock looked at Jimmy sternly. Bending forward, he set his glass of Scotch down between his boots and then unfastened a cargo pocket on the leg of his jumper. After removing a red bandanna, he draped the bandanna over the top of the tumbler and lifted the sample. It was something to note, the cautionary measure so as to not leave fingerprints. Jock scrutinized the chunk.

"You've tested this?"

Jimmy said, "That I have."

"And?"

"And it's real. Non-auriferous gold with ninety-eight percent purity, more or less."

Jock snorted. "Piss and wind—*ninety-eight percent*?"

"At troy weight. And there's more."

"More?"

"Uh-huh."

"Bugger all, where?"

"Shaft site in the Kappa Quadrant," Jimmy said. "I found a pocket when I was rigging the shaft for final closure."

"When was this?"

"A few hours ago. I was out there solo and was nearly finished with my shift when something caught my eye. Anyway, the gold vein… it looks pretty substantial."

"Define pretty substantial."

"Well, I might be wrong, but I've seen pockets like this before. I estimate there's at least fifty kilos down there."

"*Fifty?*"

"Maybe. I didn't have a portable CT scanner on me, but even if I did, there was no way I could've completed a full recess analysis because I needed to catch a surface tram to get back to base." Jimmy skewed his head to one side. "So, what do you think?"

Once again Jock was silent. He leaned over and set the tumbler back down on the bunk where Jimmy had tossed it, neatly folded his red bandanna, and stuffed it back in his cargo pocket. Taking his glass of Scotch from the floor between his legs, Jock rose and walked halfway back toward the hatch. Just then the fragmite incinerators beyond the wall kicked on with a dull rumble. Jock drained the rest of his drink in a single swallow and didn't turn around.

"You've some nerve exposing me to something like this," he said.

Life didn't have rewind buttons, but Jimmy wished he had one because he couldn't read the inflection of Jock's words. Jimmy then remembered Jock's earlier quip back in the canteen. Maybe his pickle-ace needed a little extra to spur his conspiratorial engine along. "Trust isn't a one-way proposition, right?"

Jock spun around. "No, it damn well is not! Good

lord, Jimmy, have you any idea what the punishment for a capital one corporate offense like this is?"

"Kind of."

"Kind of? Great, it's settled then. You're certifiably bonkers."

"No, I'm not," Jimmy countered. "Right now, this is something I want to do and, honestly, it's something I feel I have to do. And as of this second any scuttlebutt about this and it's your word against mine, Jock. Except for me, no one has done anything yet. So if you tell me right here and now that it's not worth it or possible, then fine. I'll go next door and burn this gold and the tumbler up in the fragmite incinerators and we'll forget any of this ever happened."

Jock peered at him intensely. "You're really ready to do that?"

"Hell, yes, I am."

"God, check out the swinging brass on you."

Jimmy folded his arms and waited.

"All right, Mister Big-Shot Lawbreaker," Jock said as he ambled toward him. "Let me tell you a story, all right? Once upon a time, I knew this bloke. A regular working-class stiff like you and me, but this bloke I knew—Donnie, let's call him—he had more hard road ahead of him than behind. Suffice it to say this was back during my pre-Azoick days when me and Donnie were employed by the same off-world developer. In any case, Donnie got his mitts on a mess of pills seized by the company's security bulls. Straight-up pharmaceuticals for the extended skip necrosis and aches, but after getting caught with his fingers up the company's skirt Donnie had enough on him to tip him over into a capital one corporate offense. Do you know what happened to poor ol' Donnie?"

"He went to prison?"

"No," Jock answered sharply. "That bloke was sentenced to valence-bond trials with intracerebral vivisection. It was only after his body was shot to pieces they sent Donnie to prison. Somebody cut his throat his first day inside."

"I take it that means you're not interested."

Jock puffed up indignantly and moved over to Jimmy's desk. Grabbing the bottle of single malt from the box and biting the stopper, he poured himself a generous refill. When Jimmy stepped toward him, Jock spat out the cork and it bounced off Jimmy's jumper like a cricket. Jock held out the glass and gesticulated for Jimmy to take it, and when he did Jock raised the bottle to his lips and did his best water cooler imitation. He lowered the bottle.

"Coworker invites me back to his little hothouse domestic, pours me a swanky gargle and presents me with one of the most dangerous, possibly profitable propositions of my life—one that in all likelihood could get both of us seriously fucked—and he's asking if I'm interested? God almighty, mate, I need to sit down."

Jimmy dragged out his desk chair, and Jock immediately dropped into it like a winded prizefighter. With care, Jimmy took the Scotch bottle from him and set it back down on the desk.

Jock shrieked. "Jimmy, you crazy son of a bitch! This is fantastic! Do you know what the current market exchange rates for gold are?"

"Yeah, I sort of checked."

"Oh, you sort of checked. *Millions*."

"If we don't get caught," Jimmy added soberly.

"*FIFTY BLOODY KILOS?*"

"Maybe you ought to keep your voice down."

Jock blew a curt raspberry. "Phfftt—get off that. Who comes down to this sweltering hole? No one except for you and those automated hover bins heading for the incinerators." Jock faked a punch at Jimmy's breadbasket. "You swine. Of course this is possible. It's incomprehensibly dangerous, but something like this…it might be the mother of all capers. Fifty kilos? We'll be wallowing in it, mate. Stinkin' rich!"

They exchanged fist bumps, and for the first time in hours Jimmy felt a thin sense of relief.

After a gleeful sniggering fit and another lengthy draw on the bottle, Jock finally settled down. "Okay, let's get down to the granularity of it, shall we? What kind of break are we talking about here?"

"Break?"

"Yeah, you know, break. Cut, split, my end of the take. You finding the honeypot and me handling all the logistics, a sixty-forty split would be aboveboard I reckon."

Jimmy was surprised he hadn't thought about it before. *Sixty-forty?* But hold on—which way? With Jock's unrestrained fervor Jimmy imagined an imbalance in a split could breed some resentment. Bitterness in any form was always problematical, but then again Jimmy estimated there was more than enough gold down the shaft for the both of them several times over. The thing was, Jimmy hadn't even divined how he was going to get all that gold out of the shaft yet—not in the two meager shifts Leela sanctioned. Not only that, but with their deep-sixed romance Leela had also given off a major-league vibe earlier that Jimmy wasn't exactly performing up to snuff. With her needle-sharp officiousness in her new managerial position, she might hawk Jimmy's every move, or even possibly change her mind and give the demolition inlay assignment to those two Chinese nitwits. The entire scheme could get clipped at the knees before anything even got started. Jimmy's head swam, but for now first things were first. The split.

"Look," he said, "my initial thought here is to be fair. As of now there's a ton of headaches ahead for both of us, and any plan we come up with will have us sticking our necks out equally, if only in different capacities. That said, how do you feel about an even cut down the middle?"

Jock's jaw horse-collared. If he was having any second thoughts, they dissolved completely.

"Half?"

"Yeah."

Jock cackled. "Fuck a duck on a loading dock. I'm in, Jimmy. I'm in all the way."

They shook on it.

Jimmy set down the glass Jock had given him and walked over to his bunk. Picking up the gold sample, he trekked back to the bathroom and concealed the tumbler carefully back behind the wall panel.

Returning to the main room, he asked, "Okay, so what's next?"

"Well, hold on there, mastermind," Jock said. "We need to put our thinking caps on. Believe me, without a solid strategy in all this we're as good as caught. Best thing for something this bold is to keep things simple. Amateurs, they get showy. You start doing long math and carrying the nine, that's when things go cockeyed. Let's talk about how you're going to get that much gold back to base unnoticed. It's been forever and a day since I bounced around out there on the surface, so you know better what's what about all that. So let's have it and rip off the varnish for me. How much time do you think digging out all that gold will take you?"

"Well, Fifty-Seven is the last site scheduled for demolition and seal."

"Right, so you said."

"And Leela wants me to finish up my inlays in my next two shifts."

An invisible curtain fell over Jock's face. "Did you just say Leela?"

"Yeah."

"As in Leela Pendergast?"

"You know another?"

"Oh, hell. Didn't you two use to—"

"Yeah, for like five minutes, and I've been trying to live it down ever since."

"Don't tell me that minky shrew is in on this as well."

Jimmy pulled a face. "Seriously?"

"I don't know. Maybe you two are still in cahoots, a little cheeky root on the side and all that. Got to say, I wouldn't blame you. Downright boggled my mind when I learned you parted ways with that bird."

"Leela and I are over," Jimmy assured him.

"Okay, so you say. But isn't Dickerson your regular supervisor?"

"Dickerson is sick."

"So now your zealous ex-honeybunch is watching you on the heigh-ho, heigh-ho until he comes back?"

"I know she can be difficult, but I can handle Leela."

Jock puffed his cheeks ruefully. "Hey, far be it from me to disparage your prowess as a cocksman and smooth operator, but that Sheila? She is one cold customer. If this tanks on your end or if she catches wind of what you're up to, I'm telling you right now, I'll deny knowing anything about all this to the slab."

"Okay."

Jock hoisted the bottle like a swami attempting to pull in a psychic read, and he tapped the bottle's tip against his forehead. "All right then, take your time and walk me through your thinking."

Jimmy paced. He started freestyling through a morass of possible haul-out scenarios and drifted off into several non sequiturs about negligible gravity suction ratios, laser draws, and the like, but the more he talked the more it sounded like getting any gold out was going to be tougher than he thought. On top of extraction, Jimmy still had the rest of the inlays to affix and, he realized, if like before Leela kept a thumb on his biometrics, he'd have to work more efficiently than he ever had. When the fragmite incinerators beyond the wall suddenly cut off with a muted thunk, Jimmy struck on a half-boiled idea.

"What if I did a back-to-back?"

"Out there? Fifty-Seven isn't exactly a long-distance shaft site, mate."

"I know, but if I take one of the crawlers and power through in one go I bet I could get all of the gold out in one pass. There'd definitely be less exposure back and forth. Not only that, but we won't have to stockpile things piecemeal back here at base. When I was on site earlier I told Leela I was having some trouble mounting my demolition inlays. Maybe I could convince her I need to use one of the long drills to complete the job. With their greater piston capacity, long drills are absolute beasts and have, like, these huge packing cases. If I take a crawler, I bet I can cram fifty kilos into an empty long-drill case no problem. Leela is all about timelines. Scope creep is, like, her nemesis. I could say I wanted to do a back-to-back to get the job done fast and she'll love that. She'll admire my initiative."

Jock stewed on it. "You really think she'll go for a back-to-back? Back-to-backs require pre-approval. And taking crawlers and long drills without authorization? That's chancy."

"I'll just wing it and sell her on it when I'm out there."

"Easier to beg forgiveness than ask for permission, eh?"

"Damn right."

Jock swished a mouthful of Scotch. "But fifty kilos isn't like moving a small chunk, you know, especially when you get it back here to artificial gravity. You're the surface specialist, so I can't help you with the hard labor, understand? If I start mucking around in your stomping grounds, it'll definitely look fishy."

"Yeah, but going back and forth and doing an extraction over two shifts, that's worse, right? This will keep things simple. It'll limit exposure to prying eyes."

"So what happens next when you get back? Have you thought about that?"

"I can leave the drill case with the gold in the crawler. You oversee vehicle maintenance, don't you?"

"That I do."

"When I bring the crawler back to base you could take it from there. Like, say if there was a technical issue, you could arrange a maintenance inspection and grab the gold after I arrive. If everything goes south and I end up getting nailed, you could just walk away and I'll say it was all my idea."

A wave of admiration played over Jock's face. "That's mighty large of you."

Jimmy raised a cautionary finger. "But once the crawler is back at vehicle maintenance the gold and the drill case will be your ball. If things go south after that, we'll both go down together. Agreed?"

Pouting, Jock nodded. "Agreed. You know, I think what we need on this job is a couple of sub-space scramblers to keep in touch while you're out there. I've a pair."

"Sweet."

Jock sat back. Like a teacher at an invisible blackboard, he circled his fingers through the air, detached in a muddled bout of complicated thought. Then he clapped his hands together and proceeded to lay out his tentative ideas for his part of the scheme. Pausing only to take pulls of Scotch, he outlined how he'd front all the kickbacks at his own expense, saying that Jimmy could reimburse whatever outlays he made later on with a fifty-fifty hit, only to be fair. Jimmy liked how Jock expressed his disdain for free riders, and when Jock further elucidated how he'd shift the necessary bribes through a baffling composition of forward-exchange transfers to minimize any data trail, Jimmy was once again deeply impressed. Then again, he figured a man like Jock Roscoe wouldn't have been able to manage his nefarious dealings all this time without mastering a few neat tricks.

Jimmy listened as Jock went on at length, drawing a scandalous picture of how customs and interstellar shipping inspections actually worked. Like most, Jimmy believed procedural governance to be a scrupulously intensive praxis, but Jock assured him that was definitely not the case. A paper tiger is what Jock called it, an organizational clusterfuck that had so many loopholes and so many entities taking advantage of said loopholes that those in charge, to stave off profound embarrassment, concentrated their efforts in presenting a formidable façade. He told him that cargo didn't really get evaluated or inspected until freighters returned to the Neptune Pact Orbital, and even then the oversight was minimal. The revelation was surprising to Jimmy, but Jock just laughed and said it was the way things always worked, time immemorial.

"I suppose you never voted conservative," Jock said.

Jimmy shook his head. "So, when the gold gets back to home, what then? Do you have a safe place where we can divvy it all up?"

"How's that?"

"The split. Do you have a safe place where we can divide up the gold?"

Jock massaged his chin. "Oh, um, yeah. I've just the place. A trusted contact and everything. No worries."

"Where?"

"Err-umm... Hong Kong."

"Hong Kong?"

"What's the matter?"

"Well, I've never been to Hong Kong."

Jock cackled. "Oh, once you get past all the polluted canals, slums, and leveled skyline parts of it are still quite lovely. As long as you pay liberally, my contact there doesn't like to ask a lot of questions."

"So who's your contact?"

"Generally, I don't like to divulge trade secrets, but since we're partners now, I've a regular dragon lady back H-Kongy ways. A real piece of work. Goes by the name Min-Min."

"Min-Min?"

"Yeah, Min-Min Ho. As a front, Min-Min operates a hostess club in what's left of the Wan Chai district. After we make the skip back to the Neptune Pact Orbital, I'll get word to Min-Min that the gold is on its way and then we'll grab an inner-system shuttle home. I'm telling you, that Min-Min, I bet she'll send a chauffeured stretch to fetch us and the cargo. Believe it or not, the little lady finds me irresistible."

Jimmy suppressed an urge to laugh.

Jock Roscoe? Irresistible? Irresistible like what, genital warts?

"It's been quite a spell since I partied all lethal like in Hong Kong, I'll tell you that much," Jock added salaciously.

Huh. It sounded too good to be true, and Jimmy wondered if maybe it was. No, he thought, the capital one corporate offense penalties were too severe. Not only that, but Jock had his debts to The Chimeric Circle to consider. The man was positively jazzed and was all business.

"Okay, so what happens next?" asked Jimmy.

"Well, with you planning on getting fired you'll be on the next transport back, probably aboard the *Adamant* as she's the last inbound freighter set to arrive. Me? I've a ninety-five-year-old auntie back home who's in a frail way with her life-extensions, so I'll put in for personal leave immediately with a claim that I'm the executor of her estate. We'll both ride the *Adamant* for the skip to the Neptune Pact

Orbital and from there we'll coordinate a connecting inner-system shuttle back."

"So your aunt is really that bad off?"

"Ha, that old bat. She's been trying to outfox death for decades. She's probably a goner already."

"I thought personal leave was kind of hard to get."

"You forget who you're dealing with, Jimmy."

"Jock Roscoe the Great?"

"The Great? I'm His Bloody Eminence as far as you're concerned."

Exalted epithets aside, Jimmy knew he needed to mention something else, so he took a sip of Scotch to boost his nerves. "I suppose this is where you warn me against loose lips and double-crosses."

"Well, that's assumed as hereafter it's you and me alone on this, lock and key." Jock pantomimed a locking motion in front of his mouth and then tossed an imaginary key over his shoulder. Jimmy repeated the gesture.

Jock beamed. "I have to tell you, mate, my blood is up! Up! Up! Up! This load, it'll be more than enough to square me with The CC a thousand times over."

"I'm glad."

Slugging Jimmy's shoulder in the exact same spot Leela had earlier, Jock stood and turned to leave.

"Wait, where are you going?" Jimmy asked.

Bottle in hand, Jock freed the lock on the hatch. "Me? I've got to get percolatin'. There are a slew of specifics that need lining up. But you… you should get some rest. There's heaps of work ahead, and you'll need your wits about you. With that in mind, I'm taking this Scotch off of your hands to cement our partnership. Check in with me before you start your next shift, and I'll give you the sub-space scrambler before you head out."

After Jock left, Jimmy sat down on his bunk and was at once exceedingly surprised at himself.

Well, what do you know. It wasn't that hard to pull a pin on an enormous grenade after all.

7. THE CANDY MAN CAN

Not long after he departed Jimmy's quarters, and with a good deal more of the single malt splashing in his gut, Jock swerved gleefully across the cavernous expanse of the shipping hangar on an Azoick glide-scooter. Deep within the shelving units and labyrinthine storage areas he found Zaafer Daavi way up on a mechanized ladder.

Jock hollered up. "There you are, son!"

From atop the ladder and adjoining balustrade, Zaafer Daavi looked down and swapped a fizzing grape-flavored lollipop from one side of his mouth to the other. Jock set the brake on the glide-scooter as Zaafer drew the lollipop from his lips with a wet, pronounced *schplock*.

"Oh, hello there, Mr. Roscoe."

"Come down here, son. I need a word."

Zaafer dithered. "Gee, I'd really like to come down and talk, sir, but I'm really very busy. I've been working straight through my cycle and there's over nine more items still left on my checklist. No disrespect, sir, but is this something we could talk about later?"

Jock looked up from the driver's seat of the glide-scooter. Blemish-faced, gaunt, with a wispy fuzz of a beard, Zaafer plugged the lollipop back in his mouth and resumed futzing with his air-wrench. All around them, the sundry echoes of hydraulics and powerful freight equipment hissed, whumped, and boomed. Overhead like a dreary gull an imaging drone beeped and lingered lazily. Jock watched and waited as the imaging drone registered his presence and then whisked away.

Typically Jock was tickled by the sedulous Pakistani tech's pains at addressing him formally, but after his meeting with Jimmy he needed irksome excuses from the kid like he needed a deep snifter of broken wind.

"It'll only take a minute. C'mon. Be a good sport, young Davey."

Zaafer sighed. "*Daah-vee*."

"How's that?"

"I said, *Daah-vee*. Gosh, you always do that, sir. You always mispronounce my last name, is it so hard to remember?"

Jock rubbed his forehead vigorously. "Just come down here, son."

Zaafer glanced downward once more and sucked fiercely on his lollipop. Jock noted a level of wariness seeping into the boy's watery, dark eyes. Fully understanding how much Zaafer disliked it when he mangled his surname, Jock angled his head amiably, all the while thinking, *Where is this little shit's sense of bloody humor?* He supposed that was how life doled out the talents. A whiz mechanic, Zaafer could overhaul plasma cloud stabilizers for a fusion drive, revamp a marcher lift, and troubleshoot even the most mindboggling of maintenance hiccups, but skylark around at his expense and the kid could snap pissy like a five-year-old brat.

"You don't even know what I want to talk to you about," Jock said.

A few more rachitic twists with his air-wrench and Zaafer finished whatever he was working on. He slipped the wrench into the waist loop on his jumper belt, fitted his boots into the stirrups on either side of the mechanized ladder, and rode the ladder's stirrups all the way down.

Jock took a brief swig of Scotch, jammed the bottle into a drink holder on the glide-scooter's dash, and peeled himself off of the driver's seat. Giving Zaafer his finest go at a smile, he then toddled behind the vehicle and retrieved a blue canvas bag and a radiation suit from the basket on the rear bumper.

"Come with me…" he said, cupping Zaafer by the elbow.

Jock knew it would take some luring with the boy so he promptly unslung the canvas bag from his shoulder. Zaafer kept describing all the other matters he needed to attend to as Jock waltzed him over to a pyramid of large, empty cargo containers.

"Sir, I'm really quite busy. I've been working almost twelve hours straight, and the hard men over in sorting? They're on a real tear. One of them told me if I didn't fix the caterpillar braces by the next shift cycle, he'd track me down and shave off my beard."

Jock unzipped the canvas bag and held it open for Zaafer to see. Inside was a treasure trove of bribery specifically designed to wipe even the most pressing of concerns from the boy's mind. When garnering favors from sources and collaborators, Jock understood that it was often critical to tap into the basest of tastes. Sometimes it took a while for him to figure out what these cravings were, as most people were somewhat chary about volunteering their most craven wants. Zaafer's desires were almost laughable, but Jock kept his judgment of the boy in check.

Zaafer Daavi was a sugar junkie.

For a while now Jock had amassed a candy stash in his quarters to help lubricate things whenever he needed Zaafer, but with Jimmy's discovery he felt he needed to ramp up his game. He made sure to fill the bag and to pack the kid's greatest confectionery weaknesses right at the top, a jumbo package of Super Sour Waddlee Wees.

Zaafer was stunned. "What's all this?"

"This? This is yours."

"*Misha Allah*—mine? Oh, my. It can't be. Are those really Mookoomarsh Bars?"

"That they are," Jock replied with pride. "Twelve of the runniest, the most delectable Mookoomarsh Bars still available. Check out the wrappers, eh? Part of the limited run, the ones with the scratch-'n'-sniff packaging you can savor long after you've had your fill. Plus there's four containers of Jupiter Caramels, those hard-to-get sparking taffy sticks I know you like, six boxes of Choco-Crunchy Gobblerz, and look right there crowning the whole mix, the classic: a nice, plump sack of Super Sour Waddlee Wees."

Zaafer crunched the rest of his lollipop. He coughed on the shards.

"B-but how?"

"Oh, you know, I've my ways."

"Mr. Roscoe, I know you have your ways, but this… this is unbelievable. This is more than you've ever brought me before. It's like a whole candy shop."

Jock zipped up the bag and held it out. "Take it."

"What?"

"Go on, take it. It's yours."

Zaafer stepped back warily. "But, Mr. Roscoe, I haven't done anything for you yet."

"Oh, but I'm certain you will."

"But all this? Really? For me? Goodness… what's the catch?"

"Catch?"

"Um, well, you know there's always a catch with you, Mr. Roscoe."

"Aw, now you're making me feel bad."

"I'm sorry. I didn't mean to offend you, Mr. Roscoe," said Zaafer quickly, "but it's just that this, well, all this… it's, it's—"

"It's what?"

"Well, it's a lot."

"That it be. And I reckon when you're through doing what I need you'll enjoy the second bag of goodies I have for you even more."

Zaafer blinked rapidly. "I'm sorry, but I don't think I understand."

Taking deliberate care to mold his next words, Jock placed a hand on the boy's lean shoulder and gave a light squeeze. God, Jock thought, for all the empty calories the kid consumed on a regular basis, the brown-skinned runt was practically skin and bones. He wrapped Zaafer's arms around the bag.

"Yeah, son, in commercial parlance this is what's known as tendering an advance, a mere taste. I've a whole other duffle full of sweet stuff when you do what I ask."

Zaafer clutched the bag to his chest. Delving a hand inside he lifted out one of the Mookoomarsh Bars and his face was overcome with such awe one might think he held a prized ruby. Visibly timorous, Zaafer glanced around and started to hand back the bag.

"I'm sorry, Mr. Roscoe, but I... I can't take this."

"What do you mean you can't?"

Zaafer looked down. "I'm sorry."

"God, son, stop saying you're sorry all the time. Saying you're sorry all the time is for losers, didn't anyone ever have the good sense to teach you that? And you, my boy, you are not a loser, not by a long stretch. You and me, we've worked out our little agreements before, haven't we?"

"That we have, sir."

"And in all those times have I ever jammed you up or let you down?"

"No, sir. Never, Mr. Roscoe. Not once."

"That's right, not once. But let's not dwell on our

fine history. We need to be quick about this before that imaging drone swings back."

Zaafer's eyes darted up to the shipping hangar's ceiling. "Oh, I don't believe the imaging drone will be back this way for a while, sir."

"Huh?"

"Yes, I've been watching it, Mr. Roscoe. There seems to have been a change in the sweep patterns and it appears to be on fifteen-minute cycles. I guess back here among the empty cargo containers is not an important scanning area."

Jock was already well aware that the area wasn't an important scanning locale. He was the one who'd adjusted the sweep pattern himself immediately after he met with Jimmy in his quarters. It was all part of the plan. Now all Jock needed to do was to get the cavity-ravaged young boy to do his bidding.

"See, that's what I like about you, kid. Always the sharpie. Now, then, to the reason for all the sweets. I need to get something off Kardashev 7-A for a friend of mine. Altogether it's something bigger than the usual stuff we've arranged for, but don't worry, I've an idea how to get all that bundled up. The thing is, eventually we'll need to get the whole lot of it back to Earth, en masse. Right now, for your protection, it's probably best if you don't know all the nitty-gritty specifics."

"Oh, okay. I understand. Sure, sure. So, um, how much?"

"All in all it looks to be about fifty kilos."

Zaafer went still. Jock noticed that a light sheen

of sweat had appeared on the boy's forehead and his now decapitated lollipop quivered on his lower lip like a cowpoke's cigarette.

"*Fifty kilos?!*"

"Pipe down, man… "

"Oh, no," Zaafer balked. "Oh, no, sir. That's not possible. By the Prophet, peace be upon him, *fifty*?"

"Oh, don't be such a donkey. It'll only take some minor reprogramming of the final destination on one of the tender holds."

"But, sir, my clearance hasn't been updated for those sort of adjustments."

"Not a problem," said Jock. "You see, I already updated your clearance grade a short time ago. You know the smaller quarantine holds?"

"The ones they pack the plutonic unidentified samples in?"

"Yeah. I've been thinking it over, and one of the smaller quarantine holds will be perfect for this little venture. K7-A has had more than a few unidentified kernels pulled from its guts, so what I need is for you to remove the existing samples and load my friend's materials in their place."

Zaafer's eyes jittered. "But—"

"It's daring, I know."

"No, the quarantine holds. I'll need to wear a hazmat suit, sir."

"Also not an issue. Just so happens I've got one right here in your size."

"Oh."

Jock slid his eyes to the bag of candy in Zaafer's

arms. "Son, remember what I just said about tendering an advance? The second bag of goodies I have for you when the job is complete is positively teeming with Mookoomarsh Bars *and* Super Sour Waddlee Wees."

Zaafer licked his lips. Standing there, the boy's deep jones for confectionery was something to observe. Jock imagined if he had a cup handy, he could practically fill it with the amount of drool about to spill past Zaafer's lips.

Zaafer said softly, "Oh, well, if you say my clearance has been updated, I suppose I can, well... I suppose I can find a way to make it happen."

Jock handed over the hazmat suit. "Good boy."

Zaafer shook the shiny silver suit and looked at its attached hood. Jock could see that the boy was already busy parsing what he'd have to do to misplace the quarantine hold samples, but it was also clear Zaafer was laboring even harder over selecting his next words.

"I know I shouldn't ask a lot of questions, Mr. Roscoe, but me doing this switch—when will all this need to take place?"

"The *Adamant* is the last freighter scheduled to arrive and it should acquire its primary orbit in a few hours. Once the *Adamant*'s tenders descend, they'll be docked in the armadillo bays for at least twenty-four hours. The plan is for my friend to drive a crawler into the maintenance area and on the crawler there'll be a package. A case, actually. You'll just take the case, make the exchange, and update the destination inputs per these coordinates." Jock handed Zaafer a slip of paper.

"But what about the existing samples?" Zaafer asked.

Jock held up a finger. "Ah, before you begin I want you to put a request in for an automated hover bin. No one pays attention to AHBs and those bins are preprogrammed to purge their contents in the fragmite incinerators on regular hourly clocks. Just slide the existing plutonic sample case into the hover bin, throw some trash on top to make it look legit and off she'll go. You'll leave my friend's case in place of the missing sample case and presto! No one will be the wiser."

Zaafer's eyes shifted up to the ceiling. "But, um—"

"But what?"

"But what about the imaging drone, sir?"

Jock glanced up briefly and made a show of being disturbed. "Damn, I hadn't thought about that blasted thing."

"Yes, Mr. Roscoe, don't you see? If things don't go well, the imaging drone could record me doing the switch. By no means am I saying your idea is flawed, but later on if something goes wrong, someone from the company is bound to look at those files. I don't want to get into any trouble."

Jock knew he could easily adjust the sweep pattern again, but he needed to keep Zaafer unaware of his capacity to tinker with the drone's cycles. Hanging some dramatic fire, Jock paced a bit and stamped a foot to express his frustration. "Oh monkey pus, this is a wrinkle I didn't even consider. What can we do? Do you have any ideas?"

"Well," Zaafer said sheepishly. "I think a distraction could help."

"A distraction? How do you mean?"

"Well, sir, a commotion or something. If timed right, a distractive event could draw the imaging drone's attention."

"Why, that's brilliant, son!"

Zaafer smiled. "Thank you, sir."

"Okay," Jock said. "I'll handle setting up all that. Don't worry. I'll make it loud so you know just what it'll be. But when the time comes just work fast and be ready with the radiation suit and the AHB so you can make the switch when my friend brings the crawler back, all right?"

"You got it, Mr. Roscoe."

Jock grinned and swung an arm around Zaafer's shoulders. "Oh, where would I be without you, boy? Enjoy that candy now, you hear?"

8. OF SNIDE AND INDUSTRY

Reclined on a lackluster boulder, Leela Pendergast tittered as Jimmy slipped off her cherry-red cowboy boots.

Jimmy thought Leela looked great. Nix that. Jimmy thought she looked amazing. In addition to her boots, Leela wore a stunning dark blue and white polka-dot bikini, and planting her hands behind her like a vintage pin-up, she posed as if she were dangling her firm, brown legs off the edge of a bed.

Arranging her boots beside him, Jimmy was at once confused by the thick, pressurized gloves covering his hands. As if on long dolly zoom, his focus cinematically retreated and the foggy condensation on the inside of his helmet visor gave him a start. Looking back to Leela, Jimmy screamed without sound as she drifted up and off the boulder. As he lunged for her ankle, an improbable buzz of insects hummed on Jimmy's wrist.

Jimmy shut off his wristband alarm and sat up. Man, some dream. Not the most off-the-wall hypnopompic jaunt to Neverland he'd ever had, but still—Leela Pendergast hadn't manifested in his subconscious for a while now. She certainly never made an appearance decked out in a frisky polka-dot bikini. Groggily, Jimmy tried to remember if he'd ever seen Leela in a bathing suit. A jog bra and sporty compression shorts, yeah, and a frilly black slip and matching panties she kept around for special occasions, but a bikini? Never.

Lolling on his bunk, Jimmy strained to pull together the last waning threads of his dream for meaning, but soon all the eidetic strength of the images melted away. He rubbed his face. After Jock had departed hours earlier, he'd been so keyed up about the plan to steal the gold he could barely keep still. Jock had pointed out that his getting some sleep before his back-to-back was an imperative, but all of his efforts at rest proved to be unsuccessful. Dozing, scratching his scalp, turning his pillow over and over to find a cool spot—nothing seemed to work. Jimmy took a thirsty draw from a water bottle he kept in a cubby under his bunk and wondered how much rest he'd actually got. Dull aches from head to toe told him not much at all.

His next priority was clear though.

Coffee.

Dressed and teeth brushed, he grabbed his rucksack, locked up his quarters, and made a mental list of what he needed to do next as he took the rubberized ramps and ladders upstairs to the residential spider's canteen.

Unlike during the earlier taco service, when he entered the canteen he found it wasn't all aswarm with carousing inebriates. Naturally, there were a few early birds like him pulling their tattered faculties together, but he counted only eight or ten Azoick employees milling about at most. Jimmy kept to himself. He navigated his way to the self-service area. Selecting a pre-split plain bagel from a tray, he slipped the slices into a coil conveyor and proceeded to hunt in the adjacent bowls for a tube of raspberry jam. There were honey-flavored protein cups, oily cubes of imitation butter, and for the strong palate aficionados concentrated yeast packets, but not a tube of raspberry jam was to be found in the bunch.

Disappointed, Jimmy crammed the toasted, sandwiched bagel sections into his mouth and filled an extra-large paper cup with coffee from one of the dispenser urns. After checking the readout on his wristband, he sealed a plastic lid to his cup and took a tentative taste. Well, at least the coffee was hot and he was ahead of schedule. He'd an hour's worth of grace time to get out to the ASOCC spider before his shift. Mixing chewed sections of bagel with coffee to soften the dough, he picked up a few energy bars for his back-to-back, stuffed them in his rucksack, and headed off to find Jock Roscoe.

From their prior dealings, Jimmy knew where Jock's quarters were down on deck three. To save himself some time, Jimmy elected to use a bypass chute and a few minutes later halted in front of Jock's hatch. Festooned with blue koala-shaped party lights, the entrance bore a slotted nameplate with Jock's name and Azoick ID number. Doctored with black marker ink, the doodle on the letter J was sharpened to a point to resemble a devil's tail.

Jimmy knocked twice and a minute later the lock snapped. If it was possible, when the door drew inward Jock looked even smaller in his shabby thermal T-shirt and sagging purple and black tiger-striped briefs—a bleary Rip-Van-Winkle apparition of hammered shit. Jock's face squeezed as a pungent pong of cloacal gases and sweated-out alcohol found Jimmy's nose.

"What the hell do you want?"

"Sorry to wake you, but I'm on in an hour," said Jimmy. "I need that gizmo thing we talked about."

Jock mashed a thumb into one of his bloodshot eyes and coughed. It was glaringly apparent his mind was elsewhere, someplace bad. "What gizmo thing?"

"C'mon, Jock..."

A hip scratch. "Oh, right. Right, right, I forgot." After a look left and right down the corridor, Jock stepped aside. "Get your bones in here, bushy tail."

Jimmy slid past him and entered the quarters. Jock's personal space was slightly bigger than Jimmy's repurposed utility room down below, and presented what amounted to a world-class, cluttered reflection of the man's derelict appetites. Lit by a kitschy, purple lava lamp, Jock's lair was packed with so many crates, spoiled canteen food cartons, and unspecified trash there was scant room to move or even to sit down. Given the ripe odors, Jimmy made a point to breathe strictly through his open mouth.

Jock sealed the hatch and when Jimmy turned

sideways to allow enough room for him to squeeze past, he started sifting through the piles like a half-crazed magpie hunting for a burnished bead. While Jock searched, Jimmy set down his empty coffee cup and continued to take in the dimly lit surroundings. Next to Jock's unmade bunk a busty life-sized standup cardboard cutout of Miss Jupiter 2772 smiled at him in a negligée, and at what passed for a desk he observed a large flesh-toned image of noodles on an activated workstation screen. With a quick double-take between the screen and Miss Jupiter, Jimmy realized that the lambent, flesh-tone image on the workstation screen wasn't noodles at all but a plaited knot of naked, leggy ladies going to town. Some sticky orgy in progress. It might have been a media freeze-frame or a screen-saver but either way, given Jock's profound depravities, the smutty image and cardboard cutout were hardly a shock. Crossing around the room's obstacles, Jock blundered up to him and slapped a large device into Jimmy's hand.

"There. Best scrambler available. Text only. Subspace frequency is all set on channel three. Not that it matters, but it has a range of ten thousand kilometers and a gyro-powered battery, so if you're feeling all anxious, shake it once in a while to ease your mind. Now, do me a favor and—" Jock heaved sideways and retched a stream of yellowy puke.

"Damn," Jimmy said, "you finished off all of that Scotch?"

Jock muttered. "Don't remind me."

Jimmy pressed the power switch on top of the

scrambler. On a minute oval display screen near the crown of the device a readout in digitized green indicated channel three was all set and ready to go. Turning the scrambler off, Jimmy spoke quickly as Jock gathered himself.

"Okay, I'm going to work as fast as I can to set the rest of the demolition inlays first. There's at least a hundred and seventy meters left between the pocket and the surface opening of the shaft so if I work fast, I should be able to knock the inlays out in six or seven hours, tops. Once she's on post I'm sure Leela will have a major hemorrhage when she realizes I've taken one of the crawlers and a long drill without asking, but don't worry, I'll take care of her. Once she's cool I'll then check in with you using the scrambler, so be ready. After I finish the inlays I'll concentrate strictly on extraction and then transfer it to the empty drill case."

Jock bobbed his head lethargically.

Jimmy went on. "I've been thinking it over and it's going to be a mother and a half to finish the regular work, but I'm ready. So, um, where's yours?"

"Where's my what?"

"Your scrambler."

Jock pawed his greasy forehead. "S'round here some place…"

"Shouldn't we, like, do a test?"

"What for?"

"Well, once I'm out there I don't want to be dicking around in the blind."

Jock scoffed. "In the blind. Don't be such a priss."

"I'm not being a priss."

"Yes, you are. Priss, priss, priss—"

"C'mon, man. I just want us to be tight."

Jock stifled a contemptuous belch and once more an eggish smell crawled up Jimmy's nose like a vile phantom.

"On top of my present crap-tastic state," Jock said, "I can't believe you're talking to me like this again. What, you think my gear is all bodgy? Sure, maybe I shouldn't have drunk all that fancy grog of yours, but don't you think I haven't already been busy making arrangements?"

"Okay, but shouldn't we have a special code with these scramblers or something?"

Jock sneered reproachfully. "If someone gets curious it's a lock, they'll think any message we share will be some weird communication echo. Codes? These suckers are equipped with souped-up, ultramodern octo-encryption. If some busybody like your ex-best poke happens to tap in—which is nearly impossible, mind you—both scramblers will fry out quick. And, trust me, if that happens, you better drop yours because both of these devices have fail-safe self-destruct charges."

Jimmy looked at the scrambler in his hand. "For real?"

"I'm positive it won't happen, but if it does, a default mechanism will release an acid charge inside both scramblers, and they'll disintegrate in about thirty seconds. Stuff will burn right through your spacesuit."

Jimmy pondered the possible fatal outcome. He

was glad to hear about the fail-safe measures, but he still had some questions.

"So how will I know you're trying to contact me?"

"Vibrations, mate. Yeah, I know it's antiquated, but believe it or not antiquated works."

"But if our communications get compromised, is there, like, an alarm on it or something before the acid charges release?"

"Sure. The vibrations will go berserk. Just make sure you keep yours handy. Should fit right on your work belt. See? It's got a snappy little clip right on the back. Don't go setting it aside."

"Swell. Then what?"

"What when?"

"If the scramblers get compromised."

"I guess we regroup."

Jimmy nearly shouted. "Regroup? Are you out of your mind? I'm telling you, there's no way I'll be able to get another chance at using a long drill or a crawler. Leela would never allow it. And getting all that gold out without those things—this can't be done otherwise."

"Then you best pray no one will be snooping," Jock said. "But hey, the odds of anyone picking up the sub-space frequency are minuscule, right? There's nothing to worry about. Look, I know I seem a little worse for wear right now, but remember—you're the one who approached me about this, not the other way around. This clambake is on, so don't go pussying out on me. Just do what you need to do and ping me when you're out there. Later, when you're all set to come back, just drive the crawler over to vehicle maintenance and I'll have somebody take it from there."

Jimmy undid a cargo pocket on his jumper and slid the scrambler inside. Jock was rambling so quickly he almost didn't catch it. Jimmy paused and snapped his fingers.

"Who?"

"What?"

"You just said you'll have somebody take it from there. I thought it was just you and me on this, Jock."

"It still is."

"So who's this somebody?"

"All right, you know a young Pakistani technician goes by the name Zaafer?"

"Zaafer Daavi?"

"Yeah, he'll meet you. And not to worry, he's already been taken care of."

"So Zaafer doesn't know anything about the gold?"

"Of course not. All that emaciated geek knows is there'll be a case. That boy knows better than to be a stickybeak."

Jimmy didn't like it. He knew someone would be involved and people along the way would need to be greased—he had agreed to it—but Jock being slow to mention Zaafer immediately, that was disconcerting.

"So what happens after I drop off the case?"

"Zaafer will transfer it to one of the tenders' quarantine holds and reprogram the final destination coordinates. He'll dump the existing quarantine samples he removes into an automated hover bin and then he'll eighty-six the samples into the fragmite incinerators."

"So you have this all doped out."

"Yeah. It's in the bag."

"Mind telling me which one?"

"What, which incinerator?"

Again, the evasiveness. Jimmy frowned and looked at Jock askance. "No, which armadillo bay."

"God, you don't trust me at all, do you?"

"Any trust I've got is wearing pretty thin right now. So far, all you've told me is that we divvy up the stash in Hong Kong, but you haven't been too specific about much else."

"Hey, I'm not trying to screw you over, Jimmy."

"Yeah, but if we get delayed or if we can't swing a shuttle connection back to Earth together post-skip, I don't even know how to contact this so-called dragon lady you talked about. Listen, I'm not saying you'd go so far as to stab me in the back, but now Zaafer is in the mix. You two might be planning to—"

Bristling, Jock grabbed Jimmy by the front of his jumper.

"Are you calling me some kind of a finky rat?"

Jock's outburst was startling, but from his rugby days Jimmy knew how to break a hold. With a quick upward spread of his arms he tore Jock's bony hands off his jumper and thrust him backward. The leggy Swedes on his workstation screen fell into motion as Jock crashed back into his desk and a cooing, orgasmic refrain filled the room.

"Sheesh—what's wrong with you, man?" Jimmy said. "I'm not calling you a rat or anything. We're partners, Jock, don't you get that? And as a partner I think I'm entitled to know exactly which bay you intend on using and the coordinates of the final destination back on Earth. Cripes, going and grabbing me like that, you're lucky I didn't knock your teeth out. And Zaafer, when exactly were you going to tell me about him, huh?"

Jock wiped some spittle from his mouth. "I would've gotten around to it."

"Oh, sure. You would've gotten around to it. The point is I shouldn't have to ask."

"Okay, okay... I'm sorry."

"Just give me the damn coordinates and tell me which armadillo bay. Now that I'm thinking about it, give me all the information on your contact back in Hong Kong too, that Hoo-Hoo Minnie lady."

"Min-Min Ho."

"Whatever. Just write all that stuff down."

Weaving, Jock turned and deactivated the orgy on his workstation. He pulled up several files and subscreens. It took a few minutes' worth of typing and transcribing, but he scribbled everything down on a greasy napkin. Jock handed the napkin to Jimmy.

"Armadillo Bay H, huh?"

"Yeah, Bay H as in hellfire and horseradish and humble. It'll go into the quarantine hold on whatever tender ends up being docked there."

"I'm going to check these coordinates, Jock."

"No doubt you will."

"And this Hong Kong dragon lady contact information as well."

"Oh, right." Jock chortled sourly. "And just how do you expect to do that?"

"Well, I could scan the datawells and dip into the station mainframes. If I do a rudimentary residential pull of archival news or a standard capitation-tax search, this Min-Min woman is bound to turn up somewhere."

Jock hung his head. "Jimmy, you are so out of your element."

"Huh?"

"Min-Min is part of the underworld, mate. What, you think someone in her line of trade just hangs out her shingle or is foolish enough to expose herself with stuff like paying taxes? Get bloody bent. Min-Min is a ghost."

Annoyed, Jimmy jammed the napkin into his pocket. "So I guess I just have to take it on faith you're telling me the truth about her until we get back to the Neptune Pact Orbital, then."

"I'm not lying to you, Jimmy."

Yeah, right.

Something still felt off—way off. And out of his element? What was all that about?

Then again, maybe Jock was telling him the truth. When Jimmy returned to base with the gold, Jock would be at just as much risk as Jimmy, so perhaps he should relax and give the man a break. Jock was going through some serious withdrawal and looked like he was going to be sick again at any second.

Yeah, it wasn't something he was proud of, but things slipped Jimmy's mind too when he tied one on. Jimmy figured there was not much more he could do but proceed with a watchful degree of skepticism. He made for the hatch.

"Jeez, take an antacid and drink some water or something. We're on the clock now, Jock. Be ready."

9. THE SWEATY BETTYS

On the residential spider's gym treadmills before starting work, or whenever she felt a good workout might alleviate some of her accumulated stress, nine times out ten Leela Pendergast listened to drums.

Primal rhythms. Thuds and repetitive whacks. Drums were the pulse of life, and Leela believed percussive bangs and throbs helped her modulate the salubrious intensities of her workouts. Usually she liked to keep the volume on her earbuds on high, so when the woman started running on the treadmill directly adjacent to her, Leela paid little notice. Ever deferential to her Azoick responsibilities, she kept her eyes glued on two overhead VDT screens, as earlier she'd cued the two giant displays into a locked-in live shot of ASOCC and a serial feed of all the surrounding surface sites. A full to-do list was ahead of her once she completed her run.

"Nice glutes."

Not breaking her stride, Leela quickly swiveled her head to the right. She didn't recognize the tall, regal-looking woman revving up the treadmill next to her. A lemon leotard with black stripes and matching Apoidea-themed leggings, the woman's workout ensemble was quite the eyeful. With buffed arms, full lips, and a sumptuous mane of blonde hair the woman reminded Leela of a classic movie starlet as she popped out one of her earbuds.

"Did you say something?"

The woman gave her a furtive smile and finished fingering a program into the treadmill's controls. "I said, nice glutes. I guess you work out a lot."

Leela glanced up at the VDT screens. Dabbing the back of her wrist across her forehead, she said, "Well, you know, it kind of pays off out here."

The woman nodded and matched Leela's speed and incline. "Oh, I know, right? Not everybody takes care of themselves. Why take care of yourself when you can eat it at any moment? I don't know. Maybe there wouldn't be so many health claims if people pushed themselves more often."

"Exactly."

The woman gestured to Leela's earbuds. "So what're you listening to?"

Leela unhooked the second periwinkle-sized earbud from her other ear and let the connecting wire drop to the back of her neck. "Oh, this? Don't laugh, but I'm listening to drums."

"Drums?"

"Yeah. The beats help my concentration."

"Gee, that's different. What kind?"

"What?"

"What kind of drums?"

Leela shrugged. "All types, I guess. Different time

signatures. Catchy rubato solos and quick marches. Today it's khols and idakkas synced with my pulse. My mother's relatives hail from Darjeeling. When I'm back home she likes to load me up with file samples of traditional Indian music. Are you new?"

Mirroring Leela's tempo on the treadmill the woman answered, "Yeah, just in from my skip. Solar parasols. Me and the two other members of my team are scheduled to launch the parasols post-blow for some study."

Leela didn't respond. Like most, Azoick's idea to bring in freelancers for any work left more than a slightly bad taste in her mouth. In spite of all their shareholder puffery, the cost-cutting decision seemed shortsighted and Leela felt the move undercut morale of the regular staff. Now, as an acting JSC, she realized she wasn't supposed to knock such corporate verdicts, but it was hard to shake one's convictions when it came to scabs. Giving the blonde stranger a half-hearted thumbs-up, Leela powered on and asked, "Got a name?"

"I'm Piper."

"Nice to meet you, Piper. I'm Leela."

"Leela, that's a pretty name. Is that short for something?"

Leela groaned. "Leelawati, but nobody but my mother ever calls me that, thank heavens."

"So what do you do here, Leela?"

"Junior Surface Coordinator."

"Oh. Guess I better mind my manners then," Piper said.

"Why?"

"Well, with a title like that you're not exactly one of the mopey hoi polloi."

Leela waved a hand. "Oh, pooh. It's not like you freelancers are even in my wheelhouse. Mostly as a JSC I just deal with the regular numbskulls and keep them from costing the company too much."

"Been with Azoick long?"

"Almost eight Earth years."

"Really? Eight? That's some dedication. And all that time in management?"

"Nah. The JSC position is a recent promotion, but I've worked my way up. Anyway, it beats suiting up for surface work, that's for sure. So what about you? Parasol work, that can be challenging."

"Not really. I used to be an engineer in the Pan-American Legion."

"No fooling? The PAL?"

"Ten tours," Piper said proudly, "but I had my fill of it. All that factional hot zone work and de-rigging anti-imperialist ordnance. I figured—hey, why not give deep space a try? With my engineering credentials, the parasol training program was a snap. A couple of off-world jobs on Mars and Triton and the next thing you know here I am on the beautiful Kardashev 7-A."

The two of them ran in silence for a while, breathing steadily, their gazes parallel. Leela kept glancing at the massive VDT screens and fleetingly thought about reinserting her earbuds, but decided not to as the burn in her muscles told her she was nearly finished. The treadmill would soon initiate her cooldown.

"I think I heard something about you," Piper said.

"Oh?"

"Mmm, in the canteen. I was hanging out, just getting over the post-stasis tremors when some bartender mentioned something about you and some guy called Jimmy."

Leela almost stumbled.

Did she just say Jimmy?

My Jimmy?

Leela slapped the cancel clip on the treadmill and the belt below her feet slowed.

Damn it, she hated nattering rumor-mongers. Certainly Leela knew petty gossip was derivative of extended isolation and the scant mining populace, but she really wished people on station would just mind their own damn business. Just because her and Jimmy's relationship hadn't been a quick hookup, just because it seemed to be something more before Jimmy deep-sixed it altogether, it didn't give people the right to make light of it. Leela particularly loathed the notion that people might see her as the injured party. As the treadmill's incline mechanisms lowered, she decelerated to a gawky, stiff strut as Piper went on.

"Yeah, the bartender said you and this Jimmy guy were an item. Oh, you're stopping? Gee, that was kind of rude of me. I'm sorry. I was just trying to make conversation. I didn't mean to upset you or anything."

Leela grabbed her towel as her treadmill came to a full arrest. "You didn't upset me."

"You're sure?"

"Yeah, it's totally fine."

Piper killed the power on her own treadmill. "Still, I feel sort of embarrassed."

"Don't be," said Leela. Draping the towel around her neck and gripping both ends, she then asked, "So, did you talk with him?"

"Who? Jimmy? Oh, no. I just noticed him because, well, he kind of reminded me of someone I used to fight with."

"Fight?"

"The PAL?"

"Oh, right."

Piper bunched her shoulders. "Anyway, when the bartender pointed him out he mentioned you two used to be an item. It's not as if I was looking at him, you know, in that way. I mean, don't get me wrong, he's a good-looking guy and all, but I'm spoken for. I recently got engaged."

Piper saw Leela looking at her hand and reached inside her leotard. When she dangled out a thin leather necklace, Leela saw a modest engagement ring along with a beautiful, silver amulet: an ornate triskelion design. As the amulet swayed Leela noticed a barely detectable pareidolic transformation in the amulet's carved ridges. She couldn't be sure, but the design looked to be three rabbits. But then the rabbits changed into numbers, then legs, then eyes, then something else. It was beautiful.

"Nice. I'd think you'd want to display that ring, though. Having it on your finger might keep the wolves on station at bay."

Piper stuffed the necklace back in her leotard. "Well, you know how it is when you're taking space gloves on and off all the time. Anyhow, I'd hate to lose either."

"That amulet..."

"My fiancé gave me the charm before I made my skip."

"Absence I guess makes the heart grow fonder, huh?"

"Hasn't really sunk in yet with being in stasis for six months, but if everything goes according to our spec brief, it'll be six whole months or longer before I get back, and I miss him already. Seeing that communications back home are delayed, he filled the amulet with a message."

"Oh, it's a thermal holographic? Aw, I've heard about those, that's so sweet. And expensive. It sounds like your fiancé is a terrific catch."

"He most certainly is. We met in the PAL. You're not supposed to fraternize in the ranks, but we're both retired now so everything's cool."

"Well," Leela said. "For what it's worth, me and Jimmy are history."

"I'm sorry to hear that."

"Don't be."

"Bad breakup, huh?"

"More like a lack of communication, actually."

"Well, if it's any consolation, your ex wasn't with anyone nearly as attractive as you."

"Oh?"

"Yeah... he was just yapping away with some short-stack baldie with tattoos out the whazoo. Kind of freaky."

Leela knew exactly to whom Piper was referring.

"You mean Jock Roscoe?"

"Is that who it was? Huh. Hideous-looking little guy."

That's putting it mildly, Leela almost said. It was strange, but Piper's mentioning Jimmy talking with Jock piqued some mild curiosity. Of course she knew Jimmy had solicited favors from Jock before (at the pissant's customary steep premiums), but so did a lot of people on station. Well, not everyone. Leela certainly never went near that repugnant twerp. In addition to the obvious illegalities, she didn't appreciate the way Jock exploited people being so far from home. Nonetheless, Jimmy said that even if Jock came off as a detestable piss-artist, the man did provide a valuable service. Where else could people go if not for him? It was true. It took months, even years, to process personal material requests, and most of the time Azoick shot down those sorts of requests anyway. Leela then remembered how Jimmy recently spent a load of currency units getting that ridiculous ship model kit of his and how he typically tapped Jock to help him keep his terrariums flourishing. Maybe Jimmy was angling for a new fern or looking to start a new project.

"Roscoe is kind of an under-the-table resource for staff here," Leela sighed. "But, believe me, that man is hardly trustworthy. It's best if you steer clear of him, if you can."

Piper laughed. "Duly noted."

Leela stepped off the treadmill. "Well, I'm on in a few so I've got to dash. It was real nice meeting you, Piper. Good luck with your parasol work. I'm sure we'll cross paths again, probably at the pre-liftoff assembly, if not before."

Piper hopped off her treadmill as well. When she took Leela's offered hand, Leela found her grip surprisingly strong but at the same time soft. Piper's fingers lingered just long enough to force Leela to withdraw first.

"Hey, before you head off, could you do me a favor?" Piper asked.

"Sure. What?"

"If it's not too much trouble, can you show me how to work the controls on those things?" Piper pointed to the gym's two VDT screens. "I'd like to tune in some music or look at something other than whatever's up there now."

Giving her forehead a flippant slap, Leela laughed. "Oh, that's my bad. I was just checking in on the office. No one's usually in the gym at this time, so I switched off the usual prepackaged drivel." Picking up a remote from a shelf near the weight kits Leela pointed the business end at the screens and stopped.

What the...?

She toggled the remote's enlargement button, and all at once it felt as if she were standing on unsteady air. Up on the right-hand screen, the long rectangular transom shields were open at ASOCC, and the view spread out on magnification.

Moving like a stiff-backed, scarab beetle, an Azoick crawler puttered soundlessly away from base in the direction of the Kappa Quadrant.

10. THE MINION, INEFFECTUAL

To the pious, then.

On completing his first invocation of his daily five, Zaafer Daavi shut down his pocket prayer rug projector and stashed the sugar cube-sized mechanism with its pre-recorded *imam* files in his jumper's front pocket. Moving to his desk and lifting a bottle of warm tangerine-tinted seltzer to his lips, Zaafer took a long drink to ease the dull, blunt ache in his stomach.

While he knew he should have restrained himself from eating too much, after his meeting with Mr. Roscoe the advance bag of candy he'd been given had been far too enticing. Zaafer stayed up most of his sleep cycle feverishly snacking on a good quarter's worth of the delicacies, tearing and devouring the sweets like a starved jackal shredding a newborn litter of polecats. Half-crazed on a sugar high, he spent several delirious hours salivating, eating, and compulsively organizing the remaining untouched portions of his fresh new stash. First, he chose to arrange the remaining candy alphabetically by brands and then he carefully sorted it by flavors, followed by textures, colors, and finally by molded shapes.

Overtaken with his spell of glucose-jacked elation, he then found himself inspired to fashion a tiny village out of the remaining candy and populated the hamlet with a frosted assortment of Super Sour Waddlee Wees. Once it was complete, he lorded over his creation and fashioned a narrative in his head. As the village's sultan and master, he believed the Super Sour Waddlee Wees, the clever infidels, were all guilty of plotting against him. Zaafer staged a mock trial and as punishment for their treacherous perfidy he devoured all the Super Sour Waddlee Wees by decollating each one with his teeth, aping their tiny plaintive screams.

Post-binge, of course, came the shame. Fun was fun, but noticing the time he knew a good stretch of rest was more important. Cramming two Mookoomarsh Bar scratch-'n'-sniff wrappers up his nostrils, Zaafer quickly passed out spreadeagled on his bunk, awash in olfactory bliss.

Now, having left his quarters to start a new day, he decided to get some cornbread and tea to settle his stomach in the canteen. Soon after he arrived at the shipping hangar and surveyed his to-do tasks on his dataslate. As usual there wasn't a lot of time to waste, but as he prioritized his action items he pondered idly what sort of thing was so dear that Mr. Roscoe would be so generous up front.

Indeed, it felt good to be such a valuable asset to Mr. Roscoe, but this time the arrangement seemed atypical. They'd never bothered using a quarantine hold on a tender before, and wearing a hazmat suit? That in and of itself was disquieting. Zaafer had three distant cousins who'd succumbed to severe radiation poisoning back in Karachi after the Valtoon asteroid tsunamis, and the haunting recollections of their excruciating ends were still fresh in his memory. Still, the risk of whatever Mr. Roscoe was up to couldn't equal the lure of a giant batch of Mookoomarsh Bars.

Back home, Zaafer's kindly mother used to have a saying: as men grow older their flaws and worst longings always show. His mother certainly would never approve of his associating with someone so perverse and profane as Mr. Roscoe, and briefly Zaafer wondered what was becoming of him. Although many on station liked to make fun and say he was stupid and naïve, Zaafer took pride in knowing he was neither. He implicitly understood that exchanging and destroying company property was wrong, but had Mr. Roscoe ever let him down or got him in trouble? No, not once. Mr. Roscoe protected him. He always made sure he had enough plausible deniability to avoid implication. Zaafer resolved that it might be best just to keep his mind on what he'd been asked to do and not dwell on questions, as questioning Mr. Roscoe always had the potential of rolling back on him.

Jock Roscoe had an insufferable temper and could get downright sadistic when he grew angry. One time when Zaafer asked too many questions regarding one of their erstwhile arrangements, he even backed out on paying him their agreed-upon compensation to teach him a lesson.

Two jumbo boxes of Whiplash Pogoes.

It was such a dear price to pay.

Banned and nearly eradicated for their nougats' latent toxicities, Whiplash Pogoes were even harder to come by than Mookoomarsh Bars. Zaafer had never tasted one, but allegedly the forbidden candy induced psychoactive visions that lingered for hours after consumption. Even as he'd begged for forgiveness, Mr. Roscoe decided it was high time to show Zaafer which side his rancid *taftan* was buttered on. After doing an elaborate tap dance on the jumbo boxes of Whiplash Pogoes, Mr. Roscoe cleared out the entire lot via an airlock.

Taking a solemn page from his religious convictions, Zaafer deemed that perhaps this time the correct course of action was to take a higher road and merely empathize. With his being in debt to The Chimeric Circle, Mr. Roscoe had to be under some terrible pressure, and while he'd been reeking of demon liquor earlier, Zaafer was happy to see him in chipper spirits. As large as this mysterious load of his friend's was, it had to be something that offered Mr. Roscoe some level of relief.

But good gracious... fifty kilos? Fifty kilos of what?

Right now for your protection it's probably best if you don't know all the nitty-gritty specifics.

Right.

Whatever the material in question was, when Zaafer accepted the bag of candy Mr. Roscoe had presented a fairly ingenious plan. With his clearance updated and a hazmat suit it'd only be a minor inconvenience for Zaafer to arrange a swap-out on a tender. And with a well-timed diversion, the imaging drone issue would be no issue at all.

Zaafer stuck a hand in his pocket and caressed the smooth rectangular edges of a carton of Choco-Crunchy Gobblerz. Giving the carton a thoughtful shake, he whistled a short, happy tune and got to work.

11. TEAMWORK (*SIGH*)

Post workout, Piper Kollár changed into a form-hugging red bodysuit with a modish, black weskit and then met her solar parasol team in one of ASOCC's padded low-ceilinged conference rooms.

The conference room was a cramped, inauspicious affair and stank vaguely of dirty socks. Like almost every other nook, passageway, and deck on the Kardashev 7-A station, every last centimeter of the room and its bolted-down polyethylene furniture was covered with a film of soft, dunnish dust. Mining operations... no matter what cleansers were used, everything on station seemed to be soiled with grime somehow. Piper shivered at the thought of it, but wondered just how pure the processed air circulating on the station actually was.

In baggy, blue canvas coveralls, the two other members of her freelance team, Østerby and Stormkast, arrived late and looked pretty rough. After their getting-to-know-each-other session in the canteen, Piper had left Østerby and Stormkast to their inebriations, and their present states were hardly a shock. For all their tough talk and scruff the two men were lightweights, as bad as teetotalers.

Piper had never worked with either man before, but the two's dossiers filled out a reasonable picture of expertise. With long stints on the Saturn belts, each labored intensely to present the bored look of an old pro who'd seen it all before. At first, back at the Neptune Pact Orbital, when they were being prepped for extended stasis out to Kardashev 7-A, Piper had ignored Østerby and Stormkast completely, but now after their time in the canteen she'd a feeling they at least were growing to like her. True, perhaps it was only for the way she filled out her red bodysuit, but Piper was used to that. She gestured at a three-dimensional rotating representation of Kardashev 7-A floating just above the raised plinth in the center of the table, and the two men slipped into their chairs and she began.

"Okay," Piper said, "we'll be setting our mooring pylons, here and here and here, so on this shift I want us to focus solely on deep prep. Router dry runs, hardware setups and breakdowns, and definitely remote ignition checks. A through Z and top to bottom. Management has allocated an area for our staging work in the central shipping hangar. Sorry, but I've been informed we'll be using the new diamond-caliper cables on this gig. I know, I know… there've been glitches with the new d-c cables, so take your time and check the schematics. Both of you have limited clearance to access Azoick mainframe simulators on site, so run your analytics as outlined in the spec brief. Once our deep prep is tight we should be able to run the first series of drills before we cycle off in a few hours."

Østerby looked at Stormkast. Both men wiggled in their chairs.

Stormkast asked, "So when's the final demo? I didn't see a schedule anywhere in the spec brief, so is there any hurry on all this monkey business?"

Piper pulled up an overlay of the mining sites on the SPO. "The red Xs indicate which mining areas are completed for closure at this juncture. As you can see, it's nearly primed, laid out in the customary grid pattern. Some sloppy Swiss cheese evidently, but all said and done I think they'll be commencing their blows soon. I know what you're thinking: we all know how that goes. But remember—we get paid by the hour. They want us to sit around on our butts, that's their problem. Post-demo, when Kardashev 7-A is all set, we'll use a crawler to moor the pylons and launch the parasols remotely after the final station liftoff. Any questions?"

Thankfully Stormkast and Østerby had none and pushed to their feet. God, Piper thought as she looked at them, they both must practice those unimpressed stares in the mirror for hours.

"Great," she said. "As I mentioned, our gear is out in the shipping hangar. I'll meet you in twenty and we'll go from there. Consider yourselves dismissed."

After a couple of mock salutes, Østerby and Stormkast lumbered out of the conference room.

Piper scowled. She seriously didn't like anyone playing loose with the act of saluting, least of all a couple of knuckle-shufflers who according to their files never served a day in their lives and thought they were something close to hard. She waited until the two were long gone before she shut down the projected image of Kardashev 7-A and unscrewed a bottle of water.

Earlier, in her quarters and after her workout with that woman who'd been involved with Roscoe's pal, Piper reviewed her orders from The Chimeric Circle. Before her departure her contacts regrettably informed her that efforts were still under way to extract payment from Roscoe's accounts back home, and while they believed his liquidation would likely be a go, they were still giving Roscoe the benefit of the doubt. As the last Mandelbrot skip transport was leaving, time was of the essence, unfortunately, and there was no way to verify their collection efforts had been successful before Piper was prepped and entered her skip stasis. The crux of it was, once the station was repurposed it was destined for a planetoid, not planned for parasol study, and thus Piper would have no further cover job work. Making the long trip would be a real disappointment if The CC called off the hit on Roscoe. Piper agreed to both her assignments only because waxing Roscoe would get her and her fiancé on a stable financial footing.

The Chimeric Circle explained that final approval for taking out Roscoe would be imbedded in a prepackaged paid-for political advertisement that Piper could review on her personal workstation. While not exactly a priority, to keep workers happy and reasonably up to date, the latest media and distractive amusements were the last things to be loaded into a transport's mainframes, Piper's included. At first she found the chosen mode of confirming the kill order a tad cornball, but then she warmed to The CC's twisted, secretive logic. Way out in space no one really paid any attention to the prepackaged marketing drivel bombarding them from home, let alone political ads. With the six-month skip out, by the time any media was consumed the pressing issues of the day back home were outdated anyway. And, honestly, did people's votes even count anymore? No matter. The CC instructed Piper to look for nuanced facial fluctuations in the political ads' subjects to detect the go/cancel message, raging histrionics by a candidate in particular. The more animated the movements the more likely there would be an imbedded message. It was a pain in the neck sifting through all the ads, but a flashy advertisement from the European Confederacy's lunar bases appeared promising. Using her own contraband processing chit and linking a synchronous cipher-translator to the ad's elaborate backend code, Piper scanned the long cascades until she noticed a useless hitch. Converted, the message read:

>target dismissal verified<

Hello, gondola ceremony and happy honeymoon. Piper wished she could share the good news with her fiancé, but for now she simply had to slog along

with her cover work until she arranged for Roscoe's
death and grabbed a skip transport back. Oh, well.
After having her ass handed to her day after day
back on Earth in the PAL, she reminded herself to
consider the mechanics of her job a restful blessing.
With the contract killing compensation coupled with
the pay for her parasol work, it looked like her new
life with her future husband was going to commence
in splendid fashion.

After gathering her paperwork, Piper took a
moment and fished out her necklace. She looked at
her ring and considered stroking the triskelion amulet
to activate the message imbedded by her fiancé. Part
of the gift was a required meaningful exchange. If
she activated the message, the memory inside the
amulet would be erased, and as agreed she would
eventually fill the memory with her own love note
and hand it back to her lover for him to wear. It was
trite and nostalgic, and she wasn't ready to come up
with something to say. But with Roscoe's eradication
a go, Piper felt a full-color thermal holographic of
her fiancé would give her some focus.

She tweaked the amulet and a cone of soft light
glimmered out from the triskelion designs. Her fiancé
spoke softly, with that husky growl she adored.

*"Hey, baby… this is for you. Yeah, I know it's
going to be tough out there being apart, but you've
been through worse, right? Anyway, I'm counting the
minutes, hours, and days until your return. Go get
'em and all my love, always."*

A hokey message, but still it made her smile. Piper

tucked the necklace back under her collar and with a spring in her step she headed off to the shipping hangar to rendezvous with Østerby and Stormkast.

12. JAUNTIN' JIMMY

Jostling to and fro in the frigid oxygen-enriched cockpit, Jimmy shifted gears on the crawler and listened to the toothy hum of the vehicle's tracks beneath the scooped bench.

Back at ASOCC's equipment stores, things had gone much easier than he'd anticipated. Turned out no one said boo about him packing the extra-large long drill, or even asked why he was taking one of the crawlers parked outside ASOCC instead of catching one of the usual surface trams. Commonly, surface trams delivered specialists to their designated work areas, and Jimmy attributed the lack of concern to either general boredom or to crashing the gate at a party. Act like you know what you're doing and before you know it you're as good as, well, gold.

Altogether the bumpy trip out to the Kappa Quadrant from base chewed up about a half hour. Navigating the augered directional beacons and pre-carved ruts, Jimmy kept the vehicle's speed swift and steady, and his stomach was in knots. He thought about the work ahead. The commitment to stealing the gold was surreally realer than real now and there was no turning back.

You can do this.

Glancing at his helmet and rucksack on the bench next to him, Jimmy thought about what his vitals were reading back at ASOCC. There hadn't been a word from Leela yet, which was good, so he took a few deep, purgative breaths and concentrated on driving.

He took a slight bend behind a jagged, pyramidal butte and out onto a low plain, and soon the talus-strewn opening of shaft site Fifty-Seven appeared in the crawler's forward headlamps.

Under a trio of expendable tower lights, a large anchored sandwich-board marker stood with five-seven on each of its opposing faces. Parking close to the trio of towers and marker, Jimmy engaged the stability thrusters and neutralized the crawler's controls.

To save on oxygen and extended battery stores and to avoid accidents, it was standard practice to equalize both the cockpit and the rear compartments on the crawler simultaneously. The crawler was a relatively new model and Jimmy hadn't piloted any crawler in some time, so he pulled a binder from beneath the bench and flipped through the rest of the proper procedures. In minutes everything looked good, so he ran additional checks on his spacesuit and helmet. There were automated safeguards for everything, but edgy as he was he knew even a minor slip-up and he could kiss his ass goodbye. The squashing, merciless threat of space and a few thousand swings in temperature necessitated caution. When all his readings appeared good, Jimmy secured his helmet and glanced at the synced readout on the inside of his visor. Suit stores and auxiliary life processors gave him an immutable exposure window of fifteen hours before he'd have to return to the crawler in order to restock.

Jimmy gripped the scrambler in one glove and finished flicking a series of switches on the forward console with the other. There was a barely audible hum before equalization was confirmed with a green light and a ping.

After climbing out the crawler's cockpit, he sealed an outside lever counterclockwise on the forward hatch and bounced around back to retrieve the long drill from the rear compartment. When he released the lock and opened the hatch, other than the long drill's case the insides of the aft compartment contained two angled banquettes above which a host of supplies were stored in wall-secured cages. He removed the long drill from its case, shoveled out the memory foam, and laid the long drill on top of the foam to keep it secured. Being in marginal gravity, it was always a nuisance to keep things from floating off. After hauling out the emptied case, Jimmy retrieved a satchel full of demolition inlays from one of the wall-secured cages. Minutes later he descended into the tenebrous maw of Fifty-Seven and activated his suit lights.

Inside the shaft, affixing the inlays from the top areas down a hundred and seventy meters to where the gold pocket waited was the call, because if Leela thought something seemed off and insisted on sending out someone else to see what he was doing, his less than honorable intentions wouldn't be immediately evident. Jimmy's fear, though, was if someone did get sent out and checked the rear compartment on the crawler first and found the drill without its case, they might call him out on it. He guessed if that happened he'd have to come up with some excuse.

Navigating his way down to a ledge near where he'd found the pocket, Jimmy secured the large case to an outcropping with two heavy straps and proceeded to slowly hand-over-hand his way back up the shaft. He was well into setting his second demolition inlay up near the shaft opening when the comm link inside his helmet crackled.

"What the fuck do you think you're doing?"

Oh boy… here we go.

In his mind's eye he pictured Leela's little ears growing hot. With her passing on the sugar and going straight for the salt Jimmy assumed there wasn't anyone else on duty yet back at ASOCC.

"This is Specialist Vik, on-site in Fifty-Seven, ASOCC."

"No shit, doofus. Please clarify why you've taken a crawler unauthorized, over."

Jimmy paused. He'd thought about this. He'd imagined what he would say, how he would say it, what buttons he could push with Leela, all in an effort to make sure what he was doing appeared truly reasonable. Not overly partial to lying, Jimmy was, however, a decent card player and fairly skilled at the bluff. Keep it short and sweet, he told himself. Short and sweet, but not too sweet.

Project poise and keep your cool. Be professional.

"ASOCC, Specialist Vik has given the timeline discussed earlier with management some thought. At present demolition inlays are being attached in reverse sequence."

Leela responded tersely. "I repeat, crawler use was not authorized."

"Can I at least explain?"

"Oh, this should be a pip."

"The crawler was necessary to pack a long drill. The screwbolts that were finicky before are now holding, over."

"Say again. Did you just say you took a long drill too?"

"The flaking," Jimmy clarified. "I thought a long drill could free up the troublesome layers I told you about, and it's working. I'm positive I can finish up the inlays with an extended shift, back-to-back protocol. The way things are going it might not even take that long. How's that for a tidy completion forecast?"

Leela didn't respond, so Jimmy counted to ten.

It was, as they say, an eternity.

"Specialist Vik, this initiative was not, repeat, was not approved by ASOCC. Do you copy?"

"Yeah, I copy. Have you had your tea yet?"

"What?"

"I said, have you had your tea yet?"

"Never mind my goddamn tea, you jerk. Taking a crawler and a long drill and setting off on a solo back-to-back without proper authorization is—"

"I know, audacious of me. Look, I'd really like to

elaborate but, gee, is there any way we could do this off the record, over?"

"Nothing is off the record, Specialist Vik. You know that."

"All right, but let's just say I'd rather not be airing our dirty laundry over the comm link. All this lobbing back and forth, conversations like this are permanent. My guess is you don't want that."

A second, horrible eternity. Times two.

Maybe three or four.

Jimmy suddenly became aware of a thickening sensation in his bladder and remembered the extra-large coffee he drank earlier. Stupid diuretic. He should have peed in the crawler's waste sleeve before equalization and heading off. Jimmy really hated relieving himself in his spacesuit.

"ASOCC, Specialist Vik requests an offline conference, over."

"Goddamn it, stand by."

"Standing by, ASOCC."

Jimmy kept drilling with his portable and retrieved another screwbolt from the satchel tethered to his waist. Each inlay needed seven of the titanium screwbolts in order to be set properly, and the screwbolts needed to be tested for strength before he could move on. He turned his head and let his suit lights flood the shaft's crevasse below him. A couple of hundred meters down, he could barely make out the outcropping where he had secured the empty drill case. From where he floated, the straps looked like they were holding, but the distance down there and the work ahead of him—he'd another twenty-plus inlays to set before he could work on cutting out the gold.

Jimmy's thoughts waffled. This was so crazy. There was no way Leela was going to be good with what he'd done. Right now, with her telling him to stand by, in all likelihood she was probably wigging out back at the command center and thinking of nine different ways of torpedoing his and Jock's plan. For all he knew she might be getting those Chinese brothers to come out and take over for him. *Oh man*, Jimmy thought. He was so toast.

"Specialist Vik, ASOCC agrees to your request for a private dialog. Switch comm link over to channel six immediately, over."

"Roger."

Jimmy reset the comm channel on his wrist pad. When Leela's voice intensified to a sharp screech he winced.

Wow, if you think space is cold…

"You idiot!"

"Before you say another word, Leela, corral your ponies for a second." Jimmy secured another screwbolt and pulled on the head. "I've been thinking. You're right. I'm ashamed to admit it, but all this time you've always been right. I know this might sound strange, but I got to say… I'm feeling a bit put out admitting just how right you've always been."

"What in God's name are you talking about?"

"Me."

"You? What do you mean *you*?"

"Me. My attitude and behavior. Me."

"Oh, for the love of—I'm not your priest, Jimmy."

"No, you most certainly are not. Come to think of it, do people still have priests?" Jimmy lined up another screwbolt. It slipped and started to drift off, but he caught it and lined it up again. "Never mind. What I'm trying to say here, Leela, is... call it conceit, call it me being a typical testosterone-crippled jackass, but you've always known me better than I've known myself."

"Well, gee, la-dee-dah. Bite me and so forth, okay? What's that got to do with anything?"

"Well, I can't count the number of times when you've told me how I never really applied myself or even tried to live up to my potential. Anyway, after we talked in the locker room I got to thinking. Maybe it's time I did better."

"Totally irrelevant."

"No, it's not."

"All right, so you want to do better. Hooray and hurrah for you. So you want to do better at what exactly?"

"I don't know. I want to be a better person, I guess."

Leela's voice tightened. "I don't see how any of this has to do with you pulling this unauthorized nonsense."

"Please, Leela, just let me finish." Jimmy bent forward and rested his helmet against the shaft wall. "Look, I know that lately I've been at the top of your shitlist. Lord knows, you've got your reasons and the right. Man... I thought all this would be easier for me to say, but you and me? Our relationship, before and now, the way I've been so distant and scattered? There's no question I've been a complete ass."

"No argument here."

"Okay, so I want to prove to you I'm capable of doing better. Not only doing better as an Azoick employee, but I want to prove to you that I'm capable of doing better by others in general. I know I sidestepped the proper procedures, but I'm out here now and things are going great."

Leela sighed. "You've really put me in a very difficult spot here, Jimmy."

"No, I haven't."

"Yes, you have! This is way, way out of line. And now is definitely not the appropriate time for a discussion like this. Confidential dropouts are looked down on, so what am I going to say, huh? Sorry, but my ex-boyfriend had a moral crisis? God, this is so typical of you. So selfish."

Man, if she only knew the half of it.

"I know," Jimmy said, "but all this... couldn't you, I don't know, put some sort of managerial shine on it? For old times' sake?"

Leela hit the comm's squelch button. Jimmy winced again.

"Managerial shine? I can't believe you! You know what this is? This is nothing but a grade A pile of bullshit, that's what this is. What, you think I'm going to put my job in jeopardy just because you've had some long-overdue personal revelation and suddenly feel now is the time to announce you want to be a new man? Holy creeping crap, Jimmy, get over yourself. Azoick regulations are clear. And I am not, repeat, I am not going to cover for you. Get off site and return to base at once, over."

"Negative."

"*WHAT?*"

"I said, negative. Look, I'm setting up my fourth inlay now."

Being barely on his second, this was, of course, a brazen lie, but Jimmy needed a break to pull Leela off of her recalcitrant position. The subsequent pause on the other end wasn't exactly another eternity, but as the length of time grew Jimmy had a sense that Leela's hidebound mental wheels might be turning in his favor.

"Did you say you're on your fourth inlay?" she asked.

"Affirmative."

"God, just how long have you been out there?"

"Not long at all," Jimmy replied. "I had an extra-large coffee before I set out, and I've been ripping right along."

"But you're on your fourth inlay? That's, why, that's outstanding."

"Thanks."

"But even so, that still doesn't excuse what you've done."

"Done to who? To you or to the company guidelines?"

"You know what I mean. Stop playing games."

"But I'm not playing games, Leela, I swear. And

don't order me back to base. Look, you want to reprimand me? You want to bust me down to some chuck bucket detail, punch my ticket with Azoick or kick me off this damn rock, then do it. But don't order me back to base. And don't dump all over my aspirations and tell me I'm incapable of change."

The next eternity was the absolute worst—a throbbing void of tenterhooked nothingness with only the feathering in-and-out *psshing* sound of Jimmy's breath. Like a stunned mule, a slow minute plodded by until eventually Jimmy thought, *well, that's it. Game over.* Any more pleading with Leela on his part and she'd probably assess his resolve as weak. If she didn't elect to cover for him, so much for Jimmy's tentative secondary plan of ticking her off further and getting himself canned from Kardashev 7-A and Azoick altogether. Jimmy grieved over how he'd have to pinball down the shaft and fit as many demolition inlays above the gold as he could before heading back to base, and the vivid knowledge that his new life as a rich man was now kaput was gutting. Of course Jock would be completely cheesed that everything went tits up, but screw Jock. Who ever said life was fair? All evidence proved otherwise.

"Leela, do you copy?"

"Stand by, you son of a bitch."

"Son of a bitch standing by."

Jimmy stayed on task and kept drilling and testing the screwbolts as the last shreds of his hopes withered away. When at last he heard a lengthy, exasperated breath in his ear he imagined the sound being a gust of karmic wind sucking him off a cliff.

"Oh, all right," Leela said grudgingly.

Jimmy repressed a laugh and his whole face contracted.

Whoo-hoo!

He couldn't believe it! The jubilation that Leela had been coaxed into cutting him some slack prompted a quick happy jig and tight fist pump. "Really?"

"Yeah," Leela said. "I must be out of my gourd to agree to it, but if what you're telling me is true and you're already on your fourth inlay, well, I guess I could think of something to make it look good."

Jimmy's face relaxed. "Oh, man, that's great, Leela. That's just great."

"But I want updates, you hear? Updates on the hour and by the book while I'm on shift. For the rest of your back-to-back, if it comes to that, log your hourlies per procedure and forward all your time files to ASOCC. Don't futz with those hourlies because you know I'll check."

"You've got it."

"I suppose I could put it all on what's his name—Dickerson. Shouldn't be too hard to pin it on that goldbricking dolt. I'll say you two cleared all this baloney verbally and Dickerson neglected to file the proper authorizations before he pulled his medical."

"Hey, sounds good to me."

"But listen up, Renaissance Man," Leela warned. "If you have the slightest problem out there, and I mean the slightest, or if you can't finish the work on your back-to-back, or if you fail to log in your hourlies after I'm off shift? You'll be cleaning vertical trapezoid mills for the remainder of the Kardashev 7-A operation, as well as your next Azoick assignment, wherever that may be. Got it?"

"Copy that. Gee, thanks, Leela. I really owe you one."

"You owe me nothing. Just don't screw up."

"I won't."

"Good. Switch back to the primary comm channel now, over."

Jimmy knew he needed to cherry the sundae, so to speak, so he quickly deterred Leela from going back to the primary channel.

"Leela, hold on…"

"God, what is it *now*?"

Jimmy took a sip from his hydration tube and swallowed. His next fabrication was going to be a doozy. With his plan of getting fired, Jimmy believed it was necessary to gussy up the circumstances a bit to ensure believability. No doubt in hindsight it might have been easier to break some other regulation to get canned, but to really sell it and get himself bounced for good Jimmy felt he needed to fashion a pattern of behavior. He needed to cozen Leela's perceptions. Despite outward appearances, Jimmy knew Leela's feelings were still tender, and admittedly at first he'd some hesitations about manipulating her in such a cruel way. But then he reminded himself of his soon-to-be new life and wealth. Perhaps somewhere down the line he would make it up to her. Send her an anonymous gift or something. Roses on her birthday.

"Um, I was thinking, you and me… maybe later if you're free, we could, I don't know, maybe we could, like, talk."

Alas, there were no more eternities.

"What did you just say?"

Jimmy screwed up his face. "Um, yeah. Like, I was thinking. Perhaps I could stop by your quarters, or if that's not cool, maybe we could take a walk out to the observation bubble or something like we used to. This new man stuff, it's kind of funny, but there's been a lot of other things on my mind lately too."

Leela hit the squelch button again, and Jimmy dreaded that maybe he'd taken things too far. Oh man… would Leela change her mind and renege on covering for him?

Oh, please… no.

Leela responded, "You're a real piece of work, you know that? You want to talk after the way you've humiliated me? I mean, why? Why now?"

"I told you, I've been thinking."

"Oh, well, if you're all disposed to go on and on about mending your shortcomings maybe you ought to take it up with your buddy Jock. I'm sure that maggot has plenty of regrets with his fucked-up life."

What?

"Jock?" Jimmy asked.

"Yeah, I ran into one of the solar parasol scabs in the gym before I clocked in. She said you two were as thick as thieves in the canteen. Maybe that slimebucket has some insight into your new reinvention, though I doubt it."

Blinking rapidly, Jimmy pushed back from the shaft wall. "What does me talking with Jock have to do with anything?"

"I don't know, but I've told you a thousand times, Jimmy. You really ought to stay away from that guy."

In retrospect it may have been foretelling, but like so many admonitions Jimmy chose to ignore in his life at that point he'd no way of knowing just how right Leela would turn out to be.

13. TOP UP, HOMUNCULUS

After lassoing the loop of an IV bag around the neck of the life-sized cardboard cutout of Miss Jupiter 2772 and piercing his left arm with a properly gauged catheter, Jock lined up a hypodermic, inserted the twelve millimeter needle, and released an enriched trans-amphetamine elixir into his distressed system.

Jock had a number of pilfered medical supplies in his quarters. Anesthetics. Top-notch antibiotics and anti-depressant mood euphoriants. He'd set aside several vials of his current specifically fabricated concoction for those times when judiciousness failed him and he didn't have the stamina to lard his way through. He was getting on in years, and with senescence it seemed Jock's limits at elbow bending had once again failed him. Not being able to hang out the cat like he used to was getting to be a real drag.

Minutes later, however, the IV cocktail worked its magic and he felt reborn. Not as bright as a waking baby, per se, but alert enough to be hungry. Picking up a package of barbecued-flavored soy jerky, he fed a leathery staff into his mouth. With his vim on the mend, at least now he could think straight.

Ninety-eight percent purity at fifty kilos...

Good God almighty, how fortunate was he? Of all people, Jimmy Vik dropping this propitious salvation in his lap—it was as if Kismet had at last set its light upon him and now it was up to Jock to make it all work out in his favor. Of course with Jimmy he'd paraded keen savoir-faire and excitement, because he knew better than to show trepidation with such an opportunity in play, but holy hell—a score like this? This sort of thing only came along once in a lifetime. Ten lifetimes. Eager as he was, Jock was still a pragmatist at heart. Most of the time, with intrigues and schemes of lesser bents, he knew that these things unraveled without due diligence. There were so many quirks and budding snafus to consider.

Poor, deluded Jimmy. There wasn't a cold chance in hell he was going to let some hump like him come out on top with all this. It was a shame, Jock supposed. Essentially he liked Jimmy (as much as he liked anyone, which wasn't saying much), but with so much profit before him Jock needed to keep up the "uff" in his buffaloing. Hell, fifty kilos of gold was a king's ransom, a fortune with zeroes stretching out like a long string of shiny balloons.

Swallowing a rough portion of the jerky, Jock thought about how he and Jimmy had gone on about trust not being a one-way proposition. Ha. To Jock trust wasn't a proposition at all. With Jimmy out at Fifty-Seven doing all the hard work and banking on Jock playing fair that was Jimmy's biggest mistake. The man's half-share grandeur dreams of *la dolce vita* were on borrowed time.

Back down at his quarters, when he'd shared the somewhat shady ins-and-outs of getting the gold back to Earth, Jock had mentioned a reliable associate in Hong Kong, and once again he admired his own skills at the anecdotal cha-cha. When crafting a good con, it was essential to bowl over an unsuspecting mark with liberally strewn mercurial half-truths and exotics. Maybe it was because he was all starry-eyed about becoming well-heeled, but Jimmy had lapped up all of Jock's talk about Hong Kong like a champ. Despite societal upheavals, conflicts, and geopolitical collapses, for centuries Hong Kong had held on to its enigmatic repute for being a mercantile haven. The fact was, however, Jock had never set foot in Hong Kong in his life. He was shocked he even remembered the name of the bloody interstellar skyport. But he reckoned with a suggestive double-entendre name like Chek Lap Kok, the skyport's name must have stuck in his memory somehow. Certainly he'd read about the seamy hostess club offerings in the Wan Chai district, but the closest Jock had ever come to the city was picking up a takeaway order. Steamed spring rolls and maybe a side order of deep-fried tank prawns.

No, Jock had already worked out the gold's final destination, and the terminus was someplace where Jimmy Vik and his tiny mind, if he lived long enough, would never know. Going forward all that was needed now was for Zaafer to load the gold and adjust the coordinates into a quarantine hold.

Bloody Zaafer. By all measures, that dumb kid was clueless. Surely before he made his skip back Zaafer would be another wretched chore that Jock would have to scratch off his list, and while he had an inkling on how to take care of the young tech, Jimmy Vik presented a more distinct problem. Jimmy was a grown man. While he was affable, from experience Jock knew that a grown man (certainly a former rugby halfback like Jimmy) if dicked over could turn violent. Blowing sunshine up Jimmy's arse would only go so far, and after a hungover Jock had blown up at him, Jimmy seemed tense and suspicious. Yet with Jimmy voicing his intention to get fired from Azoick proper, it shouldn't be too hard to lose him completely, possibly before Jock and the gold made it back to Earth. So much booty, if Jock got it all back home, not only could he pay off The CC, he could hire a private army of bodyguards and build himself a fortress. If Jimmy did try to track him down to seek retribution, then, sadly, a more sinister end would be required.

Jock looked over his shoulder and noted the IV hung around Miss Jupiter had wilted. After carefully removing the catheter needle, he swabbed the puncture in his arm with a couple of crumpled tissues. Then he traipsed to his bathroom, squirted some cologne on his face and armpits, and got dressed.

Bah, it could be all conjecture at this point anyway, Jock thought. The gold wasn't actually secured and in hand just yet.

Perhaps Leela Pendergast had already put the scrap on things.

14. SCRAMBLIN' RAMBLIN'

As he completed the seventh demolition inlay, the scrambler on Jimmy's spacesuit hummed. After holstering his portable drill and unhooking the scrambler from his waist, Jimmy stared at a flashing green prompt on the device's oval screen.

: status?

Okay, Jimmy thought. Jock had said to keep things brief, but he hadn't specified whether they should use standard operative responses or Q-codes, so how was he supposed to reply? Jock was insistent no one would pick up on the sub-space frequency, yet at the same time Jimmy didn't want to give anything away. He poked in a message and then tapped the SEND key.

: all +.

Jock responded quickly.

: xclnt.

Jimmy killed the link, secured the scrambler back to his belt, and began attaching the next demolition inlay. Since smoothing things over with Leela it'd been slow going down the shaft, so to pass the time he tried picturing his new life back home with a wide-open future. Lots and lots of teasing images. Jimmy saw himself slicing long laps in that condo pool near the monomictic shores of Lake Titicaca and wading out at the shallow end to bake in the morning sun like a fat reptile. He pictured unhassled idle time, enjoying all those things he'd never gotten around to—buying nicer clothes, actual art, and stuff he never could afford. Strangely, though, after a while Leela kept appearing in Jimmy's reveries. Damn, if all this ended up with him being caught, what would Leela even say? There was no question she would be disappointed in him and pissed off. Seismic eruptions would have more restraint. He held out a modicum of hope that if he were arrested, Leela would be terrified of what would happen to him. The terrors of medical experiments and incarceration, such things weighed against her disillusionment and heartache felt trivial somehow. Yeah, he and Leela weren't together anymore, but both of Jimmy's parents were dead. Despite her agitations, he recognized that deep down Leela still cared for him. He had to admit he too still had unresolved feelings for Leela. Maybe letting her go had been a mistake. If he was caught, letting her down would likely be the hardest thing Jimmy would have to bear.

Hours before, when Jock had asked him if Leela was in on the gold situation, the suggestion had seemed preposterous, but now it had Jimmy wondering. Was it so hard to picture? No, Leela didn't have a dishonest bone in her body. She was a straight shooter. A pure gem and one of the good ones, or so many said. Still, it was amusing to think about. While her pedantic qualities could drive just about anyone up a fucking wall, Leela's dogged devotion to fussy detail would have made her a terrific partner—a perfect Bonnie to Jimmy's Clyde.

People always took smug satisfaction in their touted principles, but in Jimmy's mind all that always seemed like a bunch of hooey. True, maybe he was being cynical, but anybody with a lick of sense knew the game was rigged. Go ahead, lay a sack of potential millions on a table and see just how long the so-called lofty morals held out.

As promised, Jimmy kept up with all his ASOCC hourly check-ins. Working faster than he normally would he also made sure to keep an eye on his exertions, but Leela didn't mention anything out of the ordinary so he figured that was something. Finally, he finished all the required inlays and reached the outcropping near the gold pocket. Resting next to the case, Jimmy let his spacesuit's wicking mechanisms siphon off his accrued sweat as he thumbed out another message to Jock on the scrambler.

: @honeypot.

Jock replied a few seconds later, a series of colons and right parentheses—five smiley faces all in a row.

Man, Jimmy thought.

What a dork.

15. SOME BLACK-FEATHERED NEWS

Several hours later in ASOCC, Leela was almost through her and all of Dickerson's unfinished tasks when the Azoick envoy aboard the *Adamant* requested a Priority B conference. Nearly everyone of the management team getting ready to knock off their work cycles simultaneously let out long groans.

Really? A Priority B conference?

This had better be good.

They all sat back down at their consoles as the message from the *Adamant* appeared on their screens. A man of Persian descent and somewhat obvious epicene flair stepped into the live feed and as closed translations slid beneath his visage, he spoke cheerfully.

[AZOICK VESSEL ADAMANT - 67230]
[REF. PB CONF. – SHALAD, Y. - 3.23.2778GMT]
[-START MESSAGE-]

"Kardashev 7-A station, this is Azoick envoy Yaser Shalad, and I hope this communication finds you well.

[BREAK]

As you know, not long ago per OST the *Adamant*

secured its operative orbit. While this is exceptionally good news that we are at last ready for final cargo transfers, the captain of the *Adamant* has conveyed to me a matter of some note."

[BREAK]

"Shortly after dropping out of our skip and crossing into your sector, the *Adamant*'s sensors detected a distress signal during its routine negative-parabolic trajectory sweeps of the skip corridor. Signal origin has been confirmed—an unmanned expeditionary vessel of the Omega Class identified as the *De Silento*, operated by Enlai Universal, weighing in at an estimated seventy-one metric tons. A long-range image capture of the *De Silento* is attached to this message, along with a recording of the signal, so please open both of these files for review now."

[BREAK]

"The *De Silento*'s distress signal does not specify the nature of its current problem. However, given the less than solicitous relations between our two competitive companies and the fact that the *De Silento* is unmanned, it is my responsibility as the Azoick envoy to inform you that this situation is not a matter of concern."

[BREAK]

"In due course, perhaps our company's solicitors will request further information from Enlai Universal vis-à-vis possible assistance and/or future salvage once the *Adamant* makes its skip back, but, to be candid, given the contested claim realignments in the sector, coupled with Enlai Universal's failed proxy fight with our company three years ago, the distressed Omega-Class's troubles should be considered our gain. A providential black swan, so to speak."

[BREAK]

"This concludes this message. On behalf of Azoick, the captain and the crew of the *Adamant*, congratulations on completing your extended mission to Kardashev 7-A."

[AZOICK VESSEL ADAMANT - 67230]
[REF. PB CONF. SHALAD, Y. 3.23.2778GMT]
[END MESSAGE-]

With the swipe of a finger, Leela moved the contents of the dispatch and the attached files to her pending screen and enlarged and scoured the long-range image capture. On initial perusal, the limpet-textured fuselage of the *De Silento* appeared normal, so Leela accessed secondary images of similar Omega-Class craft and laid these images over the LRIC. Funny how the skills you learned playing concentration games as a child never failed to come in handy later in life. *One of these things is not like the other.* After flopping the LRIC ninety degrees and comparing it against the specs of two nearly identical Omega-Class vessels, the nature of the problem became apparent. A whole propulsion booster on the *De Silento*'s starboard side appeared to be missing, with visible spavined scarring near its stern. It might be a fixable problem, but Leela understood that without staff aboard to address the issue the *De Silento* was pretty much screwed.

Before closing the files, she logged her analysis and included some additional observations for the record. Pushing back in her chair, she counted down from ten, waiting on the ever-predictable, quasi-allegiant grousing from her ASOCC colleagues.

"Typical," someone said. "Even money says that Omega-Class had a programming failure. Don't those Enlai cats use that outdated vectorware?"

Someone else chimed in. "Hey, what's a black swan anyway?"

Leela sighed. "In fiscal jargon, black swans describe measurable pluses coming out of perceived significant negatives. Most militaries use the term to describe an extremely unlikely event."

This was met with lots of well-impressed *oohs* and *ahhs*, and then a moment later someone else let fly some pejorative sarcasm. "Hey now, check out the smarty pants. Black quackery aside, what I want to know is: is this really the best LRIC the *Adamant* can give us? Shit, that Omega-Class looks pretty buttoned-up to me."

"Enlarge the image and flop it ninety degrees," Leela said.

"What?"

"I said flop it ninety degrees and bump up res to four hundred percent. Crosscheck the LRIC against available Omega-Class specs and then do a pull back and overlay comparison. Oh, hell, I'll just forward the analysis."

Leela waited for her chronically obtuse

colleagues to catch up and when they did she heard delighted snickers.

"Yeah," she explained, "right there. Looks like a whole propulsion booster is gone. There must've been an explosion or something before it dropped out of their skip. Systems defaults probably instigated a complete shutdown."

Leela rose and consulted with the rest of the team in ASOCC. After some speculation on what might have happened with the *De Silento*, the consensus was that Enlai Universal had a major problem on their hands, but so what? It wasn't theirs. If the Azoick envoy elected to do a Priority B conference and was dropping smack about black swans, then too bad for Enlai Universal. An all too common story. You could have the best technology at your beck and call, but it never negated the fact that in deep space you were on your own. So when something went wrong, it usually happened spectacularly. After some more discussion it was agreed that since Leela had identified the problem she ought to be the one to draft a bulletin for the rest of the personnel on station. In all likelihood the bulletin would be ignored, but Leela acquiesced to the task only because her mind was elsewhere.

16. JOCK ON THE CLOCK

Ensconced in his crescent-shaped console, itself encysted in a tall, thick-glassed platform kiosk at the hub of the shipping hangar, Jock Roscoe gave off the overall impression of an ascetic stylite. Camouflaged behind the eerie, bluish aquarium-like glow of projected data screens, he surreptitiously glanced at Jimmy's message on the buzzing scrambler resting to his right thigh.

: 0.10 complete.

Ah-ha. It looked like Jimmy was ten percent of the way done with the extraction. It was fantastic news and immediately Jock's thoughts tracked back to his outstanding issues with The Chimeric Circle.

Those animals, them and their unappeasable reach. Jock wondered if he hadn't been such a dipstick, would he still be doing all this?

The source of Jock's woes with The CC had been a sure thing that turned out to be anything but. A football club wager with odds locked in at fifty-to-one. Jock had secured inside information that a goaltender on one of the clubs was looking to throw the match because he had foolishly made a bargain to cover an immense medical bill. While football club professionals were outrageously salaried, like a Trojan horse a crippling virus had afflicted the goaltender's extended family back in his birthplace of Cabo Verde. The virus was nearly impossible to cure (not without evacuation to premier medical care facilities) and, as was typical of someone coming from impoverished means, the goaltender hadn't been careful with his compensations or his marital fidelities (six divorces in eight years). The goaltender was desperate. The governing bodies of the Greater Africa Alliance, European Confederacy, and elsewhere had blockaded the small island to ensure the contagion was contained, so on top of expensive medical treatment the goaltender needed to hire a team of mercenaries to extricate his family, and the staggering costs had him in a bind.

Confident that the fix was in, Jock leveraged nearly three-quarters of his savings on the wager. However, in the fury of play the goaltender's muscle memory spoiled everything. As the final seconds of the match ticked down, he blocked a freakish kick by the opposing team and that was, as they say, that. Jock couldn't have cared less when later he heard the goaltender had committed suicide by hanging himself from a streetlamp outside the stadium. The Chimeric Circle had Jock dead to rights, and they expected him to pay up.

So now, even if The CC purportedly did have someone on station keeping tabs on him, with things so far going according to plan Jock believed it was nearly *auf Wiedersehen* and *sayonara* to all his troubles.

Jock typed in his approval of Jimmy's update and then hit SEND.

Now it was time for a little schedule tweaking on Jock's end.

Using Zaafer's Azoick identification number and password, Jock immediately accessed the timetables for surface crawler maintenance and deliberated what exactly, if any future scrutinizing came to pass, would appear routine. Jock supposed he could move up a seal inspection on the crawler Jimmy took, as seal inspections on crawlers happened all the time. As he modified the timetable and appropriate data, Jock made certain to pepper in some of Zaafer's painfully repentant syntax and some bad spelling to make things look good.

MAINTENANCE AMMENDMENT: Plenty complant w/ Crawler 4's forward operationl seels. Regret overhaul of seels recomended. Est. labor time ½ hr., befor vehickle reuse. Deeply sorry for trouble. Daavi Z.- 3.23.2778GMT

Too bad Jock couldn't work a few more "sorrys" in there.

As it was hashed out, once Jimmy returned the crawler to base he'd drive it right into the maintenance area for the final transfer of the gold in the drill case. By the time Jimmy completed his back-to-back, the *Adamant* would be locked into one of the SPO's greater orbital patterns and most of the tenders would have already descended to the shipping hangar's armadillo bays. Once the tenders were docked and loading had commenced, Jock would wait an appropriate amount of time and then implement the diversion.

Zaafer could take it from there.

17. WHAT NOW, NOW WHAT?

Strenuous hours later, Jimmy pulled the drill case inside, yanked the crawler's aft hatch closed, and engaged the rear compartment's atmospheric seals. After sliding sideways onto one of the two padded banquettes, he looked upward, caught his breath, and waited for the rear compartment to pressurize. When the whirling aerosol blast of decontamination vapors abated, an indicator light opposite him finally switched from red "thumbs down" pictogram to green "thumbs up" with a sprightly C-sharp note.

Jimmy removed his helmet and gloves and threw them to the floor with disgust. Squeezing his temples with the heels of his hands, he screamed until his lungs burned.

"This is soooooo fuuuuuucked!"

Within the first half hour of his cutting into the shaft pocket, the larger promise of a significant gold seam proved to be a bust. At first Jimmy thought he'd made an error and speculated that maybe he wasn't cutting at the correct angle or wasn't even at the proper spot. There was limited visibility below the surface and, yes, if he was disorientated it wouldn't be the first time, but he double-checked his orientation and depth. There was no question he was in the right place and for that first few minutes he'd extracted hunks of the gold out of the shaft wall as easily as if he was drawing out supple pats of butter. But then nothing.

Of course, hitting a void in a mineral deposit wasn't all that uncommon. After all, moons and SPOs weren't some neatly layered tub of Neapolitan ice cream. Disturbingly, though, the more Jimmy pruned away at the surrounding rock the more the void grew. And soon he was cutting into absolute zilch.

Jimmy wanted to scream, but with Leela keeping an eye on him he knew he couldn't. Holy hell, how could he have misestimated the size and depth of the pocket? Did he simply imagine it altogether? Bearing down, he cut deeper for another hour until the muscles in his arms stung, but no matter what he tried, no matter how much loose rock Jimmy pulled away or even how much he increased the laser cutter's power, the fact was undeniable. He was unequivocally and majestically boned.

No wonder the trace scans had missed the shallow anomaly.

Oh man...

Jimmy felt like a world-class boob. So much for his grand plans to check out of the mining life, so much for the Cordillera Real grottos and kicking it poolside with the lovely señoritas along the filtered, lapping shores of Lake Titicaca. Brother, kiss all that goodbye.

Prudently, Jimmy had not directly communicated the devastating developments back to Jock at base. Holstering the laser cutter instead, he'd quickly examined the small amount of gold he'd already placed inside the anchored drill case. All in all, an eyeball estimate of what he'd extracted if you trimmed the excess clinging rock and adjusted for weight was maybe three and a half rough kilos at the most. Halved down the middle as agreed and at estimated market evaluation it was still a respectable score, but it certainly wasn't anyone's idea of a fortune. Well, maybe a small fortune for one of them. Before Jimmy told him there might be fifty kilos' worth in the shaft, Jock was fairly put out by the consequences of a capital one corporate offense, so he wondered if Jock would be down for all this chicanery if the payday was whittled down to a ridiculous nub. Not likely. He had his debts to The Chimeric Circle to consider.

Jimmy then speculated on Jock's earlier evasiveness regarding which armadillo bay was going to be used, his failure to mention Zaafer, and the supposed scribbled-down coordinates in Hong Kong. Between their first discussion and when he'd picked up the scrambler, his partner's bearing had shifted significantly, so vein bust notwithstanding, Jimmy started to wonder if Jock was already hustling him. Frankly, it wouldn't surprise him in the least that he was being bamboozled. He'd laid a lot of foolish faith on the line with Jock.

You're so out of your element…

Crap, this was supposed to be a simple and straightforward scam, a way of getting clear of this mining life forever and starting over, but now, with less than four kilos extracted, things had become very cloudy indeed.

Jimmy then had an idea.

For his own protection he'd better take steps and hedge his bets.

18.BAITING THE TRAP

On her haunches, Piper verified Stormkast and Østerby's data and operational checks on a portable CPU.

"Okay," she announced, "everything is looking real good. Remote ignitions are clean and the diamond-caliper cables are tight. Everything seems set. Good work, people."

Stormkast and Østerby crossed their arms.

Piper looked up. "Is there a problem?"

"Mind if we, like, knock off, chief?" Stormkast asked.

Piper dropped backward and sat on her butt. Like a Zen monk, she crossed her legs and welded her gaze on the two men. "You two in some hurry to be someplace special?"

"Well," Stormkast said, "me and Østerby here have been working straight through, so we were thinking about catching a bite to eat."

Piper checked the time on a floating digitalized orb just below the ceiling of the shipping hangar. Funny, even with the calliope riff of Einsteinian relativity in space, time sure did fly. Stormkast and Østerby had done everything she'd asked of them without complaint or fault. Now that their parasol gear was all packed up and ready for their assignment, grabbing a bite to eat wasn't an unreasonable request, she supposed.

"You two must have cast-iron constitutions," Piper said.

Stormkast shrugged. "Hey, it's not the worst grub we've ever had. Slather on enough hot sauce and down enough drink and anything can be palatable."

Piper flapped a hand. "Have at it. I'll check in with you two later in the canteen."

To save herself the aggravation, Piper elected not to supplement her approval with a "dismissed" and Østerby and Stormkast headed out.

It took her a few more minutes to properly close out all the open files on the CPU before Piper was able to reset the hard drive's security measures and pass codes. When finished, she clammed the portable computer together and rolled a pair of mortise locks along its side as a final protective measure. Bowling forward onto her stomach, Piper did a short set of twenty push-ups and a long "downward dog" yoga stretch and then leapt to her feet. Somewhere overhead a brief three-count horn sounded, and then an advisory over the hangar's PA system garbled with distortion:

Notice: Azoick Vessel 67230 *Adamant* has successfully acquired orbital pattern. Tender descents now confirmed and on schedule. Designated

personnel, please prepare armadillo bays A through Z
for cargo loading.

Looking around, Piper realized not far away in
a tall kiosk at the center of the main hangar Jock
Roscoe was watching her. Hmm, she thought, maybe
it was time to finally introduce herself. Work up a
little coquettish chit-chat, make the cue-ball deadbeat
see her in a friendly way so when it came time to take
down his sorry ass she could draw him in close. Piper
tucked the CPU under her arm and ankled her way
across the hangar. Approaching the kiosk, she gave
Roscoe a nod and a wave.

Jock keyed a bone mic hooked to his ear, and
his voice spat like a sizzle of hot fat from an
external speaker.

"Can I help you?"

Piper batted her eyelashes. "Oh, no. I'm fine. I was
just saying hello is all."

Jock keyed the bone mic again. "Oh… well, hello
to you too. Hey, you're one of the subcontractors
Azoick brought in for the parasol studies, aren't you?"

*Duh, like you haven't been watching me all the
livelong day, dead man.*

"Yes, I am," Piper acknowledged spryly. "I hope
you don't hold it against me. Lots of people around
here, well, they've been sort of giving us the cold
shoulder ever since we arrived."

Jock pushed to his feet. "Well now, you're just
doing your job. I can't really take issue with anyone
trying to make a living."

"Seems like you're the exception, but thanks. My name is Piper, by the way."

"Oh, I know."

"You do?"

"Sure," Jock replied. "Word gets around. And a dandy handle like that? A name like yours is hard to miss. But I'm happy to say it's a pleasure to finally make your acquaintance. People on station know me as Jock."

Piper smiled. "So, do you run the whole show out here?"

"Oh, I wouldn't say run," Jock said, angling his head with affected modesty. "I merely keep things functioning as they should. You know, make sure the designated cargo gets to where it's intended to go, some occasional machine maintenance and inventories, that sort of thing. Pretty much easy-peasy-lemon-squeezy, but don't tell anyone I said that. I like to keep people mystified." He pointed to the packed-up parasol gear behind her. "So, are you folks out for a long haul or is this just a one and done posting for you?"

Following his gaze to the equipment and then turning back, Piper said, "I'm afraid it's a temporary duty yonder for me. After the parasols get deployed I'm going to catch the next available ride for a skip back. Actually, this is the furthest I've ever been out. The other two guys on my team, I don't know. They might have other plans, but I'm not sticking around." After a pause she added, "Must get real lonely out here."

"Lonely?"

"Yeah."

"In what way?"

Piper tossed her blonde hair flirtatiously. "Well, you know, deep space and a remote station, same faces all the time for months and months and months. I mean, I know it's my job and all, but I like the proximity to Earth and the quicker turn-and-burns out and back of my own solar system. Don't get me wrong. It's a thrill to be way out here in deep space, but being so far from home is kind of freaking me out."

"Aw, you just have to put it out of your mind."

"Easier said than done. It'll be months before I get back." Detecting a mild flutter in Jock's throat, Piper intentionally decided against mentioning anything about her fiancé. "You know, I don't normally like to comment on such personal things, but I really like your tattoos. Looks like you went all in."

Jock peeled a palm over the crown of his inky dome. "Oh, you're a fan of art, are you?"

Turning sideways, Piper pulled back her weskit and unzipped her red bodysuit. Underneath she wore a supportive black tank top and, baring a shoulder so he could see, she gave Roscoe a good view of one of her own tattoos. God, Piper thought, if her fiancé saw him ogling her like that he would beat him to pulp. Oh well, when in Rome…

"Been in the wars, I see."

"Yes, sir. Joint-engineering corps, PAL."

"One of the demagogic oligarchies or the Southern Alliance?"

"Splitting hairs, but the Southern Alliance. Argentine."

"Funny, you don't sound like you're from Argentina."

"They kind of beat inflections out of you during boot camp. Did you serve somewhere?"

"Me? Nah." Jock removed his bone mic. Opening the kiosk door, he tottered down a twelve-step staircase fixed to the side of the structure and moved toward her. Up close Jock barely came up to Piper's shoulders. "May I?" he asked.

Ewwwwww.

Every nerve in Piper's body buzzed with revulsion, but she steeled herself. When Roscoe traced a tattoo on her shoulder with a light caress she tried hard not to cringe. Her PAL tattoo was monochromatic and sharply defined—a canine skull with two cross-boned pulse carbines.

"I've more," Piper confided, "but those are a bit more private, if you know what I mean."

Jock retracted his finger and pumped his eyebrows. "I bet."

Covering herself super-quick, Piper zipped up and smoothed her weskit. "Say, speaking of accents... yours is pretty cute. You wouldn't happen to be from New Zealand, would you?"

Taking umbrage, Jock leaned back. "Me? A bloody Kiwi? Never. I'm a proud son of Oz— Brisbane, to be more precise—and my relations go back twenty generations. So... have you ever been to the sweaty continent?"

"Australia? Oh no, but I've always wanted to visit."

"Well, don't believe all the hysteria about the wacky weather. Personally, I can't wait to get back."

Piper nodded. "You know, I think I've seen you before."

"Oh, is that a fact?"

"Yeah, post-skip. That taco service in the canteen? More than a little gross, but the bar seemed like quite the lively place. A girl has to wonder, though. Is that it for all the fun out here?"

"Mostly," Jock concurred, "but there's other amusements. Your arrival on Kardashev 7-A is fortuitous. You're just in time for the big party."

"Big party?"

"Yeah, post-blows we cut loose with this huge hoedown before the spiders take off. A bottom of the bottle sort of an affair, but people tend to go all out. Dancing. Lots of loud music. We piggyback the shindig right here just after the pre-liftoff assembly. They don't like to advertise it, but management even has special food set aside as a treat. Tell me, are you of the carnivore persuasion, Piper?"

You dumb Aussie fucker… you have no idea.

"Oh, definitely," she replied.

"Well, you'll love the big party, then. There's stuffed sausages, stacked terrines, and these amazing little pointy fried rice dumplings I can't seem to get enough of. A total feast. You almost forget all the identifiables you've been scarfing down for months."

"Sounds tempting."

"I wouldn't go as far as tempting, but it's tasty.

It almost makes you feel like you're back on the big blue dot."

"Gosh, I haven't been dancing in, like, forever. Are subcontractors invited?"

"I don't see why not. You'll be at the assembly, won't you?"

"I think attendance is stipulated in our contract, but no one said anything about a party. I don't know. The staff on station, like I said, they seem a little resentful of us being here."

"Listen," said Jock. "If anybody gives you any lip about taking part in the festivities, just say you're with me, all right? People here on station, they know better than to mess with Jock Roscoe. And not to skite about it or nothing, but I do cut a mean tango if you're up for some dancing."

Jock held out a hand and reluctantly Piper took it. When he leaned down for a beau geste kiss of her flattened knuckles, she made a mental note to wash off her hand with bleach as soon as possible.

Yuck.

"Well, maybe I'll see you at the big party, then," Piper said, retracting her hand.

Waggish eyes a-twinkle, Jock lowered his voice suggestively. "Count on it."

19. SPOON MAN

Long ago, back when Jimmy Vik's weekends were an endless haze of rucks, dodged tackles, and swiped post-game cases of cheap beer, his favorite rugby coach had a ritual of handing out spoons.

The spoons, a mix of second-hand utensils of varying size and wear, were pulled from a mesh sack, and, bloodied and bruised, each of Jimmy's teammates took one as they were distributed. Jimmy's coach was a real hard case and rarely said anything during such moments. Not a word about Jimmy's botched passes, the team's accrued penalties or even the abysmally lopsided score displayed on a set of flip markers posted on the far side of the pitch. After all the spoons had been handed out, his coach would then raise his arm and Jimmy's entire squad would drop to their knees with the somber resignation of dogs.

"Spoon it up, men," his coach would say. *"Spoon it the fuck up."*

It was a hell of a lesson.

Filling out the limits of his back-to-back, Jimmy sullenly recalled each of at least a dozen times when he'd spooned turf into his mouth. Oddly enough, the memory of fresh dirt and crabgrass on his tongue gave him strength as he drove the crawler back to base. As he ground his way over to the surface ruts, Jock sent several messages via the scrambler for an update. Jimmy ignored Jock as long as he could until finally he sent a message that he was on his way back to base.

Jock responded:

: status/hp?

: +++

Jock was ecstatic and reminded Jimmy in short bursts of text that once he cleared the shipping hangar's massive dual-sectioned airlock he would be met by Zaafer—or, more succinctly, in Jock's blinkered verbiage:

: our darkie in the dark ;)

When the gargantuan doors on either side of the second airlock section retracted, Jimmy powered toward the vehicle maintenance area. He saw Zaafer and, with a pair of green safety batons, the young man directed Jimmy to a jersey-walled slot.

Being on edge as he was, the procedures for shutting down the crawler eluded Jimmy briefly, but eventually he powered everything down. He climbed out of the cockpit with his gloves bowled in his helmet, and approached the young tech. Zaafer didn't look directly at him.

"I understand you had some forward seal issues."

Jimmy cradled his helmet under one arm. "Um, as a matter of fact, yeah. Standard warning light kept flashing on and off. To tell you the truth, I'm glad I made it back in one piece."

"Sorry there's been a problem," Zaafer offered as he made a note on a dataslate. "This will be taken care of right away, not to worry. Do you have anything still stowed in the crawler's rear compartment, perchance?"

Jimmy looked Zaafer over. He still couldn't process that this pimple-faced, skinny kid was in league with someone like Jock. He hardly came across as a formidable henchman. Jimmy knew a lot of people made fun of Zaafer because of his oral hygiene issues and how he stuck to his devout Muslim beliefs. Still, Jimmy couldn't help but wonder just how much Zaafer knew about the gold. Given his supposed partner's prejudiced commentary and the amount of ill-gotten profit involved, for his sake he hoped Zaafer knew very little. Jimmy speculated on exactly how Jock had paid Zaafer off. Like everyone on station he knew there had to be some compulsion or vice involved. When Zaafer motioned his head at a metal case identical to the long drill case nearby, no additional hint was necessary.

Wow, Jimmy thought, a second case was a detail he'd overlooked. He was relieved Jock had arranged the matching case for the swap, but still he had a feeling something was off. Picking up the second case by its handle, Jimmy hooked around to the rear of the crawler and quickly placed the long drill in the second case's vacant memory foam. Jimmy left the original case used out in Fifty-Seven inside the rear compartment and sealed the hatch.

He'd slipped the three and a half kilos of gold into his rucksack before he headed back. The original was full of rocks.

Bets damn well hedged.

"Well, you've got things from here," Jimmy said. "Anyway, I need to get this and my suit back to the ASOCC equipment stores on the a.s.a.p."

"Mmm, yes, right, you do," Zaafer replied.

"So, I assume we're good here?"

Zaafer shook a box of candies against his mouth and munched. "Oh, yes. Very good. Very good indeed."

Jimmy looked toward Jock's kiosk in the center of the massive hangar. He noted that Jock wasn't inside so he started to move off toward the hangar's exits. Near one of the far walls he saw a blue tarp covering a large pile of plastic drums and quickly he slipped out of his spacesuit. After sliding the second drill case, his helmet, spacesuit, and rucksack under the tarp next to the barrels, Jimmy took up a concealed position, behind the legs of an unused marcher lift, to spy on Zaafer.

The young tech made a good show of examining the seals on the crawler. After a few dallying minutes, however, he took the loaded drill case from the crawler's rear compartment and secured the case to the bumper of a glide-scooter. As Zaafer skittered off, Jimmy followed and did his best to remain out of sight. Taking cover behind shelving girders and assorted secured cargo bins along the way, when Jimmy saw Zaafer sail past Armadillo Bay H and continue on to the farthest reaches of the hangar he felt simultaneously vindicated and pissed off. Well, what do you know… Jock *had* lied to him about which tender he intended to use, that little, backstabbing weasel.

Skulking closer, Jimmy watched as Zaafer parked the glide-scooter outside Armadillo Bay X next to an automated hover bin. Zaafer jumped off the scooter, retrieved the rock-laden case from the bumper, and pulled on a shiny hazmat suit. Just as he finished zippering up his protective gear, a crashing sound erupted from the other side of the hangar and Zaafer craned his head toward the sound.

Jimmy plunged out of sight just in time. The sudden clamor at the other side of the hangar—it didn't take a brainiac to put two and two together. The noise must have been intentional. A distraction. Made sense. Jimmy knew, of course, that the shipping hangar was constantly monitored by an imaging drone. The drone would certainly zoom over to investigate whatever the ruckus was about and leave Zaafer to load the bogusly filled case onto the tender unnoticed.

Sneaky son of a bitch, that Jock.

Two can play at that game though.

After making his way back to the tarp where he'd left his gear, Jimmy saw the reason for all the noise. A bundle of drafting pipes had spilled off a shelf as, handily, the belts securing the pipes had unexpectedly come undone. Jock was standing close to the mess with a few curious onlookers. Keeping an eye on Jock and the imaging drone hovering above, Jimmy took his rucksack full of gold and the rest of his gear from under the tarp and hustled off to the equipment stores in ASOCC.

20.NEWS FOR THE HORDE

In the canteen, Østerby and Stormkast were taking copious turns with a squeeze bottle of hot sauce on their soy-burgers when an announcement appeared on the VDT screens above the bar. The announcement, read by a woman identified as JSC Leela Pendergast, appeared after an image of the Azoick arrow-in-midflight logo. For legal purposes and further lucidity, a crammed synchronous crawl in multiple languages flowed beneath the woman's face as she began.

Attention all personnel, the following message is an official ASOCC bulletin. As you know, Azoick's last scheduled freighter, the *Adamant*, has secured its orbit and commenced initial tender descents for final cargo transfers. While this is good news, station management recently received word from the *Adamant* of some note.

Shortly after the ship dropped out of its skip and crossed into our sector, the *Adamant*'s communications detected a distress signal. The signal's origin has been confirmed as emanating from an unmanned, exploratory Omega-Class vessel identified as the *De Silento*, operated by Enlai Universal. While further assessments are pending, it is the view of the *Adamant*'s onboard company envoy that no aid and/or salvage conventions be initiated at this time.

In other news—all peripheral grind quarries, strip bores, schist and shaft sites are at long last ready for final demolition blows. That concludes this bulletin. See you at the pre-liftoff assembly. ASOCC, out.

21.MADE, MOVES, MAKE

Jimmy's whole body throbbed.

After taking what might have been the longest shower of his life and after he dropped off his gear at the ASOCC equipment stores, he moped his way back to his quarters with his rucksack strapped to his shoulders like a millstone. He had finally reached the lowermost level of the residential spider when he saw Leela sitting and waiting for him down the passageway next to his quarters. Jimmy nearly reeled around and hightailed it back up the ramp.

Leela looked up. "Oh, you're back. Everything out there go as planned?"

Huh?

Go as planned?

Jimmy blurted, "What're you doing down here?"

Leela blew out a breath and tilted her head. "Now that's a good question. To be upfront, I'd a mind to completely blow you off and get some shuteye, but it turns out I couldn't get to sleep. Then I thought about maybe going to the gym for a run, but I figured—oh, what the heck. Now's as good a time as any for you to spill the beans."

Ladies and gentlemen, behold the vortextual drop into the well of despair.

Oh no, Jimmy thought.

Did Leela actually know what he had been up to?

Feeling faint-headed, Jimmy looked behind him. He half-expected a throng of deputized station personnel to suddenly appear, chuck him to the floor, and slap him in irons. Drawing a hand across his face, he turned back and eased his rucksack from his shoulders, lowering the heavy pack down onto the floor in front of him.

"What beans?" he asked.

Leela stood and stretched from side to side. Bending over, she picked up the hardcopy binder she'd been reading and jogged it in her hands. "Well, as I was saying, I was having trouble sleeping, and so with nothing better to do I cruised over to ASOCC and scanned the logs. Well, well... you finished up your back-to-back a mite early."

Jimmy glanced over his shoulder again.

No marshaling heavies.

Yet.

"I just came straight from—"

"A locker room shower. Yeah, your hair is still wet. I must say, it's kind of strange that you didn't return your crawler back to its usual spot outside ASOCC, Jimmy."

"Oh, that," Jimmy said. "There was a warning light flashing in the cockpit. It seems a seal inspection was way overdue."

"Ah, I see. A seal inspection. Smart to take care of that."

"Right."

"So I guess you think your luck is still holding out then, huh?"

"Oh wow."

"That's all you have to say for yourself? Oh wow?"

"Well, I'm... uh... I'm kind of at a loss here, Leela."

Shoving the binder under her arm, Leela started stalking toward Jimmy like a tiny lioness. From where he stood, her eyes gave away nothing and her gait was so self-assured that he imagined she was just making him sweat before she pulled the damn plug on his moral turpitude. Defensively, Jimmy stepped in front of his rucksack.

"If you could, I mean, if you could just, like, give me a chance to explain."

"Ooh, mansplaining. Goody. I love me some mansplaining."

"I can't possibly imagine what you must think of me, Leela."

"No, you most certainly cannot."

"Damn, I swear I know what it looks like, but I thought I could—"

Leela looked down at the tips of her red cowboy boots and inhaled deeply. "Look, do me a favor and just shut the hell up for a minute. Maybe my sandbagging you like this after a back-to-back isn't the best thing for me to do, but what you said out there? When we were on the private channel? It really got to me, Jimmy."

Jimmy's world yielded. "It did?"

Moving closer, Leela reached out and tenderly gave his left arm a squeeze. "Of course it did, silly. But we don't need to go to the observational bubble or to my quarters or anywhere else for that matter. I'm right here. You're right here. We're both right here."

"Oh."

Ohhhhh.

While Leela wasn't there to call him out on taking the gold, Jimmy realized that back on the private channel he should have kept his big mouth shut. Goddamn, Leela expected him to explain himself! All of his purported misgivings, all his reasons for breaking up with her, and lord knew what else. The sudden downshift in his circumstances had Jimmy's thoughts tangled and his mind was fricasseed. Holy moly, he needed to maintain.

"Um, Leela..."

"Yes, Jimmy?"

"I really don't think I'm up for this."

Leela let go of his arm. "You're *not*?"

"Well, I mean, in principle I guess I am. But I'm, like, totally wiped out on my feet right now. But hey, the demolition inlays? They're all set to go in Fifty-Seven."

"Oh, Jimmy," Leela replied softly, "I could give a hang about Fifty-Seven."

"But—"

"I know I was all freaked out before, but you promised you were going to get it done and you did. I'm so proud of you. See? I told you ambition isn't so bad."

No, it's not, but…
Oh man.
Oh wow.
Oh shit.

Gulping and pulling himself together, Jimmy finally managed, "It was stupid of me to take all that equipment and the crawler without the proper okays."

Leela moved closer. "Uh-huh, but not to worry. It's all good now."

Jimmy tried to shuffle back and when his heels bumped into his rucksack he almost tripped. *Sweet mercy*, he felt totally despicable. Despite all his premeditations, he'd never dreamed Leela would be so easily persuaded that she'd jump ahead and confront him on all his so-called changes of heart. Theoretically, yeah, he wanted to wrangle her into an intimate talk so that he could ultimately goad her into firing him, but he wanted to do it later after some rehearsal, and in public so people could witness it. It was a halfway decent plan, but now Leela had him off balance. He needed to reconsider his strategy and think quickly. First Jock pulling a fast one, now this. Once again, Jimmy heard his old rugby coach in his head.

Spoon it up, men… spoon it the fuck up.

"Gosh, Leela, there are so many things I really wish I could undo."

Nodding and giving his arm another patient squeeze, Leela turned and sauntered toward his quarters. From a sleeve on her jumper's arm, she pulled an ASOCC bypass stick and slid it into a slot on the wall. All station management staff had bypass sticks, and the sticks, unless there was a dire lockdown emergency, enabled management to drop in unannounced just about anywhere on station. When the lock to Jimmy's hatch clacked free, Leela turned back with a provocative smile.

"I can think of a few things you could undo," she said.

Oh boy.

Like a soldier condemned to a firing squad, Jimmy slowly lifted his rucksack from the floor and followed Leela inside.

22.THE CANTEEN SCENE

Stormkast and Østerby were chugging their third round of ale when Piper sat down with them in the canteen booth. Unapologetically, Stormkast let out a belch foghorn-loud.

"Hey, chief. Have you heard the latest?"

Piper settled in her seat. She rested her CPU on the table and folded her hands. "The latest? The latest what?"

"About Enlai Universal," Stormkast replied. "One of their ships is, like, totally hosed."

Østerby groused something indecipherable. Grabbing Stormkast's empty cup and his own from the table, he motioned out of courtesy to Piper to see if she wanted anything, but Piper swiped a hand across her throat. Shrugging, Østerby wandered off toward the bar.

Stormkast continued, "Yeah, apparently Azoick's final inbound picked up a distress signal from one of EU's Omega-Class Explorers. Looks as if the Omega-Class went all kaplooey either just before or after they dropped out of their skip and crossed into the sector."

"Oh really. And where'd you hear all this?"

Stormkast put a fist to his mouth to suppress another belch and then amiably gestured toward the bar. "A talking head has been cycling on those VDT screens every, like, twenty minutes. Take a look, the message is up there now."

Piper turned. Above the bar on the large VDT screens, the woman she'd met in the gym earlier was speaking. The immediate din in the canteen was noisy and she couldn't make out what the woman was saying, so she tried to read the crawl.

Stormkast laughed. "Anyway, it's like this huge crate called the *De Silento*. Man, oh man, I can't imagine what that kind of screwup is going to cost Enlai Universal."

Piper turned back around. "I'm sure the crew is addressing whatever issue their Omega-Class is having."

"Ha, right. You'd be no less than a hundred percent wrong on that one, chief."

"Oh? And why's that?"

"The *De Silento* is unmanned."

"Get out."

"No, it's true."

"And they're all the way out here?" Piper raised a thoughtful eyebrow. "Huh. That is a problem. I suppose now you're going to tell me there's some cooperative rescue-slash-salvage mission in the works."

"Nope. The talking head up there claims the Azoick envoy aboard the *Adamant* says that's a no-go. Guess there's too much bad blood between Azoick and Enlai Universal. I'm telling you, man, these mining companies... bunch of cutthroats, don't you think?"

23. THE SWEET PAYOFF

On the balls of his feet with the hazmat suit folded in a protective pouch, Zaafer Daavi beamed. Everything had gone according to plan, just as Mr. Roscoe had said it would. When his hatch at last opened Zaafer gushed proud.

"The whole thing is set, sir."

Jock glanced left and right down the passage outside and then stared down at his boots. He didn't reply.

"I followed your instructions," Zaafer added. "Just like you told me. The AHB disposed of the quarantine materials and I checked. If you don't mind me saying, I must compliment you on the, um, the ah—"

Jock looked up. "The what?"

Zaafer whispered, "The diversion."

"Bah," Jock frowned. "Stacked and bound as they were, those drafting pipes were an accident waiting to happen."

Zaafer rubbed his hands together expectantly. "So?"

"God, you can't hold your vinegar for a second, can you?" sniped Jock balefully. "Fine. I suppose a deal is a deal, so here you go."

Taking the second duffle of promised candy, Zaafer was so excited he began to tremble. *Oh heavens… Mookoomarsh Bars and Super Sour Waddlee Wees!* The bag was stuffed to the point of bursting. When Zaafer pinched the bag's zipper, Jock reached out and slapped his hand.

"Not here. We must keep up appearances."

"Oh, of course, Mr. Roscoe. I forgot. Right."

"Wait until you're back in your quarters. Swear to me by your god."

Stunned, Zaafer paused. Swear by his God? Swearing by the Lord of the Worlds was something no devout man of Zaafer's faith should ever take lightly, and under such false and mendacious circumstances swearing as such might be considered a sin of irreparable consequence. Oh why, why must he have to swear? Had he not done everything that had been asked of him? Here he was, everything completed and moments away from succulent pleasure, was it truly necessary? Zaafer made a quick promise to himself. He pledged he'd be stronger next time and would refuse to do favors for Mr. Roscoe ever again. Feeling so helpless and humiliated, he told himself he'd pray extra special hard for forgiveness and devote hours to seeking expiation. Zaafer lifted his eyes and mumbled.

"All right… by Allah, I swear."

"Again," Jock demanded.

"Pardon?"

Jock cupped a hand to his ear. "Say it again. Swear on your useless excuse for a god."

Blasphemer!

"Mr. Roscoe…"

"You cherry-picking monkey, I said say it!"

Zaafer sniveled. He curled his toes in his boots and repeated his oath. "By Allah, I swear I will wait until I am in my quarters."

Jock turned his head and spat. "Beat feet, candy-boy."

Minutes later, Zaafer tore into his quarters, locked his hatch, and opened his second bounty at long last. Packed right at the top were the most forbidden and most difficult sweets to come by—a pristine two hundred and fifteen gram box of Whiplash Pogoes.

Zaafer danced in a circle and leapt up and down.

Slitting open the box with a finger, he slid two Whiplash Pogoes into his damp palm. Fascinating. The candy was just like the pictures he'd seen. Each Whiplash Pogo portion was curled in on itself like an immaculately spiraled wheel and the frosted shells of each successive band were of a different kaleidoscopic color. The candy was more beautiful, delicate, and enticing than he could have ever imagined. While he was aware of the candies' latent toxicities, Zaafer was so overcome that he hastily slapped both portions into his mouth.

The taste was fabulous.

So explosive and intense. It was as if a dozen different sugary tangs were bathing his tongue all at once. In utter ecstasy, his knees actually jellied.

But when Zaafer bit down to release the promised nougat inside the Whiplash Pogoes a second later, something tasted unbearably wrong and off.

His esophagus constricted.

Taken aback and dropping the box, Zaafer felt his pulse take off fast, and soon the awful contractions in his muscles grew so acute that gray dots began to score across his vision.

Astaghfiru lillah! What is happening to me?

Doubling over in pain, Zaafer spat out bits of the candy still in his mouth and tried jamming his fingers down his throat. *The latent toxicities*, he thought, *ohhhh…* he should have known better. He probed his fingers farther down and gagged, but the cloying fragments he'd already swallowed wouldn't come up. He smelled a bitter scent of almonds, and his throat swelled completely shut. No longer able to take in air, he fell to the floor writhing in agony. After a minute and a half of frothing at the mouth, a cool and empty darkness slipped over Zaafer like a long, black cape.

24.OH BOY (CONTINUED...)

After Jimmy followed her into his quarters, Leela sealed the hatch. Allowing him to slip past, she watched as Jimmy jammed his rucksack into a cubby beneath his bunk and didn't turn around.

Jimmy, Jimmy, Jimmy. Leela had always admired how he looked from behind. To be perfectly honest, for a dude he hadn't much of a caboose, but his shoulders were broad and he was tall and lean and Leela always liked that. She thought possibly she was rushing things again, but then thought, so what? The tiny lights over Jimmy's terrariums were throwing everything in the narrow room into soft shapes. With the balminess of the fragmite incinerators next door, the room was so warm and cozy. Even Jimmy's dumb ship model with its broad stripes, black cannons, and ridiculous plastic sails seemed romantic.

"Jimmy?"

A low and oblique response. "Yeah?"

"Come here."

Jimmy turned. "Leela, this isn't exactly what I had in mind."

"I don't care. Don't make me say it again."

With his chin down, Jimmy mooched his way across the room to her. Placing one of her hands on his hip, Leela lifted his chin with the other and smoothed a wet lock of hair back from his forehead.

"Listen," she said, "this isn't what I had in mind either. And I know you said you're dead on your feet, but why waste an opportunity like this, am I right?"

Once she kissed his lips whatever reluctance Jimmy was holding onto fell away. It wasn't long before he had his arms around her and soon his hands feverishly began to roam. When Jimmy lifted her up, Leela experienced a slight vertebral stretch in her spine and felt his cock thickening against her thigh. Impatiently, she tugged at the talon zipper on the front of his jumper. Sweeping around, he lowered her down onto his bunk.

"Undo, undone…"

Jimmy lifted his head. "What?"

"Get this jumper off me!"

Jimmy grabbed the zipper and yanked it down.

"Boots! Boots first!" Leela cried.

"Oh, right." He pulled her cowboy boots off. "Got 'em, just a sec."

Leela sighed. It was all so awkward. A small part of her always despised how undressing and getting down to the act never seemed to be as dreamy as one hoped it would be. Working together, though, the two of them removed the rest of their clothes lickety-split and then she pushed Jimmy over on his back. Her breasts now bared, Leela pressed her body against Jimmy's heat as he reached around for a good ten-digit knead of her ass. Sliding a hand down between them, she took hold of him and briefly considered if some slickening was required. It wasn't like she wasn't up for a little extended foreplay, but what the hell—she was already wet—why mess around with a preamble?

As if reading her mind, Jimmy licked his fingers and stretched a hand down as well, circling his moist fingertips across her damp, puffed clit.

"Um, Jimmy?"

"Same spot."

Condoms. They were in the top drawer of his desk, same as always, and again an awkward necessity. After kissing the tip of his nose, Leela let go of him, jumped up, and deftly secured a shiny condom packet from the drawer. It wasn't something she liked to crow about, but Leela was pretty good at executing a gentle incisor rip. She unrolled the protection on Jimmy in five seconds flat and, spreading her knees and straddling him, she drew him quickly inside.

A small moan escaped Jimmy's mouth.

Leela tittered. "Guess you missed this, huh?"

"Damn, I think—wait. I think I'm going to—"

"Oh c'mon. Already? Don't you even *dare*."

Leela swept her dark hair across his face. It felt so good to feel him straining beneath her again, trying to push away his physical urge to be sated. With a pace slow and deliberate, she started riding him and briefly she wondered if she was being cruel. Hell, yes, she was being cruel. Tormenting him felt good. It felt sexy and empowering. And after the emotional meat grinder he had put her through, dominating him and keeping his forthcoming eruptive seizures in check felt unstintingly deserved.

Out of slit eyes, Leela looked at Jimmy's face as he wriggled through his pleasure-soaked vacillations. Like imbedded cords on vibrato, the tendons of his neck grew tight and it wasn't long before she too felt a long overdue release surging inside. Rising and falling on his hips, she rode him faster and faster.

Jimmy jerked his head. "No, I can't—no! NO! I CAN'T!"

"What?"

With an outrageous heave, he pulled out and threw her off. There was a split instant of nothing as she landed back against the wall, and Jimmy scrambled off the bunk. Swatting at him as he bolted behind the frosted partition to the bathroom, Leela quickly clambered to her feet, baffled.

Naked, buck-wild freak throwing her off, what was he? Sick or something? Leela didn't hear any form of discharge behind the partition, so right then and there she'd half a mind to follow him into the bathroom and claw his eyes out.

"Jimmy? What's wrong?"

When Jimmy returned from behind the partition he shoved a translucent, latched radioactive-proof container into her hands.

"I can't do this," he murmured. "I'm sorry, Leela, but I just can't."

Angrily Leela stared at him. Then she looked at the container in her hands and did a double-take.

Wondering if what she was seeing was real, she shook the container up and down. The oversized pit inside clanked. It was unmistakable.

Gold.

25.EASY ONE DOWN

Jock swung his hatch closed and left it unlocked. After picking his way to his workstation, he plopped down into a chair and lifted a ten-millimeter vial next to a spent syringe. The syringe was still gooey with traces of nougat. Counting the minutes, Jock estimated that any second now Zaafer would be back in his quarters, so he re-read the fine print on the vial's label.

WARNING
Upon ingestion—lethal within 1–10 minutes.

Onset symptoms include tachycardia, acute headache, serious and rapid metabolic acidosis, powerful seizures, disorientation, coma, and eventual cardiac arrest. Treatment (speed vital)—immediate removal from cause; 100% O_2 respiratory support; inhalation of amyl nitrite (1 ampule) for 30 seconds of each min.; 3% Na nitrite 10 mL at 2.5-5 mL/min. IV; furthermore...

Furthermore?

With the amount of potassium cyanide Jock had injected into Zaafer's Whiplash Pogoes, furthermore was no longer a concern for that soppy wanker.

Sweet dreams, indeed.

26. MEANY-WHILE (INTERMEZZO)

With the fathomless, black desolation of space and considering the events about to unfold, one might consider the *De Silento*'s christened moniker to be a misnomer of unspeakable, shattering irony.

The *De Silento*'s reconfigured core drives having been prepped well before it made the skip out and its recent calculated subterfuge successfully implemented, the Omega-Class's navigational inputs deemed the vessel's forward velocity could finally be increased. To avoid being misconstrued as anything other than routine system reengagement, the vessel's rekindled momentum was accompanied by a transmission advising its previous distress signal had been unwarranted.

Meanwhile, back on Earth, a fine-tailored cadre of Enlai Universal executives were finishing off their coffees and a tray of *pains au chocolat* in EU's board room. The results of the cadre's agreed-upon efforts still months out from being substantiated, it seemed a tad premature to celebrate, but in-house counsel and the company's weapons consultant assured the executives in attendance it was not. Twelve magnums of champagne were ordered and delivered. Flutes were poured, clinked, and downed.

Intercept with Azoick's Kardashev 7-A station was, as in-house counsel and the weapons consultant described it, "a foregone conclusion."

27. PINK SLIP

"Leela, please. Will you just calm down."

Leela refused to acknowledge Jimmy and finished dressing. After tying off her hair in a knot, she grabbed the tumbler with the gold sample and shook it at Jimmy like a huge clacking maraca.

"Calm down? Calm down!? You freaking imbecile! What were you thinking? Do you realize what you've done?"

"Look, I'm sorry."

"Don't even start with that. You can't even begin to apologize, Jimmy. The way you've been acting, I should've known you were up to something. You are so fired."

Jimmy hadn't put his boots or jumper back on yet and was leaning against his wall full of pictures in his boxers and socks. "As expected," he said. "And?"

"And what?"

Jimmy pointed at the tumbler. "Well, that. That's, um, like—"

"A capital one corporate offense? Oh, I am well aware of that, buster. And while I should report your sorry, thieving hide immediately I'm not exactly enamored with the idea of hiring a lawyer to defend myself about being in the same room as this right now." Leela shook the tumbler at him again. "You know, if you really wanted to screw me, Jimmy, you should have finished with the real thing because at least then I could've gotten off. I could lose my job over something like this. Goddamn it, and you said you found this where?"

Jimmy looked up at the ceiling briefly. "Along one of the surface schist sites a few weeks back."

"So you didn't think that maybe you should've told someone?"

"All the trace analytics said there wasn't any gold on K7-A. I didn't find any more, and believe me I looked. Basically I thought it fell from space or something."

"Fell from space?"

"Yeah, I mean we're talking billions upon billions of epochs here, Leela. There could've been meteor fragmentations, random panspermia—"

"Oh, don't give me that. For falling from space, this piece looks like a pretty clean cut to me."

"Well, I tidied up the dross."

"Liar."

"I'm not lying to you, Leela. And if you don't believe me, I don't know what else I can say." Cautiously, Jimmy picked up his jumper and stepped into it. "Anyway it's not like it's really quote-unquote stolen at this point. You could just choose to ignore it. I mean, doesn't me having a crisis of conscience count for anything?"

Leela set the tumbler down on Jimmy's desk and cracked an open hand right across his cheek.

"OW!"

Reaching up, she grabbed the HMS *Victory* model from the shelf and flung it at him. On reflex Jimmy stepped aside and the ship model smashed against the wall. Deducing that it might be better to not say anything more and just let her vent all at once, Jimmy zipped up his jumper. Next door the fragmite incinerators switched on, and Leela looked to the wall. She grabbed the tumbler and made for the hatch.

"Don't you move," she said icily.

Earlier, when he told Leela that she knew him better than he did himself, Jimmy had been thinking the knowledge exchange was more the other way around. He knew exactly what Leela was going to do. About a minute and a half later when she returned from the fragmite incinerators with an empty tumbler, she didn't even bother to look at him.

"The *Adamant* has secured its orbit and the tenders have descended. After the cargo is loaded on the tenders and the upcoming blows in a few hours, and once I finish filing your termination paperwork, I'll make arrangements for one of the *Adamant*'s transfer modules. You'll make the skip back with the *Adamant* right after the final assembly. All expenses for your passage back to the Neptune Pact Orbital will be docked from your accounts. Pack your shit."

"Leela…"

"You're fired, Jimmy. No ifs, ands, or buts."

"Okay, okay… so what do I tell people I'm getting canned for?"

Leela stepped right up to him and planted a

finger on his chest. "Your contract is an 'at will' agreement, so you're not owed anything in the way of an explanation. God, Jimmy, do you think people actually care what you're getting fired for? The only reason anyone would want to know is so they can adjust their own behavior so they don't get the ax too. Tell people what you want. Tell them you fucked up. Hell, get blitzed off your ass at the post-assembly bash and whine about the injustice of it all, but your career with Azoick is over."

"But—"

"I said no buts, Jimmy. Not another peep."

28. THE BLOWS/A BASHO MOMENT

AZOICK PROGRESS REPORT
SPO Ref. Code: 234.6
SOURCE: K7-A Station, ASOCC, Sector 34-T
DATE: 3.25.2778GMT
SUBJECT: Final inlay and surface area demolitions.
MESSAGE: Commencing primary and secondary charge blows at 0:800 hours, OST.

In a domino arrangement, each interconnected charge below and above Kardashev 7-A's surface cut loose on a controlled frequency-cued mark.

The primed yield areas, including strip bores, grind quarries, and all shaft and schist sites, upon their hundreds and hundreds of muted detonations, quietly collapsed inward, moving outward in a circular pattern. The rippling progression looked similar to the aftereffects of a frog leaping into a lifeless pond.

For their own amusement, the ASOCC management team synced the blows' countdown and detonations to music.

'Entry of the Gladiators' by Julius Fučík.

29.GETTING THE J-O-B DONE

Piper was supervising Østerby and Stormkast as they piled the parasol gear into a crawler parked in the shipping hangar maintenance area when the automated voice from the overhead PA system verified that all inlay blows had been completed. There was only one last pylon case to be lifted into the rear compartment when, suddenly detecting the odor of hickory, Piper turned and saw Jock standing directly behind her eating a strip of jerky.

"I suppose it's a good thing that crawler you're using just got its seals checked," said Jock. "Now you don't have to lug all your elaborate equipment over to ASOCC."

Piper resumed her observation of Østerby and Stormkast. The two men closed the crawler's rear hatch and made twirling motions with their index fingers. Like Piper, both were wearing spacesuits. They picked up a couple of helmets from the hangar floor and headed for the crawler's cockpit. Piper spoke impassively.

"All our pre-deployment checks were solid. With the blows now executed, we should be out there five, maybe six hours, max."

"Ah, you'll be back in plenty of time then."

"In plenty of time for what?"

"The pre-liftoff assembly and party."

"Looks like it."

"I downloaded a merengue tutorial by the way."

"What?"

"Merengue. You know, as in dancing?" Jock took another masticating rip of his jerky and chewed loudly. "I trust you're still up for some fun."

Even though she knew he couldn't see her face in full, it took some effort for Piper not to grind her teeth. She still had her cover assignment tasks to conclude before she could kill him, but with Roscoe reminding her of the upcoming pre-liftoff celebration the cauldron of her mind began to smolder with ideas.

Grisly, heinous ideas.

"Oh, I'm up for some fun, all right," she replied. Heading for the crawler and not looking back, she added, "In fact, I'm looking forward to it."

30. THE BOTTOM GOTTEN

Somewhat red-eyed, sniffling, and quite beside herself, Leela sat at her ASOCC console. She was on the third edit of Jimmy's termination order when one of her colleagues in the command center spoke up.

"Hey, check it out, guys. That Enlai Omega-Class is on the move again."

Leela flicked her eyes to an adjacent screen. On the display, a luminous blip slid by and registered a less than normal measure of speed. While slow, a comprehensive analysis of the Omega-Class's renewed momentum appeared in a gray sidebar and a secondary guidance file showed the *De Silento* was shadowing the *Adamant*'s previous heading before it secured its orbit around K7-A. Leela did a brief digest of the numbers. Weird. The course heading differential was scant—a mere ten thousand kilometers.

"Is the *Adamant*'s crew aware the *De Silento* has re-engaged?" Leela asked.

"Checking on that now, stand by."

A pause.

"Oh, yeah," her colleague continued. "The *Adamant*'s bridge confirms."

The fine hairs on the back of Leela's neck prickled. She wondered if it was only because she was always cold in the command center or whether her instincts were telling her something. She'd been so mad from her encounter with Jimmy that when she arrived for her work cycle in ASOCC she'd neglected to put on her fingerless wool gloves.

"What's the nearest EU spheroid claim in our sector?" Leela asked.

"Why? You looking to trade up, Pendergast?"

"Don't be a jackass," she snapped. "Just check for me, will you?"

"Okay, hang on. Hmm… all right, I think I've got it. The nearest Enlai spheroid claim looks to be on a large moon nine days from here called Alardo-9."

Clicking a pen, Leela made a note on a scrap of paper, put on her fingerless gloves, and went back to editing Jimmy's termination order.

To flush out the rest of her slowly diminishing rage, she resolved to highlight select words in the document with bold italics and underlines.

Words like *inadequate*, *reckless*, *inattentive*, and *flagrant disregard*.

After proofreading what she wrote, Leela printed out two hardcopies for her backup binders and hit ENTER on her keyboard.

It was a huge pain, but since Jimmy wouldn't be on Kardashev 7-A for the final spider liftoffs now, she had to make special arrangements for a personnel transfer module to be dispatched from the *Adamant*. When she saw an advisory statement that a personnel transfer module had already been ordered from the orbiting freighter, Leela reviewed the code signature on the request. Jock Roscoe's name and his approved application for personal leave sprung a trapdoor in the bottom of her stomach.

It took less than a half a second for Leela to connect the dots.

Jimmy.

Jock Roscoe.

The gold.

No, could it be?

Please, Jimmy, for the love of God, no...

31.SHAM-A-SCAM-A-DING-DONG

Changed into his well broken-in black leathers and best flight boots to go home in, Jimmy dumped the rest of his gear into a large, green, stitched-seam burn bag. Knowing he had little time, he disposed of almost everything he had and worked as quickly as he could. He chucked in his terrariums, the shards of his ruined HMS *Victory* model, his desk contents, his pictures, and all the rest of the miscellaneous paraphernalia he now knew he had little use for. The only things he decided to keep on his person were the straight razor his father had given him and his deck of playing cards with his secreted-away processing chit, both of which he stashed in the breast pocket of his jacket. He'd requested an automated hover bin for the burn bag, and the AHB was lingering just outside his open hatchway.

When Jock appeared next to the bin, Jimmy glanced up.

"Oh, hey, Jock…"

"Hey there, my man. I assume you got your walking papers."

Jimmy crammed a wad of unwashed towels into the

burn bag. "Yeah," he replied. "Turns out getting canned doesn't take all that much. Leela has a short fuse."

"So how'd you work it?"

"Let's just say I called Leela a few choice names."

Jock hooted his approval. "Nasty. So, are we all set to ride the same transfer module up to the *Adamant*, then?"

"Seems to be the case," Jimmy said. "I take it your gambit with personal leave worked out okay."

Jock stepped over the threshold and into Jimmy's quarters proper. "Smooth as polished marble. FYI, the transfer module is already on the landing pad and engaged with the ASOCC airlocks. I just dropped off my own strongbox there a short time ago. All we have to do now is climb aboard and the next thing we know we'll be getting prepped for our six-month pajama nap back to the Neptune Pact Orbital."

"Great."

"So, are you still planning on showing your face at the final assembly?"

"I thought I better bear through it and stick around for a few pops afterwards. Maybe say some nice-knowing-yas."

"One last hurrah then, huh?"

Jimmy sighed. "Yeah, for the both of us. Anyway, I need to finish clearing everything out, and I still have to take my strongbox down to the transfer module. So if you don't mind…"

"Oh, sure, sure," Jock said. "Hey, a quick thought before I amble off, though. Do you still got that original sample you showed me knocking around back there in your privy?"

Jimmy slapped a palm against his forehead. "Oh, damn. I totally blanked on that."

Jock tsked and shook his head. "Ah, you're lucky your partner is here to remind you."

Jimmy hurried back to his toilet. Returning a moment later, he handed over a second sample he had taken from Fifty-Seven. The sample was almost the same size as the first piece of gold he'd showed Jock and was wrapped in a blue washcloth.

Jock said, "Say, what happened to the tumbler?"

"Oh, that. I needed to return it to the ASOCC equipment stores," Jimmy explained. Leela had actually returned the tumbler after their fallout. "Company property, you know. Figured we've filched enough already. So, uh, what're you going to do with that? Are you going to make sure it goes in with the rest on the tender docked in Armadillo Bay H?"

Jock unfolded the blue washcloth. He gave the sample a superficial look but didn't seem to notice any difference. "Nah. Best we eighty-six this wee tidbit with the rest of your belongings." Jock dropped the second sample and the blue washcloth into the open burn bag.

"Kind of a waste, don't you think?"

"Yeah, but it's a pittance comparatively. No second thoughts now, you hear? Don't be taking that along with you as some kind of souvenir."

"I won't."

Jock peered at him. "Hey, are you feeling all right? You don't look so hot."

Jimmy shrugged. "I feel kind of bad about using Leela."

"Oh, you'll get over that minx soon enough, I reckon. In no time with your end you'll have ladies crawling all over you." Jock pointed a finger gun at him and dropped the hammer. "Well, I'll leave you to clean up your clutter, then. See you at the final assembly, okay?"

Once he headed off, Jimmy counted to sixty before he poked his head outside his quarters to see if Jock was really gone. Not seeing him in the corridor outside and closing the hatch, Jimmy slipped back toward his bunk. He hooked a foot beneath and slid out his strongbox. Stooping down, he tapped in a ten-digit succession of numbers on a keypad on the container and lifted the lid. Inside the strongbox was his rucksack.

Jimmy went back to the burn bag. After finding the sample in the washcloth Jock had disposed of, he stuffed it into his rucksack with the three and a half kilos of gold he'd taken from Fifty-Seven.

Jimmy sealed his strongbox.

32.PARTY TIME, EXCELLENT

Later, at the pre-liftoff assembly, all station personnel including Piper and her freelance team convened in a restless, murmuring mob in the middle of the shipping hangar. All twelve of the ASOCC management team, including a ghastly-pallored Dickerson with a sick basin on his lap, sat in folding chairs on a slightly raised, skirted temporary stage. Each member of the management team, taking turns, presented an exhaustive forty-eight-minute review of the Kardashev 7-A operation. A quartet of giant, projected holograms displayed qualitative pie charts, graphs, area diagrams, and allocated time-series summaries of the SPO's mission, and as was usual the presentation was a lethal-grade, soporific snoozefest.

All the while Jock stood in his kiosk and surveyed the gathering. Already well into his cups and taking nips from a flask of gin, he noticed Jimmy enter the hangar and sail casually over to the set up food and drinks tables. When Jimmy finally looked up he gave Jock a succinct nod in his perch. Alas, Zaafer was nowhere to be seen. Further relieved his cyanide-laced Whiplash Pogoes had done the trick, Jock chuckled to himself.

When the longwinded speeches and critiques at last concluded, the quartet of projected data holograms consolidated into one, large image of Azoick's arrow-in-midflight logo. The concluding applause was half-hearted until someone cued the music.

The pre-liftoff party began with a violent screech of gnashing Kryp-Bop guitar.

33.PRIMED TO A-GO-GO

Seated on their packed-up equipment crates, Piper observed Stormkast elbowing Østerby in the ribs as Østerby pointed at the food tables. Next to the ten tablecloth-draped buffet tables there was a massive, heavily stocked bar replete with three help-yourself taps of dreg stout, ale, and pulp cider. The two men stood and started for the gathering when Stormkast stopped and looked back at Piper.

"You coming?"

Piper studied her nails. "In a few. You two run on ahead. I've still got to submit our final situation report on our work out there."

Stormkast grinned and he and Østerby joined the party.

Looking around, Piper saw the hangar bash was quickly turning into about what she had expected: a moiling, drunken bee full of phony camaraderie commemorating the completion of the station's long-haul objectives. What a joke, she mused. Jovial loudmouths taking self-satisfaction in their so-called skills, most of which could have and should have been handled by robotics if Azoick wasn't so stingy. Sadly, a blind squirrel knew the score. While people might have sufficient brainpower to fix routine issues, the real reason men and women were still utilized in abundance for deep space labor was because they were cheap and replaceable. Perhaps in her freelance capacities Piper was part of that stone-cold equation, but she, of course, had other and more lucrative concerns.

Now all she had to do was get Jock Roscoe alone so she could pull together the right kind of accident.

The method of Roscoe's demise was up to her, and the only caveat The Chimeric Circle insisted upon before she agreed to the contract hit was that there should be no overt suspicion of foul play. Shouldn't be too hard to arrange. Nevertheless Piper did find The CC's stipulation a little peculiar. One would imagine a criminal organization like The Chimeric Circle would relish taking credit for eliminating someone who so willfully bucked their collection efforts, but it was not the case. The CC knew speculations had an insidious way of forming all on their own. They realized Roscoe's misfortunate death by accident would be strong enough to demonstrate a message.

Piper floated a look across the hangar. Leaving his vantage point in his kiosk, Roscoe descended the adjacent stairs along the structure and swaggered into the gathering like a drum major.

Showtime.

"Hey, you…"

Getting up, Piper did an about-face. It was the pintsized firecracker from the gym, the one with the tight buns who had the mother from India who sent her drum files.

"Oh, hey. Leela, right?"

"Yeah, that's right," said Leela. "So, did your parasol setups out on the surface go okay?"

Piper breezily motioned to the packed-up equipment around them. "Just like we planned. All I need to do now is send along the summary situation report to your station management group and execute the launches once the station lifts off. Busy work at this point, but you know how that goes. I take it everything is still on schedule?"

"Yeah," Leela said, looking around. "In a few hours all the loaded cargo tenders will be released from the armadillo bays and once the tenders safely rendezvous with the *Adamant* there'll be a station-wide announcement with a two-hour countdown. I understand you'll be joining us in ASOCC for your remote parasol implementations."

"Uh-huh."

"Guess I'll see you there, then."

Leela moved off, squeezing her way through the rabble, and Piper watched her as she steamed straight toward that guy who'd been talking with Roscoe just after Piper's arrival—Jimmy Vik. It was strange. Unlike the rest of the clods throwing back drinks and stuffing their faces, Leela's ex-beau wasn't wearing a bright yellow Azoick jumper.

Piper dug his black leathers, though.

34.CONFRONTATION

"Jimmy?"

Swallowing a mouthful of foamy ale, Jimmy mopped his lips with the back of his wrist. "Oh hey, Leela," he said. "Need a drink?"

"Not now, thanks."

Jimmy took another sip. "Suit yourself."

Leela grabbed his arm gruffly. Jimmy rolled his eyes at some fellow coworkers, who laughed and booed as he clownishly puckered his lips and allowed himself to be dragged away. When the distance from the rest of the party seemed adequate, Leela gave his arm a stiff, downward wrench.

"Whoa, take it easy!"

"What do you think you're doing?"

Jimmy shook his arm. He waved to someone and took another pull of his drink. "What am I doing? Well, let's see. Right now I'm taking in some suds and then I plan on saying a few goodbyes. Anyway, all my stuff is cleared out of my quarters and my strongbox is on the transfer module out at ASOCC, so once I'm done here you can relax. You'll never have to see me again."

"Jimmy, look at me."

"What? What do you want me to say? You fired me, Leela. Sheesh, you want me to grovel, is that it? You want me to moon on and on that I'm grateful you didn't report me over a tiny little piece of nothing that wouldn't have meant anything to anyone, let alone Azoick? All right, fine. I'm grateful and I'm sorry. Satisfied?"

"Goddamn it, stop being glib. Whatever it is you think you're doing, just use your head and think for a second."

"Think? Think about what?"

"Jimmy, I may be mad as hell at you right now, but even so that doesn't mean I want to see you get into trouble."

"What're you talking about?"

Leela got right up in his grill. Her lips were drawn tight and her brown eyes searched his. Oddly, the anger from before had been supplanted with a look of genuine worry and concern.

"That gold wasn't the only piece you found out there, was it? You dumb son of a bitch. Are you and Jock up to something?"

Oh shit.

35.DANCIN' FOOL

The volume of the music intensified as someone took Piper's wrist from behind.

"Hey, there you are, blondie. I believe you owe me a shimmy."

God, that accent...

Piper spun around and stretched her sunniest thousand-watt smile. Jock slipped a cup into her hand, and she glanced down at it. "What's this?"

Jock's nose twitched vigorously. "That, is a Jock Roscoe specialty. I call it a Selectron Shooter. It's just the right bevvy to put you in a social mood, missy."

Missy?

No way.

Did he actually just call her "missy"?

"Mmm," Piper replied, taking a sniff of the drink. "Smells kind of fruity. Can I ask what's in it?"

"Ooh, this and that. Just about everything."

Piper let out a disingenuous giggle. "I have to tell you. I'm really not much of a drinker."

"Oh, well, you're still up for some dancing later, right?"

Ugh.

Dancing on your scumbag throat, maybe.

"I don't know," Piper shied with a roll of her shoulder. "This garish Kryp-Bop music isn't exactly my taste. It's way too loud."

"What?"

"I said this Kryp-Bop music isn't my thing."

"Oh, so what kind of music are you into?"

"Something a little softer."

Jock exhorted, "Hey, me too!"

Double ugh.

Still, Piper thought, it was high time to get on with killing this prick, right? She hipped forward and narrowed the social space between them. Reaching out, she then pitter-pattered her fingertips on the crown of his head. "Gosh," she purred, "up close your ink is really incredible. Such craftsmanship. And these raised markings along your neck, they're so colorful. What are they?"

"Aboriginal hieroglyphics."

"Really?"

"Yeah, I've got some of that feral bush blood in me somewhere, so I thought I'd tip my hat to the ancients." Jock held up his own cup for a toast. "Down the hatch."

Piper faked a requisite taste from her drink. Hell, given the unspecified contents of the concoction and Roscoe's overall lecherous air, who knew what kind of elephant tranquilizer the little chimp might have slipped into the drink. It was always a delicate balance beguiling the weaker sex. Certainly Piper didn't want to come on too strong, but seeing that Roscoe was already looking loaded she forced herself to conjure up some compulsory misdirection. Picking up her portable CPU, she let out a long, fatigued sigh.

"Well, thanks for the drink, but I need to shove off."

"Shove off?"

"Yeah, I have to submit my parasol summaries to those in charge."

"But things are just getting started."

Oh, look at his crestfallen face. This was too easy.

"Duty calls," Piper professed.

"Yeah, but can't duty take a back seat for once? I mean, you really should stick around. You haven't had anything to eat yet. You need to try some of the pointy fried dumplings."

Piper placed a hand on his shoulder, leaned in, and spoke in his ear so Jock could feel her breath's heat. "You know, I think I'm going to head over to the canteen. With everybody carrying on here, it'll be much quieter there. If I finish things up, maybe I'll come back for a dance later."

She handed Jock her drink. Jock finished it in a single gulp, finished off his own, and flipped both drink cups over his shoulder. "Hey, you know what? I think I've a better idea."

"Oh?"

"Yeah. If you're really after some peace and quiet to get your work done, you ought to hit the observational bubble."

"The observational bubble? Where's that?"

"Over near ASOCC. The observational bubble

is quiet as a tomb usually and has a terrific three-hundred-and-sixty view too." Jock crooked out his arm. "Here, I'll show you."

"I really don't want to be a bother."

"It's no bother at all. I insist."

For real? He insists?

This was way, way too easy.

Rubbing her neck with just the right amount of dalliance, Piper took Jock's arm.

"Well, if you insist, why not? Lead on, my liege."

36. BLINDSIDED

Meanwhile, aboard the *Adamant*, ninety-seven percent of the freighter's complement were busy making its final preparations for the Kardashev 7-A cargo tender transfers. The captain and Azoick's envoy, Yaser Shalad, were playing another epic game of backgammon in the captain's ready room when a lone ensign assigned to orbital watch interrupted over the comm.

"Captain? Sorry to disturb you, sir."

"What is it, Ensign?"

"Well, um, I really think you should come to the bridge, Captain."

"Is it an emergency?"

"I'm not sure. It's the *De Silento*, sir."

"The *De Silento*?"

"Yes. She's—oh. Oh. Oh my. Um, you really need to come to the bridge now, sir."

Looking up from the game board, Envoy Shalad said, "Mind if I tag along?"

The captain threw the envoy a stony look. What the hell, the mincing twerp was rolling doubles like it was going out of style and betting one hundred credits. It was time to stop the bleeding.

"Whatever floats your boat," the captain said.

37. MANY OUT OF UNO

In the inky realm of space, one could observe all sorts of astonishing phenomena.

Vast supernova nebulae with magnificent bruise-like clouds expanding across unspeakable rips of gravity...

Flawless planetary rings shaped by magnetic-electrostatic forces and gargantuan, eternal quasars, angelic and pulsating...

On the bridge of the *Adamant*, however, what the captain, Envoy Shalad, and the ensign bore witness to were none of these things. The transfixing spectacle was a *tableau vivant*, inexplicably defined by diabolic treachery and ruin.

Like a husk peeling apart and remodeling in on itself, one by one the *De Silento*'s component parts reassembled in an efficient, mechanized progression. Seamlessly reconfigured, the Omega-Class core spread out and the exploratory craft took on a resemblance of a large wedge or boomerang. There was a momentary pause prior to a sequential separation as the *De Silento* subdivided into seven distinct sections—a wing formation. Each section in the new alignment propelled forward in the direction of the *Adamant* at an alarming rate of speed. Dropping out of formation, the flanking three sections on either side of the largest core banked off toward Kardashev 7-A and commenced thruster burns. The largest core section did not alter its course and accelerated.

The captain looked at the ensign.

The ensign looked at the captain.

Somewhere behind them an alarm went off and Envoy Shalad wet himself.

Sensors advised immediate disengagement of the vessel's operative orbit, but it was too late.

Like Michelangelo's iconic fresco, the captain reached out for the ensign's hand in cold comfort and Envoy Shalad screamed.

Everyone aboard the *Adamant* met oblivion.

38.YIKES

Jock was nowhere to be seen in the hangar.

"Jimmy? Answer me."

Jimmy looked down at Leela and finished the rest of his ale in three huge swallows.

Oh man.

Jimmy dropped his cup and took off running toward ASOCC.

39. SCHMOOZE AND LOSE

As they navigated the passages and ramps out to the residential spider, Roscoe kept yammering and shamelessly snuck glances at Piper's breasts while she coolly stared straight ahead.

Goddamn, Piper thought. What a disgusting little motor-mouth. Jock went on and on about his past work postings, his varying malcontent sentiments on a broad range of topics, and did his utmost to regale her with his rather wearisome knowledge of the Kardashev 7-A station. Piper strove to appear enthralled and took extra care to concur with each of Roscoe's bigoted opinions and laugh at every single one of his crass jokes. It was an excruciating ten minutes, but at last they arrived at a caged ladder leading upward into an overhead duct. Jock let go of Piper's arm and bowed chivalrously.

"Is this it?" Piper asked.

"Yes, indeedy-do," Jock said. "Observational bubble. Up you go, ladies first."

Piper looked up the duct and handed Roscoe the portable CPU.

Ladies first… oh sure.

It was time for ass-show.

Piper took each rung slowly, and like a weasel prowling after a savory pot roast, Jock trailed behind her. It was a climb of nearly ten meters and when Piper reached an oval hatch with a crank arm she turned her head and studied a rectangular sign affixed to the duct's wall.

ASOCC – OBSERVATIONAL CHAMBER
(Capacity 2–4 persons)

Shield retraction duration 0:20 min, max. Exposure longer than 0:20 min can result in significant Azoick property damage and possible employee injury.

"Use that crank," Jock called up.

"Is the bubble equalized?"

"Of course. Just turn that handle counterclockwise and the hatch in front of you will pop free."

Piper did as Jock instructed and the oval hatch opened with a gentle, mechanized click. She pushed upward with one hand and then crawled inside next to the levered-open hatch. Getting to her feet, Piper saw that the observational bubble was small, no bigger than a round walk-in closet, and suffused with orange safety lighting. There was an operational panel on a supportive cambering beam. Looking up, she perceived a thick metallic plate covering a canopy of dense pressurized glass in two halves. The supportive cambering beam cut straight down the middle of the bubble canopy.

Jock pushed the portable CPU across the floor

and pulled himself inside the chamber. Catching his breath, he gestured to the operational panel and then stood. "They keep the shields on when this little gem isn't in use," he explained.

Piper rubbed her hands together and flexed her fingers. "Kind of frigid up here, don't you think?"

"Sensors take a moment or two to warm up. Just turn that knob there on the left and the heat will adjust. You'll see."

Piper did as Jock suggested and a whirring hum commenced as the shields retracted like the jaws of a great whale. The orange safety lighting switched to a bright circumference illumination with just enough strength to permit a view outside. Piper took in the incalculable frogspawn of stars. A welcome blow of warming air flowed up from vents in the floor and fluttered her blonde locks.

"Cosmic," Piper said.

"See? Nice and quiet. And private as all get out too."

Not looking down, Piper thought about the duct and the ladder the two of them had just climbed. The levered-open oval entry was under a meter wide and might end up being a little fiddly, but the drop to the deck below seemed like just the ticket. People fall all the time in the workplace, and any post-mortem analysis would show that Jock was completely sauced, so now was as good a time as any. Moving across the chamber and stepping behind him, Piper crossed and wrapped her arms around his neck. It took a split second for Jock to realize the gravity of the prehensile maneuver.

"What are you doing?"

Piper locked off her arms and squeezed. "Greetings from The Chimeric Circle, cheesedick."

Jock clawed at her forearms. He tried reaching behind him to grab hold of her hair, but Piper leaned back and buried a knee in his spine. Jock convulsed, his face darkening with constricted blood.

"HhlgkIcccanrrrncannnn—"

"Can't breathe? Well gee, that's the entire point, isn't it?"

Paper-thin   rattling. "Noocannpaayouuiiivvvffgggggot—"

"You've got what?"

"Ggggggoolmppff…"

Piper eased up slightly. "Last words, deadbeat. Make it count."

"*GOLD!*"

Piper paused.

What the hell? Did he just say what I think he said?

Did he say gold?

No, it was some kind of a trick. Piper had seen plenty of desperation with enemy prisoners during her time in the PAL, and any lowlife under lethal duress was likely to say anything. One time she saw an old woman with half the skin flayed from her legs offer up her grandsons to be castrated if Piper and her squad of engineers would just stop torturing her. She'd seen battle-hardened extremists wilt like beaten wheat during enhanced interrogations, and she once watched a hardcore cleric forswear his superstitions to avoid being set on fire. But gold—that was another cup of soup altogether. After all, Kardashev 7-A was a mining operation. What if the wiggling sack of shit wasn't feeding her a line? Operating at a loss, The CC would be thrilled to recover any sort of financial windfall. And if what Roscoe was saying was true, The CC might even elect to increase Piper's liquidation bonus. Then again, what if she got a hold of this purported gold and The CC never knew anything about it? Big risk, true, and if The Chimeric Circle found out, she'd probably find herself targeted for erasure as well. The thing was, Piper was a subcontractor. Azoick had no jurisdiction over her team or their parasol equipment. If the gold Roscoe was talking about was even a minor amount, would it be so hard to disguise it with the rest of their parasol gear? It was worth considering either way. Piper elected to let the unctuous twerp speak.

"What gold?" she demanded.

Jock thrashed. Breaking her hold on him and spinning him around, Piper threw him into the dome's glass siege-engine style—*POCK!*—and Jock slithered to the floor in a heap. Grabbing him by the collar of his dingy jumper, she smashed his face into the glass three times until his upper lip split and his teeth cracked. Jock's eye pinwheeled, and Piper threw him down on his back. Dropping onto his chest, she beat his skull against the deck.

"I! Asked! You! A! Question! What! Gold?!"

Battered and bewildered, Jock attempted to

throw a mediocre cross, but Piper knocked his arm away easily. She banged his head on the deck twice more and then, reaching down between his legs, she gripped his privates. Jock shrieked, and Piper clamped a palm over his ruined mouth to quell him.

"Scream again and I swear I will squash this infected fruit of yours into paste."

"Mmmph!"

Piper removed her hand.

"Please!" Jock gibbered and drooled. "I'll pay you! I'll pay, I'll pay, I'll pay!"

"Forget about what you owe The CC, a-hole. Tell me about the gold."

Lips quivering, Jock turned his head and spewed up a gluey sluice of gin-reeking barf. Specks of detached teeth plinked onto the deck.

"You have three seconds to reply, Roscoe. One... two—"

"Please!" Jock cried. "Jsssststop, all right? There's... there's this load I'm getting off rock. It's... it's on one of the tenders. No one, nobody knows about it."

"What do you mean nobody knows about it?"

"Azoick. It's totally off the books. All of it, it's headed back to Earth. Secured transit in a quarantine hold. Nobody—*God*—nobody knows!"

"How much?"

"F-f-fifty..."

"Fifty what? Fifty grams?"

"No, fifty kilos!"

No way.

"Bullshit," Piper hissed. "Where did a scumbucket like you get his paws on fifty kilos of gold? You're no bit-head."

"Somebody else found it. They needed me and my connections to move it."

"I thought you just said nobody knows. Who found it?"

"Jimmy. Jimmy Vik."

Leela's ex-boyfriend in the sweet black leathers.

Man, Piper thought, *talk about your fucking serendipity*.

Despite the repellent stench of his puke, she leaned closer to Jock's face. "Does Vik know where the gold is headed?"

"Not exactly. Jimmy thinks it's headed for the skyport in Hong Kong, but I had the destination on the tender's quarantine hold altered. And I told him the tender was docked in Armadillo Bay H. It's not."

"So you lied to him," Piper said as she squeezed his testicles tighter, "which makes me think you're not above lying to me."

"Gah! I bloody well am not! The CC, you—you all can fuckin' have it! You can have everything! I swear, just let go of me!"

Piper let go of his crotch and wrapped both of her hands around his throat. "Which armadillo bay, then? Where's the gold really going? What are the coordinates?"

"Whaaa?"

Piper dug her thumbs into his windpipe. "Tender, armadillo bay, coordinates…"

"Uglkkmhpp—"

A few more head pounds.

Gurgling, Jock made one last effort to wrestle out from beneath her, so Piper jacked three quick jabs into his ruined face. Instantly, she realized that her punching him was a bad move as she'd put a little too much mustard into it. Jock slackened beneath her like a dead eel.

Piper wrung his neck. "Answer me, damn it!"

Jock's eyes rolled white.

40. A CHANGE OF PLANS

Oh fiddly-fucking-sticks, Piper thought.

After slapping Jock's cheeks several times to rouse him from his stupor, she discovered it was no use. The noxious turd was knocked cold and the intel on the gold was now inaccessible.

Piper sat back on Jock's legs and took a few calming breaths. She was debating what to do next when a rapid series of sparks lit up the observational bubble's canopy.

She looked up to locate the source, but the scintillating streaks of phosphorescence that had drawn her interest vanished in the blackness above. Huh. It could have been anything, one of a thousand different stellar phenomena. What really mattered right now was the gold, and who knew when Roscoe was going to come around. He was effectively useless to her now.

Getting up and grabbing his ankles, Piper fed Jock head-first through the open hatch. Without catching any of the rungs in the access duct, his body dropped like a side of beef and his skull met the deck below with a squishy crack.

Piper grabbed her portable CPU. She hit the switch on the cambering beam to close the canopy metal shields and started climbing down.

41. PLAN B—JIMMY

Jimmy knew he would never survive prison.

Good ol' Donnie couldn't.

Good ol' Donnie got his throat slit on his first day inside, and that was *after* medical experiments.

What chance did Jimmy have?

None at all.

Since technically he was no longer an Azoick employee, Jimmy speculated that the zeal with which he would be prosecuted for the theft of the gold would be far, far worse than he could have possibly imagined now that Leela was onto him. With her destroying the gold sample he'd shown her, he didn't know exactly how she sussed it all out, but she was as smart as they came and his big idea to tug on her tail had totally backfired. Now the tiny lioness, in all her persnickety glory, was licking her foam-flecked chops.

He had to get his rucksack out of his strongbox and get rid of the gold.

Like, *pronto*.

Sprinting toward ASOCC, Jimmy threw a quick look over his shoulder. While he couldn't see her, he could tell by the rapid pounding of feet behind him that Leela was no more than two hundred meters back.

Leela shouted, "Jimmy, wait!"

Man alive, that girl could run.

Jimmy hung a left and two corridors up quickly made another right. He was now in the residential spider. If he could just put some distance between himself and Leela, maybe he could lose her between decks and lock her off. Jimmy's mind ran through his options. He could still hear Leela gaining on him and for a brief second he hoped she was assuming he was having some kind of nervous breakdown. Workers lost their mental strings all the time on mining operations, and now he was what? Trying to run and hide like a little boy caught up and overwhelmed by his disgrace? It seemed plausible. Would assuming she thought he'd lost his marbles be all that far of a stretch? No, Jimmy couldn't chance it. He had to get to his strongbox and chuck the gold into the fragmite incinerators. New life be damned.

He took a bypass ladder up.

Rung! Rung! Rung!

Rung! Rung! Rung! Rung! Rung! Rung!

Rolling out of the bypass onto deck three, Jimmy spied the shores of deliverance in the form of an over-saddled automated hover bin idling nearby. He couldn't believe his good fortune. Pushing the hover bin toward the bypass ladder access, he killed its power switch and with a flat thump the bin dropped to the deck right above the bypass opening. Large, rectangular, and immobile, the bin effectively trapped Leela like a mouse corked off in a pipe.

Jimmy heard Leela's muffled cries and pounds beneath the AHB, but there was no time for reconciliation or reassessment and an unavoidable whirlwind of regrets swirled through him as he ran, leapt, and cut through the station's passages. He felt like such a failure. He should have come clean on the gold vein being a bust. True, he'd his doubts about that sneaky son of a bitch Jock, but unwisely Jimmy had thought he could finagle his own deception or call Jock on it after he saw Zaafer load the drill case dupe onto the tender in Armadillo Bay X. Shit, he should have never dreamed he could get away with something like this or even solicited a partnership with Jock in the first place. And now, not only had he gotten himself fired, not only had he deliberately hurt the only person who actually cared about him, but now Jimmy had an enormous three and a half kilo problem on his hands to get rid of.

Reaching the peripheral corridors of ASOCC, he charged through the central locker room and took a bisecting, diagonal passage that cut through the equipment stores out to the airlock vestibules. The third marked vestibule was connected to the *Adamant*'s transfer module parked on the pad. Working the controls, Jimmy released the secured airlock and entered the attached gangway that linked to the module. The portal was strafed with fringe lights like an illusion tunnel, and Jimmy scrambled his way up the gangway. He released the lever on the linking airlock hatch at the far end and just inside the module, right behind the cockpit and extra passenger seats, there was a caged locker.

Jimmy threw two latches, slid his strongbox out, and punched in his ten-digit code.

Then, hoisting his rucksack over one shoulder, he turned around and hauled ass.

He started parsing out the fastest way to reach the fragmite incinerators to get rid of the gold without running into Leela. He was nearly clear of ASOCC and passing the caged ladder that led to the observational bubble when a crunching, wet thud made him stop. Just off to his right, like a lopsided doll, was Jock Roscoe. Upside down, Jock's head was split open and his neck was bent at a gruesome, fatal angle. Punched free from its socket, one of his lifeless eyes ogled Jimmy like a novelty gumball, and he scarcely had a moment to process the situation when Piper Kollár dropped from the laddered duct carrying a portable CPU.

"Oh, what a pleasant surprise," said Piper. "Just the man I was looking for."

42. THE CORKED MOUSE

Leela pounded on the underside of the AHB.

"Jimmy? Listen to me, we can fix this."

No response.

"Jimmy, can you hear me?"

More pounds and slaps.

"Jimmy, I promise. Nothing will happen to you, okay? Just move this thing and we'll sort everything out, I swear. I know this is not you. This all has to be some mistake. I can help you, Jimmy, and I want to, so just move this thing out of the way so we can talk."

Still no response.

"GODDAMN YOU, JIMMY!"

43. A LITTLE CHAT

Piper seized one of Jimmy's arms brusquely. "We need to talk."

Jimmy stared at Jock's smashed skull and then back at Piper.

"Holyshhhhh—"

Piper jerked him forward. "Oh, him," she said dismissively. "Forget that loser. He's no longer part of the big picture. You, on the other hand, handsome, totally are. You see, I'm all about the shining dawn at this point. Atomic number seventy-nine and the aurum to be precise."

"The what?"

"The gold."

Jimmy tried to pull away. "You're joking."

"Mmm, don't think so."

"What gold?"

Piper pinched Jimmy's elbow and his whole arm twanged as she crushed a cluster of nerves. "I'm former Pan-American Legion, meathead. If I wanted to, do you know how many ways I could kill you right now?"

"Listen," Jimmy said quickly, "I haven't the

vaguest idea of what you're talking about."

Piper hurled him into the wall and backhanded his face with the CPU. She hit him with the device twice more, once from the left and once from the right. Dropping the CPU before he could recover, Piper grabbed Jimmy's leathers and headbutted his nose three times in quick succession. The consecutive blasts were all-consuming, like someone had repeatedly jabbed a garden spade into the center of Jimmy's face. Blood and snot poured from his nostrils. Piper leapt back into a ready stance as Jimmy bent over and lowered his rucksack.

"Look," she said, bouncing hither and yon, "we really should do this civil and polite, because if I go full-bore on you, I'm going to hurt you real bad. So, what do you say? I'll give you a moment to think about it. But just so you know, make no mistake. If you try to run, I will catch you, and when I do I will break both of your shins and bend them until your skin splits."

Jimmy stared. He considered charging her waist, but then he fully realized with whom he was dealing. Pan-American Legion? *Screw that*. Piper Kollár may have been rocking some dangerous curves, but she was a trained killer and totally out of his league. "You, you're the one from The Chimeric Circle, aren't you?"

Piper raised an eyebrow. Moving fast, she grabbed Jimmy's throat with her right hand and slammed him back into the wall.

"And where'd you hear that?"

"Jock mentioned someone connected with The CC might be on station."

"So Roscoe knew it was me?"

"I don't know. All Jock said was there was a rumor."

Piper steadied her grip. "Huh. No matter. Seeing that you and the late Mr. Roscoe were all buddy-buddy, let's stick with the matter at hand."

Jimmy started to speak but stopped himself. His brain was a tempest of questions. If Jock told this freak about the gold, did he throw said freak off the scent by lying to her as well? The drill case of rocks… the one Zaafer loaded into the tender in Bay X… Jock had no idea Jimmy was aware of his pulling a double-cross. Piper obviously killed him, and that gutless weasel, if he'd been tortured, he probably sang like the proverbial canary to save his own hide.

Oh hell, what did it matter? He was trying to get rid of the gold anyway. Maybe he should just hand over his rucksack and let the killer swing for the capital one corporate offense. But if Jimmy did that, she'd probably kill him right then and there to cover her tracks. Cripes, he didn't want to die. Jimmy needed to push for time.

"Listen, about the gold," he said. "Did Jock tell you he was conning me out of my share?"

Piper searched his eyes. "Maybe."

"No maybes. I know all about it. That rat switched armadillo bays on me. I discovered he'd made arrangements to ship it in another tender altogether."

"And let me guess, you know where this tender is parked."

"Yeah."

"So where?"

Jimmy squeezed his eyes shut. Lord, if he followed this gnarly invention of his any further, who knew where it would lead. What he definitely knew he damn well couldn't do was tell this crazed, less than temperate sociopath that the only gold found was secreted in his rucksack right between their feet. If he could lead her out to the tender loading bays, maybe he could call for help or get away. With the party there would be plenty witnesses for sure. Of course, he would end up getting arrested and going to prison, but right now he didn't want to die...

"Look," he said, "the gold, it's almost, like—"

"Yeah, yeah... fifty kilos, so I heard."

"Um, right, so you might be able to move it, but it's going to be a real pain in the ass. And the case it's in, it's in a damn quarantine hold. There are extra security measures. You don't have clearance."

"I'm an engineer, hot stuff. Security measures can be bypassed."

"Okay, sure, so you say, but quarantine holds have other dangerous materials too. You'll need a hazmat suit."

Piper resumed crushing Jimmy's neck. "The standard exposure window for quarantine holds is sixty seconds, tops, and that's if there's a significant issue. Besides, I don't need to remove the gold. If I can confirm its location, all I need to do is adjust the final destination coordinates."

"I can take you to it."

"Oh, really? You? Take me?"

"Yeah. If you allow me to take you, you can check and know I'm not just shining you on, right?"

Piper let go of Jimmy and snatched up her CPU. "Grab your pack and let's move out," she said.

44. RED LIGHT

Leela descended the bypass ladder and jumped down to the deck.

Think, Leela. Think.

Where was Jimmy headed?

He might be going to his quarters, she thought. But wait a second, Jimmy was all dressed to go home and had told her he'd already cleared out his unit, so why would he be running back there? Leela then remembered the transfer module dispatched from the *Adamant*—it was parked on one of the landing pads outside ASOCC.

Goddamn, are Jimmy and Jock that dumb?

Were they planning on smuggling gold out on the transfer module?

Leela racked her brain. Maybe it wasn't all that dumb of an idea. While it was a brazen plan, if they were choosing to use the transfer module, it was because they knew no one would thoroughly inspect the module interiors until the *Adamant* returned to the Neptune Pact Orbital. Within a few short hours the *Adamant* would take on the loaded tenders and then the freighter would immediately commence preparations for the skip back to home. Things would be chaotic aboard getting everything set for the skip, and knowing Jock he probably was counting on a lapse of attentiveness and had come up with a way for him and Jimmy to transfer the gold out of the module before the six-month trip. There might even be coconspirators on the *Adamant* or back at the Neptune Pact Orbital who were in on the whole plan, come to think of it.

But Jimmy now knew Leela was on to him. He took off running as soon as she had mentioned Jock back in the shipping hangar.

Was Jimmy trying to abort the scheme? Was he attempting to offload the gold from the module and get rid of it to cover his and Jock's tracks?

Leela hoped it was true. The possibility of Jimmy taking the long road around and finally wising up gave her a renewed sense of optimism. But if this circuitous scenario was, in fact, the case—how the hell would Jimmy get rid of the evidence?

Leela snapped her fingers.

The fragmite incinerators.

Calculating the quickest way down to the bottommost level of the residential spider, Leela started moving. If Jimmy went to the transfer module and doubled back, surely he'd almost be down to the incinerators by now. That son of a bitch, showing her that piece of gold and playing all dumb so she'd fire him. She was steamed at being used, but desperately she still wanted to believe that Jimmy was doing the right thing. Suddenly she realized if somehow it came to light that she knew about the gold and allowed it to be destroyed, she too would likely be implicated. God—was this the right thing for her? Willfully allowing the destruction of Azoick property? And she'd already destroyed that portion Jimmy had shown her. If she wanted to build an eventual case for her defense, that would probably come out under cross-examination, and how would that look?

Despite all of Jimmy's atrocious actions and her trampled emotions, Leela still didn't want to see him get hurt.

Just then a flashing red glow from an adjacent corridor drew her attention.

Making a turn and entering the corridor, she saw a station map display lit up with a red advisory light. A red advisory light always meant bad news for those in station management, anything from a breached structure lining to a generator problem to an emergency medical issue. The map display indicated the source of the problem, and the location wasn't far from where she stood.

ASOCC.

Everyone, except maybe for Jimmy, was in the hangar for the pre-liftoff party. No one of the station management team was aware of what was happening or minding operations.

Leela ran.

45.COLLISION COURSE,
PART UN—THE FIRE SHIPS

Meanwhile, the remaining contiguous sections of the *De Silento* fanned out and tracked over Kardashev 7-A. As they gradually decreased their altitude the sections adjusted their forward velocities, navigational systems on each skimming the SPO's desolate geographies. In a matter of seconds, targets were acquired and confirmed.

Azoick Surface Operational Command Center.

Processing.

Life support and gravity production systems.

Residential.

Shipping.

The spiders.

The remaining sections of the *De Silento* were a squadron of annihilation.

Fifteen minutes out.

46. FOLLOWING THE PIPER

To his left, Jimmy noticed a station map display winking a red advisory light as he and Piper entered the shipping hangar. Knowing that Leela was somewhere behind them, Jimmy assumed she'd probably seen the advisory light and was on the case. Well, he thought gloomily, at least Leela was out of his hair for now.

Although it hardly seemed conceivable, the unpleasant Kryp-Bop music in the hangar was louder and more grotesque than before—a sonorous, frenzied rumble of thick bass and distorted repetitive feedback. In a deft effort to further jack the party's Dionysian ambiance, someone had actually gone to the trouble to set up a compact lighting system on the temporary stage used for the assembly presentation. Polychromatic lasers combed the hangar like eerie fingers and the convex ceiling looked like the inner shell of a psychedelic Easter egg. One of the skirts on the temporary stage had been torn off and someone managed to cover the imaging drone, which bobbed above the party like an addlepated ghost. Working senseless *cinquain* and *ottava rima* rhymes, the Kryp-

Bop artist Lady Dragoonfly bawled.

M-skip springin' bad-truth backatchayallza
Starshot a-dreaminz
Grade prime-dead meat
Hot wine an' slickities
Alls dis cool MC's meanin'

Drop ya vaccine'd mindz
No future fo'ya cardia-o rehabilitat-ums (allitwuzz,
allitwuzz)
I needz m'baby hot bee-hind
Stellar liez lowback un-newy mutilationzzz
Body an' soul total ease
Pluto-Jupit-a tradin' corporationzzz
MIA Croatia keyzz
D'causez makeya beaker bleedzzz…

None of the congregants paid any attention to Jimmy and Piper as they scored the perimeter of the party, and together they made their way to the packed-up parasol equipment. Setting her CPU down, Piper opened the largest of the cases and checked its contents. After she closed the case, she picked up a strapped handle on its side and wheeled the case behind her like a buckboard wagon.

Jimmy asked, "What's that for?"

Piper answered, "Insurance. Keep moving and keep an eye out."

Threading the shelving stores, they reached the far side of the hangar and the long sweep of lettered armadillo bays in no time. Jimmy fingered his swollen nose and motioned with his chin. "There are twenty-six armadillo bays and the one we're looking for is way down on the far end."

"Yeah, I know my alphabet."

"Okay, but do you really know what you're doing? Because this is, like, a major deal. Stealing company property is a capital one corporate offense."

"Not for me it isn't."

"Oh, sure, *right*."

Piper stopped. "I detect a whiff of sarcasm. Tell me, do you have any idea how connected The Chimeric Circle actually is?"

"Not really, no."

"Think of nearly everyone who's ever had a shred of power at home or on any outpost or off-world colony—be it business, showbiz, politics, science, the military, or backward creed—and then times them by the power of twelve."

"Guess it pays to have friends in all the low places, huh?"

Piper sneered and gave him a push forward. "Oh, sure, like you're one to talk, conspiring with the likes of Jock Roscoe."

Passing the sealed armadillo bays with their docked tenders, less than two minutes later they were all the way down at the farthest, darkest end of the hangar near Armadillo Bays X, Y, and Z. Jimmy slid his eyes to Piper. If this ex-PAL legionnaire was going to dismantle his ass or get rid of him altogether, now would be the perfect time for her to do so. This far from the arrant jollity of the party, no one would find his body for hours. If Piper chose to murder him, she might even elect to stuff his corpse into a regular tender cargo hold and his body would rot for months before being found. Either way, death or ass-kicking, he wondered how much it was going to hurt.

"This is it," he said at last, pointing. "Bay X."

"Let's get cracking."

47.SELF-PROMOTION

Reaching ASOCC, Leela sped across the room and dropped into her assigned seat. All around her console her screens were streaked with pulsing red bars and beeping. She raked her eyes over the chirruping displays. The data showed that the *Adamant* freighter was no longer in operative orbit around K7-A.

Leela croaked aloud, "What? That can't possibly be." Inserting her bone mic into her ear, she immediately tried hailing the freighter. "Azoick vessel six-seven-two-three-zero *Adamant*, this is JSC Pendergast, ASOCC. Override alert indicates your orbital status negative, I repeat, negative. Do you copy?"

A rough, vacuous stream of static.

"Azoick vessel six-seven-two-three-zero *Adamant*, this is a priority transmission from K7-A ASOCC. We have an alert indicating your orbital status is negative, please respond, over."

Still not receiving any answer, Leela typed in a request for comprehensive perigee/apogee scans of all possible orbital tracks around Kardashev 7-A. At once a catastrophic smear of disjointed debris appeared on several of the screens in front of her. Leela bumped up the diagnostic magnification.

Oh God...

The *Adamant* was totally obliterated.

But how? How could this have happened?

With the vagaries of space, Leela understood that terrible things occurred all the time. Yet given the magnitude and outward dissipation of the wreckage, whatever happened to the *Adamant* looked positively cataclysmic. Analyzing the specific size and nature of the debris, she began to theorize. Had the orbiting freighter been hit by a rogue asteroid? Prior in-depth survey teams had methodically searched the outer reaches of the sector for such deadly anomalies, and the fragments and twisted pieces didn't bear the signature of an object hit. So no, Leela had to assume the destruction was caused by something else, possibly a devastating fusion reactor failure or worse.

Her thoughts shifted to everyone getting their ya-yas out in the shipping hangar. Oh hell, if the *Adamant* had an onboard emergency and the station lent no assistance because they were too busy getting hammered, every single soul on station would be held accountable to the company, top down, including herself. Immediately Leela called up all comm records and diagnostic readings and backtracked them from the time of the *Adamant*'s orbital lock. Scanning the analytics on accelerated playback, when she saw the *De Silento* closing in at five hundred meters per second and then divide into seven sections her mouth dropped open and she couldn't tear her eyes away. The largest section of the *De Silento* collided with the *Adamant* dead on as six smaller portions broke off and swooped away.

She was thunderstruck.

But the De Silento, its course heading was—

Leela found the scrap of paper from before on her desk and re-read her handwriting.

alardo-9

Her whole body locked up with dread. Oh no. There was that Priority B message from the Azoick envoy aboard the *Adamant*, all that talk about the so-called unpleasant Enlai and Azoick tensions, the failed proxy fight, and the nearly shadowed skip trajectory. The nearest spheroid claim in the sector was nothing but an EU lie. The *De Silento*'s booster problem hadn't been a problem at all.

Black swan, her ass.

The destruction of the *Adamant* was corporate sabotage.

Stupefied, she couldn't and didn't want to believe it. Corporations turning aggressively on each other when all other arbitrations were exhausted wasn't exactly unheard of back home, but normally those sorts of aggressions were tied to international and diplomatic power struggles. A rival mining outfit attacking a defenseless freighter? It was the worst possible situation, a lurid and terrifying nightmare, and Leela prayed that any second now she was going to wake up from it. Forcefully, she gave her face a hard slap.

Pull yourself together, Leela. Deal with the problem.

Okay, she thought, so the *De Silento* destroyed the *Adamant*—what happened to the *De Silento*'s other sections? Leela replayed the moments before the collision. Did the rest of the sections actually move off in formation, and if so, where were they headed? When she initiated sensor skims of the entire SPO, the worst part of the unfolding bad dream ripped through her like a buzzsaw.

The six remaining sections of the *De Silento* were on direct intercept course with the K7-A station.

Without a second thought, Leela hit the critical all-personnel "Code Zulu" klaxon. She feared, however, that with the moronic loud music and rowdiness in the shipping hangar nobody would hear it. No one had paid heed to the previous flashing red managerial advisory light that pulled her toward ASOCC. Hell, not a single member of the management team had even bothered to show up. The situation looked hopeless and time was running out. Even if somebody heard the Code Zulu klaxon there was absolutely no way for everyone in the shipping hangar to get to safety in time. Except for her and perhaps Jimmy, the entire station was at the party. Leela replayed the skim analytics once again just to be sure, and calculated the estimated time to intercept was less than ten minutes. Knowing that she was now effectively in charge, Leela had to make the call. A solution shot through her.

She sealed ASOCC's doors and all critical exits and passageways on station.

For the first time in her life, Leela Pendergast truly hated her job.

48. BLACKOUT CODE ZULU—OMG

Jimmy had been knocked unconscious plenty of times and coming to he wondered if Piper had somehow thrown a sucker punch. In an instant everything flashed dark and his feet slipped out from under him.

A split second later his body met the rigid certainty of the hangar deck and the sudden, tenebrous darkness subsided. Looking right, he saw that Piper had fallen too, and they both got to their feet.

Piper cried, "What the fuck was that?"

Jimmy looked up and all around. "I don't know. A power glitch?"

Someone cut the party music and above a brash klaxon could be heard. Leela's unmistakable voice echoed from the hangar's PA system.

"ATTENTION ALL PERSONNEL. INBOUND OBJECTS ON A DIRECT IMPACT INTERCEPT WITH THE AZOICK STATION! EMERGENCY EVAC-LIFTOFF CODE ZULU IN SEQUENCE! ALL UNITS ARE NOW ON LOCKDOWN PRIOR TO LAUNCH. IMPACT T MINUS NINE MINUTES! THIS IS NOT A DRILL! REPEAT! THIS IS NOT A DRILL!"

Jimmy said, "Oh, you've got to be shitting me."

Ominously and in turn, all of the shipping hangar exits immediately slammed shut. A loud roar of protest thundered from the area of the party as one by one across the hangar the armadillo bay systems came online. During the final loading process, the tenders inside the bays had been filled in reverse order, and thus A and B were the first to expel their tenders as they were the least full and were compensated with electric ballasts. Bays C and D were next with slightly more cargo, and so on. The discharging sequence moved at glacially slow pace down the line toward Piper and Jimmy's position at Bay X.

"What's Code Zulu?" Piper asked.

"All the spider's critical areas are sealed off."

"Yeah, okay. I got that, so?"

"So it's Leela," Jimmy said. "I think she's going to try and launch the station on her own."

There was a titanic rumble of hydraulics beneath them as the hangar's giant bulwark assemblies began their slithering leg retractions. A muted heavy tremor followed as booster engines initiated launch preparations.

Piper barked, "You mean we're trapped in here? And what, we're supposed to just ride the whole thing out?"

Jimmy looked at her helplessly and shrugged. "Basically. We've simulated Code Zulu drills before, but no one has ever ordered one for real."

The Code Zulu klaxon, an undulating *cha-hoo-gah*, wailed like a giant strangled goose as Leela's voice boomed over the PA system again.

*"AZOICK FREIGHTER **ADAMANT** INTENTIONALLY DESTROYED. REPEAT. **ADAMANT** INTENTIONALLY DESTROYED. PROJECTILE'S ORIGIN—THE **DE SILENTO** AND HOSTILE. T MINUS EIGHT MINUTES AND FORTY SECONDS TO IMPACT. MOVE TO SAFETY AND SECURE ALL PERSONNEL IMMEDIATELY. ASOCC OUT!"*

The Adamant *was destroyed?*

No wonder Leela was releasing the tenders, Jimmy thought. At first he presumed she was releasing the tenders because she was always deferential to the company's concerns and was trying to protect the cargo. Her being in management, that would be a lead concern. But now Jimmy understood what she was actually doing. The extra weight of the tenders would hold the hangar spider down, and Leela was trying her best to get the station aloft and out of harm's way. Jimmy admired her quick thinking, but at the rate the bays were purging their tenders, the math told him there was no way they all could be released in time. If the shipping hangar was too heavy, the other spiders might be able to break off and get up, but that could unleash additional problems. The whole station was designed to operate as a cohesive unit. If one or more of the spiders separated, they could veer off and dervish wildly out of control. All in all, the situation was, as they say, a total Charlie Foxtrot.

Jimmy turned toward the party way down the

other end of the hangar. Mammalian survival instincts were taking over, and the gathering shredded apart in a remorseless tumult of full-on panic. Fights broke out as people floundered for cover. Many were lashing themselves down to whatever they could, and in predictable anthropological fear others were frozen in place like red-handed possums caught in a spotlight. Someone yanked the stage skirt from the imaging drone and frantically waved at its indifferent lens. Meanwhile, near the vehicle maintenance area, somebody else jumped inside a crawler. Throwing the vehicle into gear, whoever was behind the controls started plowing across the deck, slamming the crawler into one of the sealed hangar's exits. When the vehicle backed up in order to ram the exit again, Jimmy heard a horrible scream as someone was sucked beneath the crawler's gigantic carnassial tracks.

Piper slid to her knees and opened her bulky case. "Oh, great. This is just great. Finally make a Mandelbrot skip out to deep space to pick up some extra scratch and everything goes friggin' haywire." From the case she removed two helmets and spacesuits with primary O_2 processor tanks attached. She tossed a helmet at Jimmy and he caught it.

"Cripes, what are you doing?"

Piper slipped into a spacesuit, removed a pair of gloves from the helmet, and put the gloves and helmet on. Bending down, she took what looked like a long white cylinder from the large case along with a black duffle. She circled a finger and gestured to the other spacesuit and stomped toward Armadillo Bay X. She called back over her shoulder, "Get dressed."

Jimmy started after her. "Dressed? Why? What for?"

"There's no way I'm riding this overgrown lifeboat. I may need an extra hand."

"Wait, do you think we're going to head outside until all this blows over? We can't get out! Everything is on lockdown. The whole station is going to lift off."

"No, it isn't."

"Huh?"

She motioned again to the helmet and gloves in his hands. "Suit up," she said. "We've less than eight minutes now. I'm going to blow us a hole."

Jimmy's eyes doubled in size. "A hole? In the hangar? Are you out of your mind? It'll depressurize! There's still people in here!"

"Relax. I'm only going to blow a hole in this armadillo bay, not the whole hangar."

"But there'll be an explosion," Jimmy insisted. "There'll be a mammoth sudden release of air and the whole structure could wrench apart. You can't predict what'll happen with an explosion. There could be cascading system failures. If the whole hangar depressurizes, it'll be—"

"What?"

"Mass murder!"

"And your point is?"

"You can't do that!"

Piper threw a switch on Armadillo Bay X's control panel and an access door retracted with a hiss. A cloud of condensation steam rolled out. "In the Pan-American Legion one of the first things they teach you in survival school is improvisation. Even if this whole shooting match manages to get up in time, the station will move like a beast. Inbound hostiles? I guaran-fuckin'-tee you those suckers are already locked in on their targets. You want to be pulverized and kiss the great beyond at forty thousand degrees below zero? Be my guest."

This was madness. Jimmy looked behind him again. A clutch of workers had climbed onto the ramming crawler. Others continued to tie themselves down with whatever they could, and some started crawling inside empty cargo containers. Obviously enraged with drink, several strip-bore specialists Jimmy knew had decided to go for broke and were choking members of the ASOCC management team. Goddamn, he thought with despair, for hundreds of years with all our revolutionary and advanced technologies no one ever found a shred of intelligent life beyond Earth. It wasn't the first time he'd considered it, but maybe it was best that humans were relegated to a galactic backwater. Pushed to their limits, people turned feral and downright savage.

On the flipside, knowing that Leela was already locked inside the ASOCC and trying to do something to save them all gave him hope. At least someone worth a damn had balls. Jimmy wished he could see Leela one last time and tell her that he was sorry for everything. Cutting back to the case, as he picked up the spacesuit he saw two men in blue coveralls pointing at him four hundred meters away.

Piper advised tersely, "Don't look now, but that suit in your hands belongs to one of those boys. If I were you, I'd get dressed on the amscram."

The two men in blue coveralls sprinted toward Jimmy and Piper cheetah-fast as the armadillo bays continued to expel their tenders. Jimmy dropped his rucksack and pulled the spacesuit on over his boots. The automatic seals and cinches pressurized to his leather-clad body and boots instantly so he secured his helmet and locked off his visor. The O_2 flow was clean—a much-needed mind-clearing rush—and he grabbed his rucksack and met Piper at the access door on Bay X. Piper's visor was locked off now as well and her voice streamed into his helmet.

"Step aside," she said.

Dropping the black bag, Piper lifted the large white cylinder she'd taken from the case, pressed a button, and a cushioned shoulder stock extension shot out. A high-pitched whine resonated and a bulb on the business end of the cylinder changed from red to green. Piper then tucked the cushioned stock into her right shoulder like a shotgun as one of the approaching men skidded clumsily to a halt. The second man kept moving, dodged left, and threw himself behind a parked marcher lift.

"Sorry, Østerby," Piper said.

There was a squelched sneeze as a lasing white twine of light flashed from the tip of the cylinder. Jimmy stared in horror as the halted man, the one Piper called Østerby, took a galvanic hit to his chest and misted apart. Piper then dropped to one knee, swept the weapon and aimed at the second man cowering behind the parked marcher lift's legs.

"Kollár!" the second man screamed. "What the hell are you doing?!"

"Sorry, Stormkast. Be a dear now and hold still."

The snout of the cylinder sneezed again and a second twine of hot light shot outward. Like trembling fingers webbed in prayer, the light wrapped around the marcher lift's legs and fizzled. Piper zapped the legs again and the upper portion of the marcher lift came down and squashed Stormkast like a bug.

Piper rose from her firing position. "Let's go. We've got one shot at this."

Jimmy swallowed hard. This was some totally evil shit, but he didn't want to be her next victim so he didn't argue. He threw the lever near the stern of the slotted tender and a second hatch in the hull retracted. Piper waved for him to get inside.

Cargo tenders typically were controlled remotely, but with the *Adamant* gone Jimmy knew it didn't matter. Once inside and twenty meters ahead down a narrow passage near the tender's faired bow there was a forward operating console used for backup. The console was covered in a sheet of plastic. Jimmy ripped the sheet off as Piper shouted at him from the stern.

"Standard manual-overdrive ignition is nearly always on the starboard side," she yelled. "Look for a key covered with a safety cap!"

Jimmy located the key. He flipped back the safety cap. "Fire her up now?"

"You have to ask?"

Jimmy engaged the ignition and the tender's systems came online. From a small lens and projected in a slanted blue haze, gyroscopes, navigational readouts, and callout screens materialized. There wasn't a pilot seat for the controls as a few thousand meters was usually the most a tender was ever needed to be moved manually, and the fact that the console was still pristine and covered in plastic made Jimmy think it hadn't been touched since the day the tender moved off the assembly line. Holy smokes, he thought. Burdened with its yield, piloting the tender was going to be like steering an overgrown refrigerator even if they escaped Bay X in time.

Two joystick controls rose from the surface of the console, and a shield just above retracted, revealing a curved forward casement window.

"We're hot," Jimmy announced.

"Wait!"

Back at the stern near the access hatch, Piper beavered. From the black bag, she attached a remote seismic detonation charge to the cylinder rig's snout and adjusted a dial on the charge. A countdown of twenty seconds. Looking right down the ribbed darkness of the armadillo bay, she took aim at the huge doors leading outside. A set of massive friction-toothed hinges just to the left looked critical and from her position it was an unobstructed shot. Piper inhaled. If this plan went tits up, maybe Vik was right. The whole place could blow apart, but with hostile inbounds she figured they'd all soon be dead anyway.

Piper steadied her aim. Goddamn, she needed to salvage something out of all of this. If the K7-A station was destroyed and she survived, there was no way of verifying Roscoe's liquidation. Her handlers with The Chimeric Circle were a bunch of cold-hearted bastards, and no doubt they wouldn't take Piper at her word and would fail to pay her fee. She needed the gold and had to get back to her fiancé. This better work.

Piper drained the stretch of air from her lungs and squeezed the trigger. The remote detonation charge flew forward with a sparkle of micro-illuminated tracers and her aim was perfect. The charge hit the middle friction hinge and latched on with scarab-like barbs.

Piper folded back inside the tender and sealed the hatch. Leaving her black bag and cylinder weapon she stormed forward to where Jimmy stood at the backup console. Shoving him aside, she swept a finger through the slanted blue arrays and released the tender's docking holds. There was a meager, weightless wobble from side to side and she gripped the joysticks. Jimmy moved behind her.

"What now?" he asked.

"Best find something to hold onto."

Jimmy put a hand on her shoulder. "But wait—"

"Not me, you idiot!"

"No," Jimmy said. "I didn't feel anything."

Piper studied the navigations. She powered up the lift hovers and onboard gravity systems. Using the joysticks, she backed the tender out of its chocks and the tender lifted off of the bay's

internal pad. "The explosive charge is on a timer,"
she said.

"So how long 'til it blows?"

"Ten seconds, maybe less."

Piper and Jimmy braced themselves.

49.THE HARD SUCK

In ASOCC, Leela smeared back her tears with the cold fingertips of both hands.

Cutting the primary station power had worked. The blackout and subsequent temporary loss of artificial gravity had grabbed everyone's attention. But having to make the call to seal everything off and announce Code Zulu—that really sucked.

Leela studied the readings in front of her. The projectiles' bearings were still on a direct collision course heading with the station and the estimated time to impact was six minutes and forty seconds. Leg retractions, station-wide, were only at sixty-seven percent, and less than half of the armadillo bays had purged their tenders. The structures' lower fusion reactors had all of the lift rockets ready to burn, but, damn, Leela knew there was no way the whole station could get aloft in time. Looking up at a monitor on ASOCC's far wall, she watched a panoptic-visual of the shipping hangar relayed from the imaging drone. Some jackass was attempting to use a crawler as a battering ram. All civility in the hangar was lost. Everybody was going apeshit.

Making sure she didn't broadcast to the rest of the station or to the panicking hordes out in the hangar, Leela spoke into her bone mic.

"Jimmy? If you can hear me, listen. I'm in ASOCC. I've done all I can, but the readings indicate the station won't get up in time. Even if we do, it looks like the projectiles from the *De Silento* are going to strike us anyway. I know it sounds bad, but if anyone can survive this, you can, so hold on, okay? Try to seal yourself off somewhere, and before you do, try to grab some water and food. With any luck, maybe wherever you hide yourself, if it's sealed, could—"

Could what? Get blown clear? Survive certain destruction?

It was unlikely. If anything, even after all he'd done to her and with the gold, Leela knew Jimmy deserved to be told the truth.

Don't lie to him.

"God, Jimmy, I don't know what else to say. I mean, I know I should've been, I don't know, more honest and open with you about how I feel... how you hurt me and all that, but for what it's worth I want you to know that I love you anyway. You hear me, you stupid jerk? I love you! Hang on!"

There was nothing more she could do.

Clenching her teeth, Leela slapped her bone mic from her ear and made for the *Adamant*'s transfer module. Passing through the connecting vestibule and grabbing spacesuit, helmet, and gloves she charged up the airlock gangway and entered the parked spacecraft. Locking the hatch behind her, she pulled on the spacesuit and clamped on the gloves. After strapping into one of the pilot seats, she secured her helmet, lowered and locked off her visor.

Five minutes and twenty-five seconds to impact.

She quickly entered her Azoick employee identification number and password.

Screw crosschecks.

Leela fired booster ignitions and a booming rumble beneath her began.

50.BLOWING A HOLE

Jimmy wedged himself along a partition. Piper gave him one last look as the charge blew with a seismic *KUH-WHUMP!*

As Bay X's door tore free and outward, a clacking maelstrom of wreckage strafed the tender's hull in a reverse squall of rushing, depressurized air. The tender shot backward abruptly, lifted and held, and then jerked from port to starboard. Jimmy crashed sideways left and right accordingly, and Piper hung onto the joystick controls.

"C'mon, damn you! C'mon!"

Gong-loud, something hit directly above the forward casement. Pitching downward, the tender bounced roughly off the pad and lifted upward again. The ale Jimmy recently consumed sloshed in his stomach and began creeping up his throat. Surfing the turbulent vibrations in a cowabunga-stinkbug stance, he watched as Piper engaged the tender's aft engines at full power. The tender rocketed forward and Jimmy flew backward.

Outside the forward casement, the ferocious gale of swirling apocalyptic carnage churned. Jimmy had suspected Piper's blowing a hole in the door would cause additional damage and regaining his footing he saw that he was right. The hangar had, indeed, split open like a rotted melon, and all manner of objects were being ripped out into space. Like a giant tomahawk a marcher lift wheeled past followed by a compound crusher lid, a whipping tumbleweed of thick cables, and a dozen men screaming and clawing for purchase.

Piper groaned, "C'mon! C'mon, you fat piece of junk! That's it! Fly! FLY!"

Riding the express elevator down to the misery department, Jimmy hated himself. On top of being culpable in a capital one corporate offense now he was an accessory, ipso facto, in the untimely deaths of hundreds. Of course, with the looming projectile impacts moments away, everyone in the hangar was pretty much fucked anyway, but that wasn't the point. The point was Jimmy hadn't even tried to stop Piper. Goddamn, if he survived the next few minutes, his doing nothing in the face of all this insanity was something he knew he couldn't live with. Sooner or later Piper would discover that the supposed gold in the quarantine hold was bogus, and then she'd find the gold stashed in his rucksack and kill him. *Oh man—* this was bad. This was way, way past sliding into the abyss. This was a lurid hell of his own making and now the only way out of it and doing something at least halfway honorable depended on Jimmy willing himself to do the worst possible thing. But fuck it, he needed to see things through to the end.

It always came down to that, didn't it? What one was willing to do? Jimmy was willing to steal. He was willing to risk imprisonment and medical experiments. Hell, he was even willing to cast aside Leela, the one decent person who cared for him, and now she was going to die too. Yeah, her death wouldn't be his fault, but why not push the chips all the way across the table? The wry old adage mocked him.

In for a penny, in for a pound...

Jimmy had to do something.

Hanging back as the tender soared forward and rose, he loosened the buckles and pressure seals on his spacesuit and removed his helmet. Still busy at the controls, Piper wasn't paying any attention and when the top half of Jimmy's spacesuit was down and folded back around his hips, he gingered his legs out of the rest of it. Taking two steps forward he reached out for Piper's helmet. Snicked free of its locking clasp, her visor rose automatically and all surprise vanished.

Piper whirled at him. "What the hell?"

Jimmy swung an arm and knocked her helmet off. Taking a stutter-step, he stomped on her left knee joint as hard as he could, and Piper's leg folded inward and wrong.

Piper howled. Releasing the controls, she gripped her damaged knee as the tender sloped upward at a vertiginous angle. Both of them lost their footing, but Jimmy grabbed the edge of the console just as Piper rolled down the flanking passageway toward the stern's hatch.

Jimmy got to his feet and took hold of the joysticks. Even with her bad leg, he knew Piper was already scrabbling her way back forward and in a matter of seconds she'd reach him. Jimmy searched the projected navigations. He had to slow her down.

Yanking the joysticks left and right, he veered the tender riotously to port and starboard and heard Piper spilling backward down the passageway. She screamed.

"ASSHOLE! I'M GOING TO RIP YOUR GODDAMN SPINE OUT!"

Shit. There was no way Jimmy could keep her off balance forever, so with his right fingers he trawled into the breast pocket of his leathers. Pinching out his straight razor, he looked back and saw Piper limping toward him like a winded mountaineer with her cylinder weapon. When she finally took aim she was barely three feet away, so Jimmy rotated and kicked out a heel. His foot caught the cylinder weapon and knocked it out of her hands.

Stumbling, Piper charged and threw her shoulder into Jimmy's side, knocking him away from the console. The tender rocked frighteningly from side to side. Jimmy flicked out his razor and slashed upward, hoping to slice something critical. Whiffing on his follow-through he spun around, fell, and slammed onto his back. The words "done for" came to mind.

Great, he thought miserably, *now she's going to kill me.*

Surging up one more time, Jimmy bear-hugged Piper's waist and plowed her back into the controls.

The tender entered a dive.

51.UPLOAD

In the transfer module, Leela made sure her orbit was secure before she tried syncing into K7-A station's relays. It was imperative that she at least try to upload all the files from the station's mainframes before the inbounds destroyed everything. The syncing upload commenced and just as she peered out a starboard porthole the projectiles at last blitzed into the spiders.

Given the module's orbital altitude the destruction below was a bit underwhelming: a half an instant's worth of brief bursts, squelched fire, and then nothing but dust clouds. Leela immediately turned back to check the upload sync.

The connection and all the files from K7-A were lost.

52. DONE FOR

Piper jabbed a four-finger spear strike into Jimmy's throat.

Jimmy dropped to his knees. It felt as if a blob of molten steel was suddenly lodged in his windpipe and he couldn't breathe. Canting to the side and rolling onto his back, he looked up at Piper as she took control and leveled the tender out. Engaging the automatic pilot, she turned.

Jimmy tried to get to his feet, but lightning fast Piper kicked him and he fell back. She leered.

"Nice try."

A merciful trickle of air reached Jimmy's lungs. "You murderer…"

Unfazed by the character update, Piper shot a boot into his kidney and glanced briefly back at the console. "Well, yeah, technically I suppose that's true." She kicked him in his side again. "But by association you're on the hook for that as much as I am. Not that it matters now. Take a look."

On the navigations a callout screen showed the spiders just as the *De Silento*'s projectiles slammed into the station—soundless fire and blooming white clouds of obliteration. There was no way anyone could have survived.

God, Jimmy wished with every fiber of his being he'd never found the gold. All he wanted was another chance, another chance to do a million things. To save Leela and everyone else on K7-A station, to say proper goodbyes to his parents even though they were long dead and gone. Jimmy realized these flashes of regret were coming to him because instinctually his brain knew the end was nigh.

As improbable as it was, just then Jimmy felt a raindrop land on his lips. His attention drawn, he licked the improbable drop of liquid and tasted warm iron. He imagined it might be blood dribbling from his broken nose, but looking up at Piper he noticed a barely perceptible swoop of red stretched across her neck. The swoop widened and when Piper saw the blood dripping down onto Jimmy's face she slapped a glove against her neck.

"Oh no—what did you do?!"

Jimmy beetled back on all fours. When he turned around, the remaining integument cells on her wound gave way and a wash of blood gushed over Piper's glove. The blood spilled remarkably fast and down into the collar of her spacesuit, and an ineffable look of terror rose in her eyes. The wound was deep. It was growing more fatal by the second, and Piper knew it. There was so much blood.

Jimmy edged toward the passageway and pulled himself to his feet. He swung his razor out in front of him like a foil. "Stand back."

Piper beat a look at the razor and then at Jimmy. Her lips parted ghoulishly. "Where did you get that thing?"

"This?" Jimmy answered. "It was a gift from my late father. Sorry, but you were going to kill me eventually, weren't you?"

Piper made a move toward the cylinder weapon, but Jimmy blocked her path. She swayed back drunkenly. "Well, maybe not right away. But, yeah, I suppose sooner or later I would've, sure."

"It didn't have to be this way, you know."

Piper regarded him. She lowered her glove from her neck and let her blood pump freely like a spring. Reaching into her collar, she jerked something free and dangled it—a necklace. Looking at a ring and an amulet attached, she caressed them both. "Listen, I know this sounds awful of me, but if… if you and the hijacked loot make it… could you do me a favor?"

"For *you*?"

Piper nodded weakly and tossed the necklace at his feet. "Get that to my fiancé."

"*You* have a *fiancé*? What the—why the hell should I?"

Piper fell to her knees and wheezed. "Just be decent, saw-grinner. Tell him… tell him that I tried. "

Clutching her chest Piper pitched forward onto her face.

Believing she might be pulling a fast one, Jimmy waited nearly a minute before he crept toward her. After kicking Piper in the temple, to be certain she was dead, he turned and picked up the necklace from the deck.

Fiancé?

Whatever, man.

As he stuffed the strung jewelry into his breast pocket, a winking light outside the forward casement drew Jimmy's eyes. It was a navigational beacon on the *Adamant*'s transfer module. The module was approaching fast, no more than three klicks out. An alarm on the navigations throbbed. Jimmy dropped his razor.

Collision course, *part deux*.

53.EVASIVE LEELA-ACTION

A threat alert squeaked blithely. Leela flipped up her visor.

"Now what?"

The module's forward displays advised:

Azoick tender closing. Bearing seven, nine-eight-delta. Three thousand meters.

Like a slab-shaped warhead, the tender was cruising straight for the module. The forward displays continued:

Two thousand meters. Emergency orbit abort advised.

Leela engaged the module's navigations. "Go for emergency orbit abort."

To engage emergency orbit abort, please re-enter your Azoick employee identification number and password.

"Are you freakin' kidding me?!"

Negative. Repeat, please re-enter your Azoick employee identification number and password to initiate emergency
orbit abort.

Leela typed as fast as she could.

"Emergency abort now!" she shrieked. "Abort! Abort! Abort!"

Thank you. Emergency abort now initiated.

Reserve ion-thrust nozzles kicked in and the module skated into a mighty slant. Leela heaved her body to the side as if moving her slight weight could help avoid disaster.

Warning. Impact probability ten percent.

Compensating for combined velocities.

Leela slapped her visor down, locked it off, and held her breath.

Correction, impact probability four percent.

Compensating...

Compensating...

54. OH, DENOUEMENT—OH,
SWEET DENOUEMENT

Well, Jimmy thought, this is it.

The big adios.

Nothing to do now but take it on the chin.

Sorry, Leela.

Sorry, Mom and Dad.

Oh, and by the way, universe?

Go fuck yourself.

In the final seconds before impact, the transfer module looked so close Jimmy thought he could reach out and touch it. When ion propulsions fired and the module listed hard to port, Jimmy remembered.

Leela made the Code Zulu announcement from ASOCC.

God—was it her?

If it was, Jimmy figured Leela must've launched the module to save herself. Never one to quit, she was alive and taking evasive action. Goddamn, that girl had some moxie. Jimmy's heart swelled.

Go, Leela, go!

The module's propulsions burned bright as they slid past the forward casement, and Jimmy hunted the console's navigation screens for a way to reverse the tender's momentum. He activated inverse power, but the tender's response was sluggish. It wasn't going to be enough.

The two hulls collided and a clangorous scraping filled the tender. Flung into a centripetal spiral, Jimmy tumbled sideways, fell, and sledgehammered his head against his rucksack on the deck.

The last thing he heard before blacking out was Leela's voice streaming over comm.

"*Adamant* tender, I'm coming about. Prepare for boarding."

55. NAPTIME OVER, 'FESS UP

Later, when Jimmy came to, he noticed that he was no longer in the forward area of the tender. He found himself enveloped in a gray wool blanket with a second gray blanket folded beneath his head. Leela was bending over him and wrapping a self-adhering elastic bandage around his head.

"Leela! I can't believe you made it! You're alive!"

He tried to pull her to his chest, but she smacked his hands away.

"Hold still, dumbass."

Jimmy lowered his arms. "Oh man, I thought I lost you forever."

Leela shook her head and smirked. "Gee, you talking all mushy like that, you must've whacked your skull pretty hard. You might have a grade-three concussion." After securing his dressing, she closed the first-aid kit and slid it across the deck. "I guess it's safe to say we can add 'throat slitter' to your resume."

Jimmy remembered Piper's slashed neck. "Oh that... that was in self-defense."

"Oh, really? Self-defense? Do tell."

"Listen, I know what it looks like but that

woman... she... she used to be in the PAL. She was an operative for The Chimeric Circle, Leela."

"Piper?"

"You *know* her?"

"We met a couple of times. I thought she was a freelancer."

"She was, but I think that was just a cover ploy to get her to K7-A. The real reason she was on station was to kill Jock."

"Kill him?"

"Yeah. Jock had, like, some serious debts to The CC. I'm not sure, but I think Piper killed him when everyone was at the pre-liftoff party. I saw his body."

"Doesn't matter," Leela said flatly.

"Huh?"

"Jimmy, the whole station was annihilated. The *Adamant* is gone. Enlai Universal attacked us on purpose and there's no active record of what happened."

"Meaning?"

"Meaning if we're rescued, and that's a pretty big if, there's no way for us to prove what EU did. We're the only survivors, don't you see? It'll be our word against Enlai Universal's until someone launches an investigation."

"No one else made it?"

Leela shook her head once more and sat cross-legged next to him. "How are you feeling?"

Taking a serious breath, Jimmy took personal inventory. "My head feels like I've been clobbered with a brick and my nose is broken and my sides are sore, but other than that I think I'm okay." He tried to sit up, felt woozy, and laid back down.

Leela continued, "Look, if Azoick mounts an investigation, forensics might be able to pull the pieces together, but with the Mandelbrot skip delays, something like that could take months, maybe even years. I imagine when they learn of the losses Azoick is going to go ballistic and they'll want to blame someone. If they don't take us at our word, Azoick might even prosecute us. They'll definitely negate our contracts, that's for sure."

"But you already fired me, Leela."

"There's no record of me doing that. Everything was lost when the station was destroyed because I couldn't upload any of K7-A's records. Phew—I tell you what, though. We better seek legal counsel if and when Azoick debriefs us."

Jimmy reached for Leela again, but she rebuffed his hand and furrowed her brow. Damn, all he wanted to do was to hold her, but seeing as that looked out of the question Jimmy decided to come clean about everything instead. The harebrained plan, the gold vein being a bust, Piper boosting the tender and blowing Bay X's door open, the supposed Hong Kong dragon lady and Jock's double-cross, everything. When Leela asked him why he fled from her when she confronted him at the party, Jimmy told her he wanted to get rid of the gold in the fragmite incinerators, but Piper shanghaied him before he had the chance to do so. Leela seemed glad to hear he'd had a change of heart, but she wondered aloud whether, if she hadn't confronted him at the party, he would've followed through with his criminal intentions. Jimmy didn't want to lie to her so he admitted shamefully that, yeah, he probably would've. Leela assumed as much. She then asked him what happened to the gold.

"Like I said, Jock thought it was all loaded in a drill case that Zaafer placed in a quarantine hold on the tender," he said, "but what little I managed to pull from the shaft is still in my rucksack."

"And where is your rucksack?"

"On the tender. We're still docked with the tender, aren't we?"

Leela rubbed her eyes. "Oh, Jimmy… we de-docked with the tender over an hour ago."

"We *did*?"

Leela glanced about. "This module, the reserve batteries don't have that much power. The tender was slowing us down and there was still tons of debris from the *Adamant* flying around, so I cut it loose. Fortunately we're now drifting toward the sector's main shipping channels, and I've activated a distress beacon. The spiders on K7-A were scheduled for repurposing. If we're lucky, the scow that was due to tow the spiders to their next location is bound to pick up our signal in a few days."

"But what about—"

"Piper?"

"Yeah, she's still on the tender."

Leela made an "ick" face and got up. "I jettisoned her body and what I assume was all her gear after I cleaned up the blood. In the long run, a salvage crew may find the tender, but I thought it best not to leave any incriminating loose ends."

"But my rucksack, that's a loose end."

Leela went still. "Jimmy, I jettisoned everything, even the damn cargo."

Jimmy went silent for a moment. "Wow," he said. "I guess… I guess I ought to thank you."

"For what?"

"For saving me from myself. I'm so sorry, Leela."

Jimmy made a go of sitting up again, but Leela wagged a finger and told him to stay down. She sighed. Jimmy had never seen her look so tired.

"I've been thinking," Leela said after a minute, "this stupid gold business of yours and all your lying, I feel it might be for the best if we just leave things as they are, you know? Stay away from each other."

Jimmy held Leela's eyes. "You really mean that?"

"Yeah, I think I do."

After everything that had happened, her words were crushing.

"Yeah," Jimmy admitted glumly as he fingered the tape over his swollen nose. "I suppose you're right. You deserve better than someone like me."

Clunking her cowboy boots on the deck, Leela traipsed away. "Lucky for us there's a nice supply of fresh water and a urine purifier onboard if we get desperate. There's some energy paste packets too, but we'll need to ration things."

"Okay…"

"Don't fall asleep on me now. Concussions can be tricky."

"I won't." Jimmy licked his lips. "Hey, Leela?"

"Yeah?"

"I really am sorry."

"I know."

"I hate to be a dick about it and all, but after all this are you still going to—"

"Tell Azoick about what you did?" Leela tilted her head. "We've both been through a lot, Jimmy, and on balance none of it seems to matter now anyway, so no. I won't tell them anything. It'll be our secret."

"Thanks."

"You're welcome."

"Guess we should get our stories straight then, huh?"

"Well, you're the storyteller," Leela said. "To keep your mind occupied and keep yourself awake, why don't you think it all out. In the meantime, I'm going to check our readings. I'll bring you some water in a little bit, okay?"

56.JUDGMENT AT THE NPO

Six months later, on the Neptune Pact Orbital, a jaundiced-eyed committee of company investigators glared unpleasantly at Leela and Jimmy.

They were seated in a rented, cubiform conference room at a round steel table, members of the committee on one side and Jimmy and Leela on the other. The chairman of the committee mumbled something into a microphone, switched the microphone off, and stood.

"What a mess," he said.

Jimmy nodded. "Yes, sir. A real mess. One for the books."

Leela cleared her throat. "So is Azoick going to do an investigation of what actually happened out there?"

The chairman frowned and didn't look at either of them. "Oh, with such substantial losses and the disastrous collateral deaths, our solicitors deliberated launching an inquiry once the scow that rescued you returned from its skip. But seeing that you've been out of pocket for so long, I believe I should make something clear to you: the entire matter is now closed."

Puzzled, Leela and Jimmy looked at each other.

"Closed, sir?" Jimmy asked.

"Mmm, yes. You see, with the extended time gap between your rescue and the scow's skip back I don't think you've been made aware of something. Enlai Universal and Azoick? Our two companies consolidated two months ago. We're Enlai-Azoick Universal Holdings now, the largest interstellar mining company in existence. Investigate ourselves? It seems rather pointless."

Leela nearly leapt up from her chair. Jimmy put a hand on her arm. "But, sir," he implored, "hundreds of people lost their lives out there. The *Adamant*, the K7-A station, all of it was destroyed. It was—"

"What?"

"Well, a massacre, sir."

"Immaterial."

Leela squeaked, "*Immaterial?*"

Grumbling peevishly, the committee members gathered their dataslates and stood as well. As they left the conference room, the chairman planted his hands on the table with contempt.

"I can't believe I need to make this any plainer for you two," he said mirthlessly, "but have either of you ever had the good sense to read the fine print on your contracts? Company indemnification clauses address fatal hazards. While I can understand this may seem like an outrage to persons of your capitulating stature, resources like you are expendable. By signing contracts, whoever perished out there accepted all risks whether intentional or not, yourselves included. Conveniently your ilk always seems to put such things out of your minds, but no matter. Effective immediately you are both released from your obligations."

Puzzled, Jimmy asked, "Our obligations?"

Leela covered her face with both her hands. "I think he means we're fired, Jimmy."

"Oh."

After the chairman left, Leela got up and gripped the back of her chair. It occurred to Jimmy she was this close to blowing her stack and he was about to say something to calm her down when she picked the chair up and hurled it across the room.

"Those bastards!"

Jimmy crossed to the thrown chair and righted it. "Looks like this fancy dog-and-pony show was just a formality."

"A formality!? People were killed out there, Jimmy! The *Adamant* was blown to bits. These starch-collared jerks and their stupid merger, they can't just pretend none of it happened!"

In an effort to fix things, and quite mistakenly, Jimmy thought some consolation was in order. "Hey... things will work out, you'll see."

Leela glowered at him. "Oh, sure. Maybe you can be all lackadaisical about everything, but I've put in nearly eight solid years with this stupid company. I've busted my butt for them. I've risked my life. I even tried to save their damn station and those snotty clowns, they didn't even bother to say one word about that. They don't care."

"Leela, c'mon..."

Leela marched out of the room without another word.

* * *

It took some arranging on his part, but Jimmy negotiated a low-cost shuttle ticket back to Earth on one of the inner-system budget carriers. With the transport shuttle employing fractional skip power and thin on amenities, the trip home would be an uncomfortable forty-seven-hour slog and he just wanted to get it over with. Post-stasis and before their grilling with the investigative committee, Leela informed Jimmy she was staying on the Neptune Pact Orbital. She said it was because she wasn't ready to go home just yet and explained her nerves needed some more time to decompress and she would make other arrangements. It bummed Jimmy out Leela didn't want to travel back to Earth with him, because he wanted to try to convince her into taking him back, but sadly he realized he had to respect her decision. After all, it was probably for the best.

In the men's room of the discount carrier's boarding lounge, Jimmy shaved with a disposable razor. Leela had apprised him that when she got rid of Piper's body and cleaned up all of her blood, she'd jettisoned his straight razor as well because it was evidence. She'd asked about Piper's necklace with the engagement ring and the amulet, and Jimmy had said that when Piper was dying he had vaguely agreed that he'd get the necklace to Piper's fiancé.

Jimmy nicked himself several times with the cheap disposable and dabbed his cuts with some toilet tissue. Studying his tissue-specked, haggard face in the mirror, he thought about his late father and mother and felt melancholic. Had he listened to his parents and stayed in school, who knew where he'd be now? All this loss, all this needless destruction and death—was any of it worth it? No, he thought, it definitely was not.

Everyone always claimed you should live for the moment, that everything could be taken away from you in an instant. Jimmy knew he used to adhere to this notion, but he made a deal with himself now. He decided he would never travel to space again, because he wanted to live for a long time and simply back home on Earth.

Live clean.

Enjoy a few sunrises.

Plant a garden. Maybe fly a kite once in a while.

He wanted to read the classic literature canons and absurd philosophies of all cultures, both vibrant and forgotten, to see if they could help him make sense of his condition, and maybe in time he thought he could begin to make amends for his actions. Jimmy the cloistered, James Barclay Vik the saint. He saw himself volunteering with a relief program or tutoring misguided kids somehow. After a long and lonely time with all these noble pursuits perhaps then he'd find someone to share breakfast with. Or not.

That last idea wasn't exactly a priority. While he'd wanted to patch things back together with Leela, after everything that'd happened it seemed like he was waving for a ship to come back for him just as the flags of the poop deck crested the horizon. He likened it to that painting by Géricault—*The Raft of the Medusa*—only Jimmy saw himself alone on the lashed-together planks. With no one left to cannibalize, it was up to him to paddle on for his own redemption.

After cleaning himself up, Jimmy threw the disposable razor into a waste bin as an announcement drifted into the men's room. The shuttle *Sultana* was boarding in ten minutes.

At the embarking gate, Jimmy shuffled his way into the queue. It wasn't a full flight, but directly in front of him two passengers were conversing about the events that had transpired on K7-A six months ago.

"Yeah," one passenger went. "I overheard a bunch of suits from Enlai-Azoick yakking over at the concession stands. Seems the whole station and one of their freighters totally bought it out there."

"No way," the second passenger said. "And everyone died?"

"Well, not everyone. There were two survivors, apparently."

Without even thinking, Jimmy raised his hand. The two passengers turned and looked at him.

"I'm one," Jimmy said quietly.

The two conferring passengers were aghast. Another passenger a few feet ahead in the line, a broad-necked brute of a man with an anvil-like head, turned and stared at Jimmy.

"Did you just say you were on Kardashev 7-A?"

"Um, yeah. I was."
"My fiancée was on K7-A."
Jimmy's face went white.
Collision course, *part trois*.

57.AFTERCLAP

And so, later, aboard the shuttle *Sultana*...

"Liar!" Piper's fiancé bellowed inside his helmet. "Don't tell me my baby died out there like the rest of them! This amulet recorded her last moments. You cut her throat, saw-grinner!"

Jimmy let his weight drag him to the floor and curled into a ball. On some pale empirical level he fully accepted that getting his ass handed to him was a rightful and just comeuppance, so what could he possibly say in his defense? That Piper was going to kill him first? If Jimmy whipped together the grandest and most profuse of apologies, would that assure him a swift and merciful death?

In hindsight, perhaps he should've waited to give his attacker the necklace until they safely landed back on Earth. How could Jimmy have known the triskelion charm recorded his and Piper's last moments together aboard the *Adamant*'s tender? But no. Once they were aboard and well under way, Jimmy's conscience gnawed at him. Eventually, when the shuttle passed Earth's moon, an announcement from the flight deck advised the *Sultana* was on approach and spurred him into action. Jimmy got up, and finding him in his seat, gave the necklace to Piper's fiancé.

"Listen, you don't know me," he said, "but I think this belongs to you. Piper told me to tell you she tried."

Piper's fiancé gave Jimmy a disconcerting glare, and when he lifted the necklace and engaged the amulet everything skated straight to hell in a hurry. A confusing thermal hologram of Piper bleeding out and calling him a saw-grinner appeared in the air between them.

"And where's all this hijacked loot, huh?! Answer me!"

Alas, the word *hijacked* changed everything.

While discount inner-system shuttle services may have been a take-your-chance undertaking, one thing that no space transportation provider tolerated, even a discount carrier, were certain words mentioned even in jest. The syllables of "hi" and "jacked" in sequence, while muffled, were picked up by a cabin mic and a small armored turret with a threat-neutralizing stun cannon descended from the ceiling. Painting Piper's fiancé as a target, the cannon zapped out a crackling blast of fifty thousand volts and he fell to the floor. Like a fat hornet, a security drone emerged from the turret a second later, and the hornet-like drone pounced and crabbed over the man's immobilized frame. After injecting a sedative into his neck, the drone took flight again and hovered above Jimmy.

"Sir, remain still."

Jimmy moaned and rolled over. "Oh, god, thank

you. I knew something was wrong and that freak attacked me. I think—I think he was trying to go for the door or something. I tried to stop him, but he overpowered me."

A camera lens on the drone flickered as it assessed the situation. It spoke with a modulated, adenoidal tone.

"Are you injured?" the drone asked.

"Would it be okay if I sat up?"

"Slowly, no sudden movements. The shuttle's countermeasures are now locked in on you."

Gradually, Jimmy sat up holding his cracked ribs. He looked at the stun cannon pointed at his head and then at the hovering hornet drone as it scanned his body for weapons. The drone initiated a secondary cursory physical scan. Registering a tally of contusions and two hairline fractures of Jimmy's right ribs, the drone gauged him a possible victim/hero in the recent altercation and dispatched a secondary message to the authorities and the flight deck.

"Thank you," Jimmy whispered hoarsely.

"Sir, authorities on the ground and the pilots have been notified. Remain still."

"Ahhh… um, have you seen my necklace?"

"Sir?"

Jimmy gestured to Piper's zonked-out fiancé. "That animal took it when he attacked me."

The drone eased back and returned to an aerial position over Piper's fiancé. While he was anesthetized, the necklace was still clutched in the man's hand.

"This necklace, sir?"

Jimmy nodded. "Yeah, that's the one. My late mother... she gave it to me. It's all I have left of her. A family keepsake. The ring was hers too."

After a second spent determining that Jimmy wasn't a menace, the drone lowered and used a pincered hook to secure the necklace. Gliding forward, it dropped the necklace in Jimmy's lap.

"For your safety and the safety of the other passengers, it is necessary that you return to your seat and remain there until we touch down."

The shuttle leveled out. Sunlight poured into the cabin.

Jimmy looked out a porthole on his right. The blue skies and clouds were so beautiful. None of us deserve this world, he thought. He got to his feet and the drone rose with him.

"I'm sorry, but would it be all right if I used the bathroom? I think I'm going to be sick."

Rubbernecked in their seats, the other *Sultana* passengers in the main cabin were looking at Jimmy. Many of the passengers had flipped up their helmet visors, mesmerized by the scene. The drone counseled:

"If you feel you are ill, please be prompt with your emesis and then return to your seat as instructed. The authorities will meet the shuttle upon landing."

Jimmy nodded. Hobbling into the bathroom, he locked the door behind him. With his damaged ribs it took some effort to kneel down, but he'd a feeling he ought to make things look legit. There was no way to know if additional security measures or even a camera was monitoring the bathroom, so faking a retch Jimmy slipped the necklace with its engagement ring and triskelion amulet into the toilet and pressed the flush button.

Per international agreements, the *Sultana* purged its waste tanks somewhere over the Arctic Ocean.

58. BACKSLIDING BACK HOME

TEN MONTHS LATER

There was one thing you could always count on in Vancouver and that one thing was a ton of rain.

It was a Saturday afternoon and a virtual cataract of minimal pH buckets poured down from a slate-colored sky as Jimmy patrolled the sidelines. Not the best day for rugby in the park, and excluding extra time there were nineteen minutes left in the day's match. The junior girls' club he helped coach was down twenty-nine to thirty-four. Despite the mucky conditions, all the girls and gathered supporters seemed to be having a good time.

After the altercation aboard the *Sultana*, Jimmy and Piper's fiancé were promptly manacled and detained by the authorities at one of the European Confederacy's largest interstellar skyports. The skyport was just outside of Paris, and it turned out Piper's fist-happy beloved was wanted in connection with nearly a dozen open murder investigations involving The Chimeric Circle. Regardless of his story and his hostile, blubbering accusations of Jimmy (not to mention the atrocious lack of corroborating evidence, seeing that Piper's necklace was flushed into the Arctic Ocean), after Jimmy was held for eleven hours the authorities saw no reason to keep him further and let him go. Piper's fiancé, on the other hand, wasn't so lucky. Taken to a cooperative government black site, he confessed to many of the crimes related to The Chimeric Circle under enhanced interrogation and was later executed extrajudicially by lethal injection.

As for Jimmy, after a week of moping around Paris's silo-cinemas, brasseries, and cafés he decided to return to his hometown for a much-needed recalibration of his internal compass. He supposed he could've started again just about anywhere or stayed in Europe, but being around all the nearly forgotten city landscapes of his hometown and easing into its congenital Canadian attitudes, he thought returning to Vancouver would even his keel. It did. He quit drinking, stayed inconspicuous, and took an under-the-table position as a night custodian at a dynamo-part warehouse in possibly the sketchiest part of town.

The night custodian work afforded Jimmy a small, storage-container apartment in a neighborhood that, like the part warehouse, would never know a rebound, and for a while, not knowing what befell Piper's fiancé, he lived day to day in fear. Jimmy knew better than to start researching what had happened to Piper's beloved, as that would mean raising his head and registering for all sorts of regulated services. However, as the weeks stretched into months he started to breathe easier and gave up looking over his shoulder altogether. Life wasn't exactly peaches and cream, but his job kept him busy from nine at night until five the next morning, and he filled most of his remaining free hours with torpedo kick drills and the like.

He'd happened into the assistant rugby coach position because one day he read a flyer posted in the laundromat around the corner from his pathetic living arrangements. Turned out the head coach who'd posted the flyer ended up being an old rugby rival and remembered Jimmy from their shared youth.

As he stalked back and forth along the sidelines, Jimmy heard a noise, and he looked up to see a bright yellow aerocab spinning down from the rain clouds. The aerocab alighted just beyond the playing fields in a fenced-in parking lot, and when the passenger got out it was as if a ball of warm, gelid light pierced Jimmy's core. The aerocab's passenger was the last person in the world he ever expected.

Leela was dressed for the weather: a glossy black slicker, matching umbrella, and boots with a pink hooded sweater and jeans beneath. Taking her time, she took up a position beneath a frail whitebark pine near the parking lot's fence. Seeing Jimmy along the sidelines a hundred meters away, eventually she gave him a small wave.

Holy shit, Jimmy thought. *What the holy hell is she doing here?* He hadn't seen Leela since they'd parted ways on the Neptune Pact Orbital, and while he thought about her constantly and sometimes even dreamed of her, he never imagined he would see her again after everything he did. Hastening over to the coach, Jimmy explained he needed a break because an old friend had just shown up unexpectedly. When he pointed Leela out beneath the pine tree by the fence, his old rugby rival told Jimmy to take his sweet time.

Circumventing puddles, Jimmy jogged over to Leela, swept back his hair with a hand, and let out a laugh.

"What in the world are you doing here?"

Giving her umbrella a twirl, Leela said, "Well, let's see. I did some research on my own, but you're one tough hombre to find. No communication service providers, no entertainment credits, bank records, or smart-tech accounts—I ended up having to hire a professional investigator. Tracking you down cost me a bundle, thank you very much."

"I've been trying to keep a low profile."

"I'll say."

"Gosh, it's really good to see you, Leela."

"Likewise."

"So what're you doing here, huh? Are you traveling? On leave? Working?"

Leela giggled. "Working? No, not working yet if can help it. I just thought, you know, now that I'm finally settled I'd take some time to look you up. I mean, really, the world wants to know. What's Jimmy B. Vik up to these days?"

Jimmy pointed at the rugby game in progress. "Coaching."

"Uh-huh. And they pay you for that?"

"Mostly in adolescent aggravation, but I've got a real job."

Leela nodded. "Mmm. A real job. My investigator gave me a full workup. You're living in a storage container like a janitor terrorist."

"Hey, it keeps me in mac 'n' cheese and out of trouble."

"Uh-huh. I guess your ambitions haven't changed."

"Guess not."

Leela took a step toward him. "I've missed you."

Jimmy's heart glowed and beat a high-speed tom-tom. His thought wound with so many apprehensions he could hardly stand still. It was rash, but sensing the liminal slipstream between them again after so many months apart, Jimmy abandoned all hesitation. Placing his wet hands on her cheeks, he leaned down and kissed her with everything he had.

Leela broke off the kiss. "Woof, easy there, bucko. You're steaming me up."

Jimmy dropped his hands and stepped back. "Oh hell, I'm sorry. That was out of line. I shouldn't have done that."

"No, no," Leela replied, fanning her fingers under her chin. She looked back at the aerocab idling in the parking lot. Its operator, a truncated silhouette, flashed the lights and honked.

Leela held up a finger. "Listen," she continued, "if you can tear yourself away from all this sloppy business, I was hoping you and I could talk."

"Talk?"

"Yeah. Do you need to stick around?"

"I'm only the assistant coach."

"Meaning?"

"The head coach is an old rugby rival of mine from back in the day. He told me I could take my time."

Leela glanced at the coach and peeked up at the dark sky from under her umbrella. "All this rain... would it be all right if we, like, maybe got something hot to drink?"

"Tea?"

"A cup of Earl Gray sounds perfect."

On the pitch, one of Jimmy's up-and-coming wingers stiff-armed her way across the goal line on a try and a boisterous cheer went up from the sidelines. Jimmy looked back and his old rival shooed him off with a hand.

Together Leela and Jimmy walked toward the parking lot.

"I was going to wait," Leela then said, "but I don't know. Now that I'm here and seeing all of the months that have passed, I think I should just come out with it."

Oh crap, Jimmy thought. He'd mistakenly misread her warm reception of their fleeting kiss and surmised she was only there because she'd some unresolved issue. When someone said they wanted to talk or come out with it, invariably it was because they wanted to express something that bothered them, usually something bad. They hadn't left things exactly cordial on the Neptune Pact Orbital, so Jimmy wondered if this was all about Leela's desire for closure. In a perfect world he believed he might be able to persuade her to take him back, but the world was never perfect to begin with. Jimmy reminded himself to keep his expectations low and prepared himself.

"Come out with what?" he asked.

Reaching the parking lot, Leela stopped and looked up at him. "You know your rucksack, the one you said you left on the *Adamant*'s tender?"

"Yeah?"

Leela gave her umbrella another twirl. "It wasn't on the tender, Jimmy. I took it."

The revelation was a sock in the jaw.

"*You?* You... *took* it? But I thought you left it on the tender when we de-docked."

Leela held out a palm. The rain that was coming down had stopped so she shook off the drops on her umbrella and closed it. "Yeah, it took some wheeling and dealing on my end after the scow picked us up, not to mention some sleight of hand on the Neptune Pact Orbital, but I got all of the gold back to Earth intact, every last bit."

Jimmy blinked. "But when? How?"

Leela smiled. "Hey, babe, if there's one thing I've a head for, it's taking care of details. Anyway, like I said, it took some fancy moves on my part, but no worries. We are totally in the clear."

"Wait a second, did you say *we*?"

Leela took his hand. "Yeah, dummy, *we*."

Oh wow.

Oh man.

Back on K7-A Jimmy had thought of it before, but holding Leela's hand he broke into a wide grin.

Leela Pendergast.

A perfect Bonnie to his Clyde.

THE END
(OVER AND OUT)

ACKNOWLEDGMENTS

The debts beholden:

Stacia Decker, Cath Trechman, Natalie Laverick, Ella Chappell, Steve Gove, Titan Books, my family, the genius of Gerry Anderson, quiet libraries, the ancient Ethiopian who came up with the idea of coffee as a beverage, and all my friends and readers.

ABOUT THE AUTHOR

Theoretically, with three books to his credit (*Koko Takes a Holiday*, *Koko the Mighty* and *Off Rock*) Kieran Shea might be considered a novelist. Professional liar might be another way of putting it. He is proud of all his crimes.

KOKO TAKES A HOLIDAY
KIERAN SHEA

Five hundred years from now, ex-corporate mercenary Koko Martstellar is swaggering through an easy early retirement as a brothel owner on a tropical resort island. Koko finds the most challenging part of her day might be deciding on her next drink. That is, until her old comrade Portia Delacompte sends a squad of security personnel to murder her.

"FAST AND FURIOUS... FUN PULP"
SFX

"WILD RIDE... BREAKNECK PACE... GREAT FUN"
Booklist

31901062760303